MW01398584

Praise For *Memory Weavers*

"*Memory Weavers* is a poignant and compelling exploration of memory, trauma, and resilience. With authenticity and depth, Muffy Walker captures the complexities of early-onset Alzheimer's and trauma-related disorders—shining a light on the profound impact of friendship and human connection in the face of adversity. As someone immersed in psychiatry, neurology, and neuroscience, I am heartened by its ability to bridge storytelling with mental health awareness. A truly moving debut."
—Husseini K Manji, MD, FRCPC, former Director of NIH Mood and Anxiety Disorders Program

"Beautiful, moving, and neurologically accurate. A rare achievement in literature! "We now know that memory and forgetting work in unison. We depend on memory to record our most cherished life experiences, while forgetting is vital for squelching those emotional experiences that can burn too hot. Literature is littered with works that focus on one or the other. Muffy Walker has written one of the first books that weaves in both aspects in a searingly moving and neurologically astute novel that is a must-read for anyone who cares about memory or forgetting. Which is to say, everyone."
—Scott A. Small MD, Director of the Alzheimer's Disease Research Center, Columbia University

"*Memory Weavers* is a poignant and beautifully crafted exploration of memory, trauma, and the unbreakable threads of human connection. Muffy Walker masterfully weaves together the lives of two women—one desperately holding onto her past, the other fighting to escape it—into a narrative that is both heartbreaking and hopeful. With lyrical prose and deep emotional resonance, this novel is a testament to the power of friendship, resilience, and the courage to confront our darkest fears. A compelling and unforgettable read."
—Dianne C. Braley, award-winning & bestselling author of *The Silence in the Sound* and *The Summer Before*

"*Memory Weavers* by Muffy Walker is a well-written, all-too-common tragic tale of the end-of-life changes in a person suffering from Alzheimer's disease. In this case it's even more tragic since the main character is a young woman in her forties who learns through genomic testing that she has inherited the rare genetic changes for familial Alzheimer's disease, or early-onset Alzheimer's disease, that can start in the thirties or forties and often progresses rapidly. Walker's engaging writing style, which feels like it could readily be adapted to a screenplay, gives us a compelling perspective through the eyes of the woman and her family and friends of the rapid disease progression. I appreciate fiction when it's based on solid science, as Walker has achieved with *Memory Weavers*."

—J. Craig Venter PhD, sequencer of the first human genome in 2000

"I am the same as Bergen, the husband/caregiver in Muffy Walker's story, *Memory Weavers*. My wife died of early-onset Alzheimer's. I could feel all the things Bergen feels and think all the things Bergen thinks. Ms. Walker writes so well that we (the readers) get to 'feel' the emotional journey from all sides—the Alzheimer's patient, her husband, daughter, son, and her friend battling memories of a terrible sexual attack. In this way, the author helps the rest of the world, those who have been lucky enough to avoid this dreaded disease, understand why we should all be gravely concerned about the growing number of Alzheimer's cases.

"Beyond raising awareness, the book is deeply thought-provoking, raising some of the biggest questions about life. Do you want to know the future? What if you could know the day or the year you'll die? As science improves, we can know things that, maybe, we weren't meant to know. The book raises tough questions about love and marriage: Do you love your spouse enough to let him/her die, or do you prolong life as long as possible with the help of modern medicine? And what is 'life' here on earth? What does it mean? Is it 'life' to have a brain functioning enough to continue certain autonomous and semiautonomous functions, like a heart beating or breathing? And, most importantly, the book raises big questions about God. Hadley asks, 'Are you even there?' In her anger, she says, 'A real God wouldn't let people suffer and die.' So we are forced to answer the ultimate questions. Does God exist to prevent suffering and death, to create a utopia for us humans (most of whom don't care about God)? Does God allow disease, sickness, suffering, and death because He actually cares about our salvation, about where we will spend eternity? If God creates heaven on earth, why would we seek to know Him?"

—Randall J. Krause, Esq.

"*Memory Weavers* is a captivating and thought-provoking book that humanizes the journeys of dementia and PTSD, offering a raw look at how these diagnoses reshape not just the lives of those affected but also those who love and care for them. Through every high, low, and unexpected turn, Muffy Walker invites us to feel the emotional weight and shifting dynamics that accompany each challenge.

"Walker does an exceptional job highlighting the reality of early-onset dementia, dispelling the misconception that dementia only impacts older individuals.

Through vivid, real-life examples—from the emotional toll of a diagnosis to the practical complexities of genome testing—Muffy Walker captures the evolving 'new normal' families must navigate. The narrative explores both the heartbreak and the small moments of grace that emerge along the way.

"At its heart, *Memory Weavers* is about acceptance and support, showing how these qualities help families navigate their toughest challenges. The story explores the slow, often painful path to coming to terms with a diagnosis and the shifting relationships it brings. Acceptance, the book shows, is not resignation, but a vital step toward finding peace and purpose in the face of adversity. More than a reflection on hardship, *Memory Weavers* is a journey of resilience, healing, and understanding through human connection. Muffy Walker seamlessly blends the good and the bad, showing how support—from family, friends, or unexpected sources—becomes a lifeline in times of uncertainty. A deeply moving read, *Memory Weavers* offers comfort, clarity, and compassion to anyone navigating complex challenges."

—Janet Hamada Kelley, Executive Director Alzheimer's Association San Diego/Imperial County Chapter

"Muffy Walker has written a smart, intriguing book that turns on two contrasting memory conditions and the impacts these have on the lives of two accomplished women and their families. In an era of increasing awareness of the importance of brain health and brainspan, it is a welcome read."

—Dale Bredesen, MD, author of the *New York Times* bestseller *The End of Alzheimer's*

"A truly lovely book. Made me cry. Muffy Walker's wonderful new novel, *Memory Weavers*, made me contemplate all things, the nature of angels. If they were to exist, what would be their purpose? Perhaps it would be to help us when we face the obligatory, harsh realities of existence. Help us discover the coexisting beauty—that of the world around us, as well as that within us. Help us to overcome, weather, or even grow despite the slings and arrows that we must face.

"If such beings existed, would they be ethereal, winged, and clad in shimmering white vestments? Or would they be more prosaic—a stranger we meet in a waiting room, seemingly suffering his or her own demons? Or a doting spouse, a distracted child, an estranged parent? Or a supportive lover, a caring therapist? Or perhaps a wizened old veteran, an abandoned pup?

"Perhaps we all need a 'village' of angels. Some taking a major role, some being supporting actors. Heck, maybe some of us are angels ourselves—unknowing angels, but angels nonetheless. Helping others through their darkest days. Perhaps we are *all* angels, or can be.

"Yes, I think that is what this poignant and lovely story made me realize—none of us can go it alone. We all need angels. And it turns out, we all are each others' angels. If a book can spur such contemplations, it's a must-read."

—Gary Simonds, MD, award-winning author of *One Happy Accident*, *Death's Pale Flag*, and *The Thriving Physician*

"*Memory Weavers* is deeply compelling, with characters so vivid and engaging that I found myself wanting to be part of their world. Their stories leave a lasting impression, forging a profound bond with the reader.

"The emotional depth is remarkable—I was moved to tears by certain passages, a testament to the book's powerful storytelling. It not only educates about the diseases the characters face but, more importantly, humanizes them, revealing the immense burden on patients and their loved ones.

"Yet, at its core, this is a story of resilience and hope. The kindness woven throughout—from small gestures to life-changing support—reminds us of the quiet, everyday acts that bring us together in compassion. This book is unforgettable."

—John C. Reed MD, PhD, named one of the top 10 "Doctors of the Decade" by Thomson Scientific

"Two women, one middle-aged and wealthy, the other young and struggling, meet in the waiting room of their psychiatrists' office. Against a background of impersonal New York City, they form a friendship that helps each other accept and transcend the trauma they carry. Hadley's life has been upended at age forty-seven by a diagnosis of familial Alzheimer's disease, and Rachel's, at age twenty-four, by the sexual assault she suffered in college. As Hadley declines and Rachel grows stronger, *Memory Weavers* teaches us that our lives do not cease when we cease, that they extend into the future through the love we give others. A deeply moving book."

—Anne Matlack Evans, author of *The Light Through the Branches*

"*Memory Weavers* by Muffy Walker takes us on an intimate journey of struggle, friendship, family, hope, and triumph. Threads of the past, present, and future are interwoven in the friendship between Rachel, a young woman dealing with PTSD, and Hadley, a middle-aged woman grappling with Alzheimer's and its impact on her family.

"We witness their individual struggles and challenges as they work to manage the effects of their conditions. The novel also explores the impact on their families and relationships, both old and new, as they seek ways to cope and escape their current realities. Amidst their hardships, we experience the joy and hope they find in an unlikely friendship, expanded networks, and small and large victories.

"The complexity of multiple experiences faced by individuals and their families confronting life-changing conditions is expertly and compassionately presented. The depth of the characters and their experiences is enriched by the author's professional expertise as a psychiatric mental health nurse and personal experiences as a caregiver.

"This novel is a must-read for professional and family caregivers and for anyone who believes, or needs to believe, in the power of the human spirit."
—Antonia M. Villarruel, PhD, RN, FAAN, Dean of Nursing, University of Pennsylvania

"Walker's strength lies in her portrayal of female friendships and the quiet, sustaining power they hold. Rachel's relationship with Mandy is a standout, embodying unwavering support and warmth. Even Rachel's occasional prickliness doesn't diminish the sincerity of their bond . . . It's a story that doesn't shy away from pain but also offers a glimmer of hope. I'd recommend this book to readers who appreciate emotionally layered stories about overcoming inner demons . . . its emotional depth and honesty make it a poignant, memorable read."
—Priscilla Evans, Managing Editor at Literary Titan

"*Memory Weavers* is a compelling and moving read. It sensitively explores the complex realities of mental health and Alzheimer's, while also highlighting the profound impact of therapy dogs on veterans facing similar challenges. Through its gripping narrative, the book reveals how these specially trained dogs provide not just companionship but also vital emotional and practical support—offering retired warriors a renewed sense of purpose and connection when navigating civilian life. An insightful and thought-provoking story . . . right to the final page."
—Gregory R. Hillgren, chairman of THE PATRIOTS INITIATIVE

"Muffy Walker, in her debut novel, *Memory Weavers*, transports the reader into the strong bond of friendship that forms between two women who meet by chance in their psychiatrist's waiting room. One, Rachel, is there to seek help in dealing with the lasting trauma from a college rape, while the other, Hadley, is dealing with an early-onset Alzheimer's diagnosis. The author gives the reader a window into the mental decline of someone with Alzheimer's and what friends and family experience as well. I really appreciated the very detailed and vivid descriptive style of the author's writing. A great read!"
—Diann Hjermstad, book club member

Memory Weavers
by Muffy Walker

© Copyright 2025 Muffy Walker

ISBN 979-8-88824-657-3

All rights reserved. No part of this publication may be reproduced, stored in a retrieval system, or transmitted in any form or by any means—electronic, mechanical, photocopy, recording, or any other—except for brief quotations in printed reviews, without the prior written permission of the author.

This is a work of fiction. All the characters in this book are fictitious, and any resemblance to actual persons, living or dead, is purely coincidental. The names, incidents, dialogue, and opinions expressed are products of the author's imagination and are not to be construed as real.

Designed by Suzanne Bradshaw.

Published by

köehlerbooks™

3705 Shore Drive
Virginia Beach, VA 23455
800-435-4811
www.koehlerbooks.com

MEMORY WEAVERS

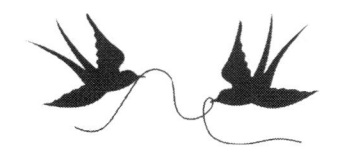

Muffy Walker

VIRGINIA BEACH
CAPE CHARLES

To Mom

CHAPTER 1
PRESENT

Rachel looked around nervously, forced herself to smile, and then gently pushed open the door. The silent room was sterile and painted in an ashen shade of white. The patient who had been in the other bed was no longer there. A lone vase of wilted daisies by her bed bowed their heads as though mourning the patient's passing. Looking further into the room, Rachel noticed the note on the rocking chair telling visitors that Hadley's husband, Bergen, had gone for coffee and would be right back.

Then, finally, she focused on her friend.

"Good morning, Hadley. It's Rachel." She gently pushed on the mattress next to her. "Can you hear me?" She wasn't sure what she was expecting since Hadley hadn't opened her eyes or responded in days. Her skin had a grayish hue and was cool to the touch. It shocked Rachel that someone as young as fifty-one could look so old.

The horizontal fluorescent light over the bed cast a sickly hue over Hadley's tired face. The furrow in her brow seemed deeper, angrier. Her lips were dry and pasty white. Above her bed, big orange letters announced DNR—do not resuscitate. The heart monitor, now disconnected, had stopped beeping. The only sounds Rachel could hear were the nurses hustling about in the station across the hall and various noises of grief and trauma from the next room.

With no acknowledgment from Hadley, Rachel felt sure her friend wasn't aware she had a visitor. She sat gingerly on the side of the bed, trying not to move the air mattress supporting Hadley's emaciated frame. It had been two weeks since Hadley ate any real food. A pink and green blanket, crocheted by hospice volunteers, lay rolled up under her left arm, helping to support an IV. A picture of Bergen and the three kids was taped to the side rail of the bed. Rachel placed her backpack on the floor and took out a small, soft hairbrush. She removed the terry cloth turban Hadley wore and tenderly brushed her friend's thinning blond hair. Knowing that musical memory is preserved right up to the end, Rachel softly hummed "Memory," Hadley's favorite Barbra Streisand song, hoping it would bring her friend some level of peace and contentment. Amid her intense sorrow, Rachel felt a profound sense of intimacy, having navigated this journey together with Hadley. Tears welled in Rachel's lower lids.

She wasn't sure what to look for as a sign of life. Hadley's chest rose and fell only eight times a minute. Rachel counted and watched, wondering if a further decrease meant death was not far away. She reached across the bed and put her fingers under Hadley's nose. A full ten seconds passed before she felt a feeble exhale. It was coming.

Rachel tried to keep her mind off the inevitable. "Hadley, I've got great news. I've been accepted to several veterinary programs," Rachel said with a touch of pride. Rachel pulled back the sheets and lovingly rubbed lavender oil on her friend's dry, cracked feet. Hadley stayed still.

Rachel picked up the beige plastic pitcher on the bedside table and poured herself a glass of water. She stared at Hadley's face—there were lines and creases she had never seen before. There was no movement behind her thin, pink eyelids or sound of breath coming from her parched lips.

Jolted out of her vigilance when Father Martin, the hospice chaplain, appeared at the doorway, Rachel stood to greet him. Since Hadley and her family had never been particularly religious, she thought it odd that the priest came each day, but any gesture of comfort was welcome. As far as Rachel knew, Hadley's attendance at church had been limited to Christmas Eve, Easter, and weddings. In her mind, Rachel added funerals to the list.

"How's Hadley doing this morning?" Father Martin asked.

Rachel bit down hard on her lower lip, trying not to cry.

"Hadley is lucky to have such a loving friend. Would you like to pray with me?" he asked.

Rachel nodded. He took both of Hadley's hands and recited the Lord's Prayer.

They sat in silence for what seemed to be an eternity; then the chaplain put his large, warm hand on Rachel's shoulder, kissed her on the top of her head, and left the room.

Rachel stared at the clear plastic catheter bag hanging from the bed. There now seemed to be very little urine accumulating. Assuming this was another sign that death was close, she texted Bergen to come back. Rachel pulled the curtain closed around the bed and lay next to Hadley, resting her head on Hadley's bony shoulder. She held Hadley's hand, rubbing her thumb gently over her fingers. "Farewell, Hadley," she whispered. A kaleidoscope of memories flooded her. Tears blurred her vision and trickled down Rachel's cheeks. She licked the salty drops from her upper lip. Joy, nostalgia, and deep sadness filled her heart. Rachel surrendered to the flood of emotions and allowed the floodgates to open, giving way to a torrent of tears.

CHAPTER 2
THREE YEARS EARLIER

After seven hours of meetings, Hadley Stanton kicked off her shoes and leaned back in her maroon leather desk chair, admiring the view of the city below. It was a crisp fall day, and she could see all the way to Central Park West. Carriages pulled by scraggy horses adorned with purple and red plumages in their bridles lined up along Fifty-Seventh Street. Joggers crisscrossed their way along the winding paths while vendors hawked bags of peanuts and paintings of New York cityscapes to tourists passing by.

Hadley opened her desk drawer and took out a pack of neon-pink Post-its. She wrote a reminder not to forget the anniversary gift and stuck it on her phone and then sent an email to her admin, reminding him to confirm the dinner reservations for the evening.

Within seconds, she had a reply:

> I confirmed the reservation this morning. You're all set. Happy anniversary. Have a wonderful dinner.
>
> Spencer.

Hadley picked up the framed photo of her husband. She had chosen well. They'd met at her friend's 1993 Super Bowl party—Dallas Cowboys versus Buffalo Bills. He wore a button-down shirt and khakis; she wore blue jeans and a Cowboys sweatshirt, her long blond hair pulled back in a neat ponytail. She noted immediately how handsome and confident he was.

Hadley had purposefully avoided his eye contact for most of the night—he seemed a little too self-assured, maybe even cocky. At halftime, Bergen approached her with a beer and asked her why she was rooting for the Cowboys and not the Bills. "I like Aikman," she told him.

Bergen stayed long after the game was over and offered to drive her home. She flushed recalling his polite peck on the cheek when she got out of his car.

Their year of dating and then engagement was exciting, full of sensual romantic evenings, long, lazy Sunday afternoons in bed, and parties every weekend. They went parasailing in Jamaica, got certified in scuba, and gambled all their vacation money on black seven in Atlantic City, making enough to pay for the trip.

Having grown up on the West Coast and taken family vacations outside the US to Europe and Asia, trips to the East Coast were novel and exciting, plus Hadley liked that Bergen wanted to show her his stomping grounds.

The phone rang, startling Hadley from her memories. She swiveled her chair in the direction of the phone and pushed line one. "Hadley, Andrew here. Our executive team call started ten minutes ago. Are you joining?" Hadley looked at her watch. She was late for her team's monthly executive call.

"Sugar," she said under her breath. There on her phone in bold black letters was the Google calendar alert. Executive Team Meeting. Today at 5 p.m. On the home screen behind it, her three children smiled at her. "So sorry Andrew. I had an emergency meeting with a client. I'll dial in immediately." Despite Hadley's tech-savvy nature, she still clung to the analog world. Her well-worn leather-bound planner sat proudly on her desk, its pages filled with color-coded appointments and handwritten notes. She still even preferred to use an address book that fit in her purse, finding comfort in the reliability and simplicity of the printed directory. She hung up and chastised herself for forgetting about the call. The third Tuesday of every month, she reminded herself. She joined the conference call and pulled up the agenda. There were several important business items that would require lengthy discussions. *If forgetting about the meeting wasn't enough, now I'll be late for my own anniversary dinner*, she silently chastised herself.

Hadley tapped her nails on the desk, willing the meeting to end. As soon as the adjournment was announced, Hadley stood and quickly retrieved her blue high heels from under the desk and slipped them on. She checked her face in the mirror, grabbed her coat, and left her office.

—

ELEGANT IN NAVY wool slacks and her mother's favorite blue cashmere sweater, Hadley arrived at the highly touted Le Renard et Le Lièvre fashionable—and fashionably late. A dark-purple velvet curtain hung in the entryway to ward off the cold. Several Toulouse Lautrec posters welcomed guests to the number one French restaurant in all of Manhattan. The restaurant was, as expected, full, even on a Tuesday night. Waiters, dressed in spotless white shirts with long black aprons tied around their waists, hurried quietly about the dining room. Brass sconces sent oblong spotlights onto the ceiling.

"Good evening, Mrs. Stanton," the maître d' offered; his Chicago accent hardened his fake French one. "Your husband is already here. May I take your coat?"

Hadley returned the greeting and handed him her coat.

He took the coat and passed it to the clerk. "Please follow me." A wave of heads, male and female, turned as Hadley walked through the room. With her shoulder-length hair, perfect pillowy lips, and Grace Kelly blue-green eyes, she was a classic beauty. As promised, the Stanton's table was next to the stone fireplace. Above it was a large painting of a red fox and a brown hare facing each other, their bodies twisted to resemble a heart. Framed in gilt, it was clearly the showcase of the aptly named restaurant.

"Happy anniversary, my dear," Bergen said, rising to greet her.

"I'm sorry I'm late. It was impossible to get a cab. How long have you been here?"

"Just half an hour," replied Bergen. "I had a martini and caught up on emails." Bergen pulled back the heavy leather chair for her to be seated. He breathed the familiar scent of her Chanel No. 5 perfume. Unlike the other tables adorned with a silver bud vase and single yellow rose, their table was resplendent with a large bouquet of long-stem red roses. Their celebration unfolded with a romantic gesture as Bergen recited the first two verses of Robert Burns's poem: "O my Luve is like a red, red rose. That's newly sprung in June; O my Luve is like the melody. That's sweetly played in tune. So fair art thou, my bonnie lass, So deep in luve am I; And I will luve thee still, my dear, Till a' the seas gang dry."

"You're so romantic," Hadley said, blowing him a kiss. "Thank you. The flowers are lovely, but I can't see you." Hadley placed her napkin on her lap and summoned the waiter to move the flowers to a side table. A moment later, he placed one of the bud vases with a single yellow rose in the center of their table.

Hadley reached into her handbag and pulled out a long white envelope. "I have a gift for you too." Hadley had racked her brain for months trying to choose the perfect gift for a man who had everything—literally. "I hope you like it," she said and handed him the envelope. "I made the card myself."

Instead of rushing to open the card, he thoughtfully read the card's inscription out loud. "Twenty-two years, 8,030 days, 11,563,200 minutes of wedded bliss." Bergen smiled. His face was warm and kind, and his eyes twinkled as he looked at Hadley.

"Open the card, honey. Your gift is inside." Hadley shivered, excited by the anticipation of his reaction.

Bergen cocked his head to the side. As he opened the homemade card, a glossy blue pamphlet fell out. "GenSeq: From Chance to Choice," he read out loud. He was caught off guard. This wasn't the gift certificate or airplane tickets he was expecting.

Hadley noticed the confused look on his face. She reached across the table and took the brochure from his hand. "Remember that article we read in *The New York Times* about genome sequencing?" It had gone into great detail about the pros and cons and had listed the top three facilities, one of which happened to be in New York City. "I made appointments for next week to get ours done," Hadley announced excitedly.

Bergen tilted his head, looking uncertain. Hadley explained how the test would look at their unique DNA sequences. "With this now readily available to the public, I thought it would be a great way to be proactive with our health. Its early identification of disease and disease risks will help us make informed medical decisions. We can be one step ahead."

"You've always had your finger on the pulse," Bergen said, smiling as he reached past the wine and water goblets and took Hadley's hand. He stroked her skin before bringing her hand to his mouth to kiss it. He reached under the table and brought up a robin's-egg blue bag tied with a white ribbon. "You didn't think the roses were your only present?" he teased.

Hadley was thrilled her husband always remembered birthdays and anniversaries. They were important to her, and he was sensitive that way. She slowly untied the ribbon and dipped her hand in the bag. She raised her eyebrows and smiled as she pulled out the matching blue box. After removing the lid, she cooed with delight at the pearl and diamond studs nesting inside. Hadley carefully removed the small gold hoops she was wearing and replaced them with her new anniversary earrings.

A tall, young man approached the table. Before he had time to request their cocktail choices or offer the wine list, Bergen ordered a bottle of the Alfred Gratien champagne.

"Do you remember we had that champagne on the flight to London last year?" he asked with a wink.

Hadley shook her head from side to side as she nibbled on her upper lip, a habit she had when nervous. "No, not really, but I don't pay much attention to those things," she answered.

Tucking his notepad into his apron, the waiter commended his choice and inquired about the special occasion.

While Hadley and Bergen filled each other in on their day's activities, waiters discreetly filled their water glasses, brought warm baguettes with various salted butters, and delivered two large black leather folios.

As if on cue, once Bergen and Hadley finished their first glass of champagne, the waiter appeared at the table and recited the evening's specials. After taking their orders, he nodded and disappeared as quietly as he arrived.

Bergen looked down at the GenSeq brochure. "Tell me again when we're going for this test?" He could feel his body relaxing from the champagne.

"Next Thursday, at two o'clock. I checked your schedule with Karilynn beforehand. I'll be coming from a meeting across town, so let's just meet there," Hadley suggested.

He stared at his wife and lifted his champagne flute. "To fifty more years together—and a spotless report card from the sequencing."

CHAPTER 3

In a whirlwind of emotions, Rachel dressed hastily, pulling on a pair of baggy gray jeans, black combat boots, and an army-green hoodie. Looking in the mirror, she wondered if this was an appropriate outfit for a doctor's appointment.

Rachel shook her head in disgust as she pinched the skin above her waistband. In high school and her freshman year in college, she had worked hard to maintain a size-four figure. She exercised frequently and rarely ate carbs. She was proud of her body and didn't mind when boys looked at her. Now she liked to keep everything covered up. She felt more comfortable that way; it was easier. "Fuck it. Who really cares what I look like?" she said to her reflection in the mirror. In the hallway, she grabbed a piece of chalk and jotted a quick note on the chalkboard to Mandy, her roommate and best friend. *At the shrink. Back at 5:30. Dinner after? R*

RACHEL ARRIVED AT the brownstone five minutes before her appointment. Yellow chrysanthemums flanked the red wooden door. *Pretty*, she thought. A shiny brass nameplate announced the practices of Monica Blanzaco, MD, and Harold L. Kopple, MD, above a large, tarnished knocker. Standing on the top step, Rachel inhaled the musty, sweet smell of the fallen leaves and watched a squirrel scamper among them, foraging for acorns from the oak tree. She hated that she was once again at this office. But Dr. Blanzaco had been kind. At least that was how she remembered her. She checked her email until there was one minute to go, then took a deep breath and turned the knob. Her hand was so clammy with sweat that it nearly slipped off.

Inside, the receptionist greeted her, took her insurance card, and invited Rachel to take a seat. Three blue tweed upholstered office chairs were lined up against the wall. Recent issues of *Good Housekeeping*, *O,* and *The New Yorker* were splayed across the square pine table, a distraction from the two large literature display racks containing brochures for biofeedback, ADHD, coping with PTSD, and various alcohol and drug treatment facilities. A water dispenser next to the door emitted a rhythmic glugging as air bubbles rose upward into the bottle.

Dorothy Taylor, as the plaque on the receptionist's desk announced, reminded Rachel of a younger version of Judi Dench. A small woman, with round, pink cheeks, a shock of silver hair, and blue, piercing eyes that seemed to have the capability to look deep within people.

Just as the clock struck four, Dorothy left her perch at the desk, holding an olive-green folder in her hand. Tapping lightly on one of the adjoining doors, she poked her head inside the office, announcing Rachel's arrival to the doctor.

"Rachel Weissman," Dr. Blanzaco repeated. "Do I know her? The name is familiar."

Dorothy explained that Rachel was referred by a social worker from St. Luke's Hospital several years before, but she only came once.

She returned to the waiting area and, smiling, pointed toward the open office door. Sensing Rachel's trepidation, she said encouragingly, "Dr. Blanzaco will see you now."

Rachel's heart pounded against her ribs as a sour taste rose into her mouth. She thought she was going to be sick. The portable heater in the corner clicked on, and its wires glowed a bright orange-red. *Breathe, Rachel, you can do this*, she told herself.

Dr. Blanzaco was still an attractive woman, but her tight chignon and thick, black-rimmed glasses added years to her otherwise youthful appearance. She wore a burgundy wool dress and was seated in a large brown velveteen armchair when Rachel entered. A small coffee table separated her from a matching couch and a brown leather chair—options for the patient. Rachel looked at the box of tissues on the table and vowed she wouldn't need them.

"Hello, Ms. Weissman. It's nice to see you again. Please have a seat."

Glancing between the sofa and the chair, Rachel opted for the former, sitting closest to its large, curled arm. "Hello, Doctor," she barely squeaked out.

Dr. Blanzaco gave Rachel the once-over, noting her attempt at androgyny. Rachel's baggy clothes and hoodie zipped to her chin made it difficult to tell if Rachel was curvy or not. Her thick, curly brown hair, pulled back and tied in a knot, and the lack of makeup and jewelry, except a black leather braided bracelet, was neither feminine nor flattering.

"You can call me Monica. Is it okay if I call you Rachel?" Dr. Blanzaco asked.

Rachel nodded.

As Monica started the therapy session, Rachel's skin crawled, anticipating what was to come.

"Rachel, I see it's been six years since I last saw you. So, you must be twenty-seven now. Is that right?" Rachel bobbed her head affirmatively. "What brings you back here today?"

Rachel stared at the Rubik's Cube on the table in front of her. She remembered from her high school statistics and probability class that there were over forty-three quintillion configurations. She was never good at math and hated that course. She wondered why it was in a psychiatrist's office. "Dr. Blan, I mean Monica, when they referred me here back then, I didn't think I needed your help," she explained, twisting the leather bracelet tightly around her wrist.

"Asking for help isn't a sign of weakness, Rachel. I'm glad you're here. What can I help you with today?" She gave Rachel a warm smile.

Rachel's eyes darted around the room. She still remembered every detail: the walnut bookshelves lined with textbooks, the titles screaming judgments at her—*Schizophrenia, Depression, Bipolar Disorder, Anxiety, Phobias*—stacks of medical journals on the remaining shelves, and framed pictures of Broadway at night on the walls.

"I'm not really comfortable being here," Rachel told her. "I just want you to know that. I saw a psychologist about four years ago, but we didn't click, so I stopped going after a few months. To be honest, I'm not sure therapy can really help me." Rachel hesitated and hoped she hadn't offended the doctor and her profession. Monica remained quiet, allowing Rachel to proceed at her own pace.

The silence made Rachel want to run out the door. Instead, she explained that a while back she had been at a party and saw a bunch of guys hitting on another girl. Not in a complimentary way, but more aggressively. The next thing Rachel knew, she was in the emergency room. Someone at the party had called an ambulance. "It all happened so fast, and I was scared shitless," she said. "They said it was a panic attack, and the ER nurse suggested I see a therapist. She gave me some dude's card. I didn't want to talk to a man."

Rachel narrowed her eyes and looked up quickly to check the doctor's reaction. Monica nodded again, encouraging Rachel to go on.

"Since that party, I've had more panic attacks. Mostly in my apartment, but also in restaurants or crowded places, like malls. And I also have really bad nightmares." Rachel took a deep breath and explained that when she told her mom what was going on, she encouraged Rachel to give therapy another try. Her voice dropped several octaves and was barely audible. "I don't know if you remember the details of my case," Rachel said, wondering if "*case*" was the right word in psychiatry. "*Nut case*" jumped into her mind, and she smirked.

"I have your chart here, but why don't you remind me?" Monica said.

Rachel turned her face away, squinted, and pursed her lips tightly. "I don't know if this is such a good idea. I mean, maybe I should just go." The room was silent except for the ticking of the glass-domed clock on the side table. "I mean, can you really help me? It's over, it's done."

"Tell me how you're feeling right now, Rachel," the doctor said.

Rachel bent down and fiddled with the lace on her boot. "I feel stupid and embarrassed and scared," she blurted.

"Okay, that's a start. Can you tell me more?" Monica asked.

Rachel rolled her eyes. "I really don't want to do this," she murmured. "Okay, I feel stupid that it's been six years since the rape, and I don't seem to be able to move on with my life. I thought maybe you could give me a pill or hypnotize me or something," she said, almost pleading. "I just want my old life back."

Rachel told the psychiatrist how different her life was then. Before the rape, she was independent but popular, with a lot of friends. She was on track to graduate with a bachelor of fine arts degree. Her poetry had been published in magazines, and she had her own blog with several hundred followers. "In fact, at the end of my freshman year, I won $1,000 in an online poetry slam contest." The memory of happier days brought a smile to Rachel's face.

"It seems so unfair that I was his target," she said. "I mean, I knew about the dangers for women and was careful when walking through campus at night. I even carried a can of pepper spray attached to my keys that my father had given me the day I left for college. I never went to bars alone and never, ever left my drink unattended."

Rachel reached for the Rubik's Cube on the coffee table and started clicking the tiles around as she explained the events leading up to the rape. "Every other Sunday evening, the first two floors of our dorm held their hall meeting. As a junior, I felt the meetings were juvenile and should only be required of incoming freshmen and transfers. I was tired that day. I had a headache from partying the night before and just wanted some alone time. But since the meetings were mandatory, I went and sat in the far back." Rachel hesitated. In her mind, she saw the fake Christmas tree in the corner and menorah on the windowsill. The RA had rattled on about exam schedules, arranging transportation home for the holidays, and the need to eat healthy food and get enough sleep during finals. When the staff wasn't looking, Rachel slipped through the door and went back to her room.

Rachel dropped the cube onto the table. She folded her arms tightly across her chest and bit down hard on her lower lip. Monica waited patiently for her to continue.

"When I got back to my room, I opened the window. There was only one thermostat for the building, so my second-floor room was unbearably hot." Rachel shook her head. "I was so stupid. It was only eight o'clock, but I was exhausted. I got undressed, turned off the lights, and got into bed. The rest, as they say, is history." Rachel's pulse quickened. She felt dizzy.

"Your memories are still quite vivid, Rachel."

Rachel nodded robotically, then continued. "I did come back for spring semester but couldn't concentrate. I had this vague sense of dread. I was always on alert. I couldn't relax. So, I took a leave of absence after six weeks in the spring semester. I meant to go back, but I just never did. Now I have a mindless job as the manager at Abercrombie in the Seaport Mall."

Monica crossed her legs and jotted notes on a yellow pad. "Where are you living now?"

"With a girlfriend in a small five-story walk-up in the East Village. I was staying at my parents' after I left school, but they've been separated for years." Sadness filled her body. She blamed herself for their failed marriage. "After my second year at school, I begged my dad to let me move into Scarlet Hall with my freshman-year roommate. It was a coed dorm, separated by a floor—guys on the ground floor for safety. My dad was dead set against it. 'Young women don't live among men; they're only interested in one thing,' he said.

I remember him banging his fist on the kitchen counter, and finally after a big blowup, with lots of yelling and tears, my mom convinced him to let me move into Scarlet Hall. But I guess he was right. After the attack—that's the word my dad used instead of rape—everything changed. We used to snuggle on the couch and share hotel rooms when we visited colleges. But then a glass wall rose between us. Even simple hugs goodbye ended.

"I know my dad blames my mom for letting me live in the coed dorm," Rachel told the doctor. "Even though I'm one-hundred-percent sure the guy didn't live in my dorm, that's where dad chose to direct his anger. In my heart, though, I know he blames me." She hung her head in shame. "Six months after the rape, he and Mom separated. He moved to the Upper East Side, and Mom moved in with my aunt Claudette, in Brooklyn Heights. I haven't seen him in four years. I don't think he can stomach looking at his little girl, knowing what happened."

Monica closed her eyes and then asked about Rachel's mother.

Rachel looked up at the ceiling and rolled her eyes. "I see my mom a few times a week. A lot of times it's a burden to be with her. I don't want her to worry, so I'm always faking it, like I'm okay. It's exhausting." Rachel snorted indignantly. "But she is a great support and doesn't judge me for what happened."

"Judge you?" Monica asked.

"*Every*one who knows has something to say about it," Rachel said bitterly. "The dorm's resident adviser intimated blame by asking why I was in my room when everyone else was at the hall meeting. The policeman who questioned me insinuated wearing only my undies to bed was an open invitation. He asked me why I had my window open in December." She paused.

"My roommate moved out after the Christmas break. She said she was just too uncomfortable living with me, as if the rape leached from my skin into the air she breathed. But it was the snickering and name-calling behind my back that bothered me the most. Overnight,

I became one thing only: *that girl who was raped*." Rachel vented the years of pent-up anger. "The stuck-up girls who paraded naked down the hall to the showers parted ways when I walked by. What, did they think the rapist was still there lurking inside me? I even heard the girls in the room next to mine refer to our dorm as Scarlet *Letter* Hall. So, to answer your question, yes, I've been judged." Rachel buried her face in her knees and pulled them to her chest.

Monica put her pad down and folded her hands on her lap, allowing silence before she broke the stillness. "I'm sorry for what you've been through, Rachel. I understand your hesitancy being here today, but I applaud your bravery for coming back and working on these issues. I do believe that we can work together to resolve the anger and hurt you are feeling. What that man did to you is over, but the aftermath still haunting you needs to be silenced." She paused. "We have about ten minutes left. I'd like to hear what you feel causes you the most distress."

Rachel stared into space and rubbed her lower lip with her index finger. This was exactly why she hadn't wanted to come. The nightmares and sudden panic attacks were bad enough, but she couldn't handle voluntarily recalling the details. Images, sounds, and smells flooded her mind. Her heart rate quickened. "I should go," she said, starting to rise.

Monica nodded and said nothing.

Rachel stood and walked to the back of the couch. She ran her fingers along the trim of the cushions. "I have a lot of fucked-up memories," Rachel blurted out. She paced back and forth until she plopped down where she had been sitting before. "They come when I'm expecting them, like at night or when I'm out alone, but they also show up completely out of the blue." She brushed her palms up and down over her thighs, wondering again if she really wanted to open the wounds. "Two days ago, I had a dentist appointment. I needed a cleaning and X-rays. When the hygienist was scaling my gums, they started to bleed, and the coppery taste of the blood brought me back to that night. I pushed her hand away and started to cry. She thought she hurt me." Rachel hesitated, trying to build courage. "I could feel the impact of his fist slamming into my jaw." Rachel's eyes grew wide, and she shivered.

"Rachel, take a deep breath," Monica instructed. "Breathe in through your nose. Then slowly let it out." Rachel followed her directions. "That's good. Now one or two more. Open your eyes and look at me. You are safe. You are in my office."

Rachel opened her eyes. Her hands were clenched tightly together, and her heart raced.

"Do you need a break?" Monica asked. "Would you like a glass of water?"

Rachel shook her head. She hated the memories. She hated how difficult it was to differentiate them from reality. She looked away and clutched the throw pillow to her chest. "I thought I was stronger than this," she said, embarrassed at her own frailty.

Monica explained how the brutal attack had caused symptoms of PTSD and the goals they could work toward to lessen them. Rachel liked Monica. It felt good to have her feelings validated. As the session came to an end, Rachel's body relaxed. "Do you think I can get better?"

Monica smiled gently, her eyes full of warmth and assurance. "Yes, Rachel," she said, her voice soft yet resolute. "You absolutely can get better. Healing takes time, patience, and courage, but I believe you possess all of these qualities within you."

Rachel's grip on the pillow loosened as she listened to Monica, and the corners of her lips lifted. "But what if the memories never go away?" she asked, her voice tinged with doubt.

Monica leaned forward, her expression compassionate. "It's natural to fear that the memories will always haunt you, but with therapy and support from your friends and family, you can learn to manage them so they no longer control you. They may never fully disappear, but they can lose their power over you."

Rachel nodded slowly, digesting Monica's words. For the first time in a long while, she dared to believe there might be a light at the end of the tunnel. "Thank you," she whispered, her voice thick with emotion.

Monica reached out and squeezed Rachel's hand. "You're welcome, Rachel. Remember, healing is a journey, and you don't have to walk it alone. If you'll let me, I'll be with you every step of the way."

As Rachel stood to leave, a newfound determination burned within her. She knew that the road ahead would be difficult, filled with challenges and setbacks, but she also knew that she was stronger than she had ever realized. With Monica's guidance and support, she was ready to face her demons head-on and reclaim her life.

CHAPTER 4

Amid the bustling city, Hadley emerged from the revolving door, out to the street, and hesitated. For a split second, she had forgotten where she was going. Oblivious tourists and harried businessmen brushed past her as she deliberated: right or left? "Coffee," she said, pointing into the air, suddenly remembering what she had gone out for and turning the corner toward Starbucks. A line of customers fixated on their phones, patiently waiting to order their favorite concoctions. The aroma of brewing coffee filled the air. Glancing only briefly at the lemon pound cake in the case, Hadley thought better and simply ordered a nonfat latte. It was nearing lunchtime, and she was hungry, but she was fastidious about maintaining her figure. She held a conviction that individuals who gained weight lacked a certain level of self-respect and that conscientious choices in diet and exercise were indicative of a person's dedication to their physical and mental health.

She chose a table in the back to avoid familiar faces from her habitual coffee haunt. They were all such creatures of habit, going to the same Starbucks every day, when there was one on almost every block. Hadley looped her handbag over her shoulder and sat with her back to the wall. While she enjoyed her latte, she thumbed through photos on her phone. She stopped briefly at one of her dog, Bear Bear. Although he'd been gone a while, she still missed him and told herself one day she'd have to get a new pup to fill the void.

The next photo was one of Bergen on a beach. She studied the tropical scene but couldn't place where it might have been. An incoming text message dinged, interrupting her train of thought. It was Ellie:

> Had, where r u?

Hadley cocked her head, shrugged her shoulders, and replied,

> Starbucks on Columbus. Y?

> Janine's surprise bday party! Where r u?

Hadley jolted up, nearly spilling her latte.

> On my way. Soooooo sorry

Hadley darted outside. The sidewalks were crowded and cars sped past. She hailed a cab and pulled up to the restaurant ten minutes ahead of Janine's arrival. She combed her fingers through her hair and smoothed on a new layer of pink lipstick before entering the dining room.

"I'm so sorry I'm late, girls," she said. "I stopped at Starbucks to get a coffee and ran into my old college roommate. We got to talking, and I lost track of time," she fibbed.

Her friends looked at her curiously and glanced down at her business attire.

"I know! I had an important meeting and didn't have time to change," she said, rolling her eyes, disappointed in herself. Hadley moved to one of the tables, brushing her hand across the lavender damask cloth. She was pleased that the florist had done exactly as she had requested; the pave of purple tea roses and green hydrangeas were in square white ceramic containers rather than tall glass vases. She examined the place cards written in purple calligraphy, then scanned the room to ensure everyone was where they should be. The room was gorgeous; everything turned out just as she'd planned.

She took a quick walk around the room, eyeing the various blown-up photos of Janine, and stopped next to her favorite: one of Janine in a peach taffeta bridesmaid dress, standing next to Hadley in her wedding gown. She took out her phone and snapped a selfie.

The ladies gossiped and complimented each other on their dresses, handbags, and shoes. Hadley felt foolish in her drab business suit and scolded herself for forgetting about the party.

"It's one ten," Janine's mother announced. "Let's all be quiet; she should be arriving any minute." Hadley pulled out the piano bench and took a seat behind the white Baby Grand. Bunches of lilac balloons wrapped in tulle bobbed against the ceiling.

"I'm so excited," whispered one of the guests.

"Surprise!" the women yelled when Janine opened the door. Hadley played "Happy Birthday" on the piano as the girls sang gleefully.

After lunch was served and Janine opened her gifts, the staff cut slabs of the three-layer chocolate mousse cake. Janine clinked her glass with her spoon and stood. "Thank you, thank you. I am *the* most fortunate girl in the world to have such special friends. I love you all."

As each woman stood to offer a special memory with the birthday girl, Hadley struggled to conjure the right heartfelt words for her toast. Images of trips, weddings, and Mommy and Me classes flitted through her mind. When it was her turn, Hadley stood and smiled. After an uncomfortable silence, she raised her glass and hesitated, then simply said, "Happy birthday, Janine. I love you." Embarrassed, she forced a weak smile and cowered into her seat.

How could I have forgotten? she asked herself in the back of the cab, biting her upper lip and shaking her head. She checked her calendar, wondering if she had made a mistake. *I've had so many meetings and business lunches, it was easy to forget the party.* She closed her eyes for the duration of the ride back to the office. It was only 3 p.m., and there were deadlines looming.

At 6:30, Hadley left the office and headed home. Twenty minutes later she announced her arrival as she entered the apartment. Their apartment was large—two apartments they had purchased and joined together by removing the dividing wall. It had four bedrooms, enormous by New York standards, three and a half baths, a large closet they had converted into a small office, barely big enough for a desk and chair, a warm, inviting kitchen, and, Hadley's favorite, an open living room overlooking Central Park, complete with a Steinway piano and a woodburning fireplace. Having grown up in a big house in San Diego, Hadley was used to space. Bergen had promised if she'd move to NYC with him, he'd make sure their living quarters were spacious.

Hadley removed her coat, slipped out of her shoes, and dropped her purse on the freshly polished floor as Bergen rounded the corner with a glass of red wine in hand.

"Where you been?" he asked.

"I was at the office working on a campaign. Today was Janine's party, so I was behind."

"Oh, that's right," Bergen said, looking at her suit. "Didn't you buy a new dress for it?"

Hadley avoided looking at Bergen and shifted from one leg to the other. "I did, but I had a very important meeting and decided last minute that a lilac silk dress would not have been appropriate. I'll have plenty of other opportunities to wear it," she said, taking her husband by the hand. "I'll tell you all about the party over dinner." She wasn't sure why she was lying again; she was always honest with Bergen, but she was too tired to open that conversation now.

Hadley and Bergen coveted dinner at home with the kids. It was their sacred part of the day to reconnect, free from cell phones and televisions. Bergen cut the lamb and placed a chop onto each dinner plate, then passed them to Hadley, who spooned cauliflower and a dollop of mashed potatoes onto each. "You know they're just babies," Brook said, pushing the lamb chop off her plate. Hadley looked at her daughter. She was the age where any topic could be taboo.

"Who's a baby?" Tucker asked, confused by the dialogue. Then, a lively debate of the pros and cons of being a vegetarian ensued. Each was entitled to their opinion. There were no winners or losers. It was what Hadley and Bergen loved about their dinner ritual with the kids.

After the table was cleared and the dishes were stacked in the dishwasher, the children left to do their homework, and Bergen and Hadley retreated to the living room to enjoy another glass of wine. Hadley sat close to Bergen on the sofa and stretched her legs out over his lap.

The sofa's pastel floral pattern reminded Hadley of spring, and springtime reminded her of her mother. She chose the fabric for that very reason. Every year on the first day of spring, Hadley's mother, Rebecca, hosted a luncheon for her best girlfriends. She covered the table with a blanket of fresh, sweet-smelling sod and decorated it with live mini jonquils, daffodils, and buttercups. Hadley was given the special job of making the napkin rings out of curly willow twigs and choosing the color of the linen napkins.

Spring also brought memories of playing the music from the Maypole dance on the piano her father gave her, deciding what to give up for Lent, and shopping for Easter dresses. Hadley smiled. Such sweet memories. What she still wouldn't do for one more hug.

She ran her finger around the rim of her glass, watching the syrupy legs of the Petite Sirah drip down the wineglass. "Bergen," she started, "today I was flipping through pictures and came upon one of you on a beach. For the life of me, I have no idea where it was taken." She scrolled to the unidentifiable photo. Hadley handed her phone to Bergen. "This one," she said.

Bergen put his wineglass on the table, glanced at the picture, and then enlarged it. "Hads, this is in Sanibel. We went there for spring break two years ago with the kids," he said.

Hadley bit her lower lip and shook her head, trying desperately to remember the trip. "Oh of course," she said, "how silly of me. How could I forget? It was a wonderful vacation." She grappled with the realization that her demanding lifestyle was taking a toll on her recollections.

"That it was," said Bergen, "especially seeing you in that black bikini."

"Oh Bergen," she said, her ivory skin suddenly taking on a pinkish hue. "I think I've had so much on my mind with work, I'm forgetting things. I need some rest. Let's go to bed."

Bergen raised an eyebrow and put his hand on her knee. "Bed?" His tone dropped low, into his sexy voice.

Hadley patted Bergen's hand and gently moved it from her leg. "Yes, for sleeping," she replied. "I'm totally exhausted."

CHAPTER 5

Rachel sat on the metal bench in the cluttered break room at work. She had been at Abercrombie for eighteen months and quickly advanced from salesgirl to day manager. Clothing boxes were stacked against all the walls, leaving little space to maneuver. The strong smell of a cheesy pasta dish lingered in the air from someone's lunch in the microwave. Her stomach gurgled. She pulled a power bar from her backpack and slid the screen of her phone to the left, searching for the heart icon. The dating app she used hadn't brought much success in the past, but since her session with Monica, she'd been feeling more curious about her life. Hopeful even.

She stared at the first photo on her phone. Joe, twenty-four, likes Van Halen—swipe left. Marcus, twenty-two, likes Navy SEALs, pizza, and marathons— swipe right. Will, twenty-seven, likes 24 Hour Fitness, Ithaca College, and Kenny Chesney—swipe right. *I need to narrow down my age requirements. Most of these guys are way too young.* Rachel wondered how long it would take to find Mr. Right in such a large pool of users.

Dating had initially come easily to Rachel. She had admirers in high school, mostly scholarly and pimply or brainless, burly jocks. So, in tenth grade, when she met Richard, who was neither, she fell. He was tall and had dark hair. He was physically mature and shaved daily. He was raised in a good Catholic family with solid values. Unlike many friends, his parents were happily married and enjoyed spending time with their kids. Richard was the oldest of three, two boys and a girl. Every summer he vacationed in the Hamptons. Although wealthy, he worked weekends and during breaks and was not given a car for his sixteenth birthday.

Rachel and Richard met in a bio lab, where they dissected a frog together. He expected his female partner to be repulsed, squeamish, but she made the first cut straight down its shiny, rubbery belly. Later, Rachel received a text:

> Do you want to grab frog's legs for dinner?

By eleventh grade, Rachel and Richard were a serious couple. For her seventeenth birthday, Richard surprised her with a small diamond pendant. That night, Rachel lost her virginity to this man who stole her heart. A month later, Richard's brother was busted for selling drugs, and the family abruptly moved away. Rachel was devastated; he never tried to contact her. Maybe it was naive, but Rachel thought they might get married after high school.

Her second boyfriend, the only other man she slept with before college, was Liam Deisseroth. He was adopted and never knew his birth mother; Liam told her his birth mother was a crackhead. Liam was studious and driven. Rachel often wondered why he spent time with her when he was often so busy. But Mandy frequently reminded her, "Guys want sex."

Unlike Richard, Liam did not have a sensitive side. He was a brick wall: solid, unyielding, and indifferent. He liked structure, rules. They only went out on Saturday nights, didn't drink, and got home by eleven, no matter what. He claimed no religious affiliation: "There is no scientific proof of God." Liam had his sights on Harvard, premed, and let nothing get in his way. After graduation, he left for Cambridge, promising to stay in touch, but she never heard from him again. Although broken, Rachel was convinced she'd find her forever man in college.

THE CLOCK SIGNALED the end of her workday, prompting Rachel to punch her timecard. She grabbed her brown wool coat and said goodbye to her coworkers. A promising match with Will showed on the dating app. "Bingo." Rachel smiled and messaged him.

> Hi I saw you like country music. Me too.

Hi Rachel what's up?

> Just got off work. Going home. U?

Will responded immediately.

Going to the gym then grabbing something to eat.

Will seemed like a nice enough guy. Twenty-seven, never married, no kids. Grad student.

> Okay TTYL

Wanna get pizza tonight?

"Finally!" she said. Her heart pulsed in her throat. The sensation was familiar, especially when she was nervous or consumed too much alcohol or caffeine. She was ready to give it a try. Rachel counted to ten, playing as hard to get as she could stand, then wrote,

> Sure. Where?

How 'bout Francesco's in the village at 8?

> K. C u there

She replied (after deleting the smiley face she wanted to send).

It was 6:10. She hurried to the bus stop. She'd have just enough time to get ready.

She laid out skinny jeans, boots, and a chunky sweater. Next, a black leather miniskirt, tights, and a loose-flowing white blouse. Then a faux fur vest and gray sweater dress from her closet. *No, that isn't right either.* "Mandy," she yelled. "Come help."

Mandy opened the door and laughed at the pile of clothes. "I'm meeting a guy for pizza," Rachel said. "What do I wear?"

"Who? Have I met him?" Rachel told her. "So just go *caj*, like you didn't put any effort into it," Mandy advised, grabbing the jeans.

"Thanks, Mand, that's why you're my BFF." They had known each other since grade school, were both Girl Scouts, took ice-skating lessons together, and had a crush on the same jock in ninth grade. Since her father was often gone on business and her mother spent time with Jack Daniels, Jim Beam, and Old Grand Dad, Mandy practically lived at the Weissmans. Mandy was the first friend Rachel called after the rape. She didn't treat her differently, saw her as the friend she first drank beer and skinny-dipped with, not as damaged goods.

Mandy was the prettier one. Her features resembled a young Snow White: perfect red bow lips, round blue eyes, and porcelain skin. She had long blond hair that reached past her butt, which was often the brunt of jokes from teenage boys. At five feet, ten inches, she was statuesque. Rachel was also tall but had her mother's athletic build, curvaceous hips, and a rather large bust, features Mandy secretly yearned for. Mandy was a fashionista and knew designers, celebrity gossip, and popular bands. Rachel was more scholarly, enjoying art, poetry, and literature. Despite their differences, they both liked cats, hated purple, never ate lamb or veal, and lost their virginity in eleventh grade. In high school, both were optimistic about their futures. Mandy had dreamed of modeling for Ford or Elite and maybe even gracing the cover of the *Sports Illustrated* swimsuit issue. Rachel dreamed of studying art in Rome, marrying an Italian, and living happily ever after, jetting about on scooters through the countryside.

Rachel pulled on the jeans and sweater and put her cell phone, twenty dollars, and ID into her black cross-body purse. As she turned to leave, she took in the mess of her eight-by-twelve-foot room. Two coffee-stained mugs on her bedside table, a stack of mail, and several tubes of open foundation and lipstick were askew on the white pine dresser she'd got from her mother. The floor was covered with clothes, both clean and dirty. Rachel hated to leave her room in such disarray. She looked at her watch. It was time to go. As a small gesture of tidiness, she pulled the sheets up on the bed and folded the pale-peach duvet she'd had since childhood. Rachel leaned a pencil against her closet door, took one last look in the mirror, and said goodbye to Mandy.

What if he doesn't like me when he sees me? What if I don't like him? Rachel walked quickly, her arms folded across her chest. *Should I let him order? Do I get a beer or water? After we're done, should I just go? What if he's a murderer?* She stopped herself dead in her tracks. *Don't go there, Rach. Keep some distance, keep your phone out, and tell him Mandy knows you're with him and where.* Rachel rehearsed these three steps whenever she went out on a first date. This date would be the fourth one since "it" happened. It had taken Rachel nearly five years to let herself keep company with a man. She hadn't met a man yet who didn't hurt her.

The blue neon sign for Francesco's was a block away. Rachel slowed her steps. It was only 7:55, and she didn't want to seem anxious. Rachel saw him round the corner, coming from the other direction. Tall, maybe six feet, two inches, quite muscular, with brown, curly hair. *Just like his Tinder picture*, she thought. *Check, so far, so good.* She took in a long breath of the cool night air and watched as Will entered the casual Italian restaurant. Her heart raced wildly.

After the initial awkward introductions, Will removed his black leather bomber and offered to take her coat, then walked toward an empty table by the window. Stereotypic of pizza joints, the tables had plastic, red checkerboard tablecloths and white porcelain bud vases with a single fake daisy. Frank Sinatra played in the background while dripping candles in Chianti bottles cast a glow on the windows. "Is this table okay?" he asked.

"Yeah, sure," Rachel replied. Something was bothering her; she felt a lump rise in her throat. She frowned and rubbed her nose, taking in thin sips of air. Her nostrils flared at the too familiar scent of the leather and clove aftershave.

"Have a seat," Will offered. "Want a beer or something?"

Rachel's face turned beet red as a wave of panic rose. She stood up, grabbing her coat. "I've gotta go," she said abruptly. "I'm sorry. I just remembered something." And out she fled.

Against her better judgment, she ran through Washington Square Park, stopping under the arch to catch her breath. Rachel startled when a gust of wind sent a plastic bag whirling toward her face. She swatted at its frayed remains, shoving it forward onto the thorny branches of a bush. Even though it was only forty degrees, Rachel was hot and perspiring. She took off her coat and retrieved her cell phone and pepper spray. While purveying her surroundings, she walked the remaining six blocks to her apartment.

What the F is wrong with me? Trying not to cry, she checked her phone. No message from Will. "He probably thinks I'm a whack job," she said into the cold night air. Rachel ran up the five flights of stairs to her apartment. She never took the elevator. It would be too risky if someone got on and she couldn't get off. Barely able to catch her breath, she unlocked the door to her apartment, entered, closed several locks, and put the chain across. As she entered her bedroom, she looked first at the pencil; it was still leaning up against her closet door. The room was how she left it. Clumsily removing her shoes, she let herself fall face-first, with arms and legs splayed across her bed. She pulled her phone out and rolled onto her back. Still no text.

"Rachel, you're home already? You okay?" Mandy asked, tapping on the door.

Rachel made the letter L with her thumb and forefinger and held it to her forehead. Mandy entered the room and climbed onto the bed. She knew most of Rachel's past and had been both a patient and sensitive friend. Rachel wiped her runny nose with her sleeve.

"Well, I fucked up another one," Rachel said. "You'll never guess what was wrong with this guy," Rachel began sarcastically. "His aftershave. I mean, aftershave, can you fucking believe it?" Rachel yelled. "It's the same one you-know-who wore!"

"Wait, what? Do you actually think Will is the rapist, that he's stalking you?"

"Oh my God, no, not at all. But that smell brought back everything. We had just sat down. And then I swear I couldn't breathe. I felt like I was choking. I was right back in the dorm room. So, like an idiot, I jumped up and told him I had to leave."

Mandy sat quietly, allowing Rachel some space to collect her thoughts; then she asked, "Do you want to call him and tell him you left the stove on or something? Tell him you're sorry, but you'll come back if he's still there." Mandy wanted to help make it right. She felt sorry for Rachel and her failed dating attempts. She deserved better than this.

Rachel shook her head slowly. She felt humiliated and defeated. "No, I'm too embarrassed to talk to him. Mand, what is wrong with me?"

Mandy understood. She wouldn't call him back either if it were her. "Nothing's wrong with you. You're battling some bad demons. I'd have left too if it was me."

Rachel looked up at her best friend and shook her head. "I'm such a train wreck. Let's forget this ever happened tonight. I'll do better on the next date, but for right now, I'm starving. Let's get Thai at the Golden Lotus." Feeling a little bit better, she got off the bed, put her shoes and coat back on, and checked that the pencil was still standing, assuring her no one had entered the closet. The two girls hooked arms and left her room.

CHAPTER 6

Hadley's cab glided to a stop just as Bergen was climbing out of his Uber, the impressive GenSeq building towering above them. The glass walls reflected the glimmering stream of cars driving down Broadway. An intercom button on the right of two huge glass doors invited guests to reveal themselves before gaining entry.

Bergen confidently declared themselves as "Mr. and Mrs. Stanton," gaining access to the high-security lab. The security guard sitting behind a frosted glass desk buzzed the door open. Bergen and Hadley signed the log and put on the plastic visitor badges.

The guard shrugged, walked them to the elevator, pushed the up button, and slid his ID card in the slot. "Stop at level three for the receptionist. Have a good day," he said.

After the short ride, the doors opened, revealing the company name and logo—GenSeq—in royal blue letters. It stood out next to a matching blue-and-green helix wrapped around the figure of a man. On the opposite wall was a large screen TV, scrolling news stories about human microbiome studies, noteworthy scientists, and genomic medicine updates. Two photographs flanked the television: one of a balding man with a gray beard, brows, and mustache, the other, a scholarly-looking gentleman with a full head of silver hair and thin metal-rimmed glasses. Under each was their title: J. Craig Venter, PhD, and Francis S. Collins, MD, PhD.

"Mr. and Mrs. Stanton, I presuma?" the receptionist inquired with a thick Italian accent. She welcomed them and led them across the hall to a small but nicely appointed waiting room. Black leather couches were positioned against three of the four walls, with a square table nestled among them. On the walls were colorful pictures of DNA helices. The nutty smell of freshly brewed coffee permeated the air.

"I did some reading about DNA and chromosomes," Hadley said. "We should remember this from high school biology, but I've forgotten most of it. DNA is the molecule that carries the genetic instructions of all living things. Did you know," she asked, "that ninety-nine point nine percent of people's genes are identical? That remaining one-tenth of one percent is where we find human variation. We'll find out all kinds of things from this test. Aren't you excited?"

"Scared is more like it," Bergen replied. "You do realize, Hads, that we might find out some bad information too?" He raised his left eyebrow and gave her a worried look.

"Oh, honey. We're healthy as oxen," she replied and lightly punched him in the arm.

A distinguished-looking man dressed in brown trousers and a white lab coat, with Dr. Green monogrammed in red over the left top pocket, entered the room. He extended his hand to introduce himself. Bergen noticed the deep folds on his face. He shuddered ever so slightly and rose from his seat to offer a hearty handshake. Hadley stood and shook hands as well. She tried not to stare at the dark hairs growing out of the doctor's ears.

"I'm pleased you have chosen GenSeq for your sequencing. Our goal is to provide information to assist your physicians in achieving disease prevention and, if necessary, accurate personalized treatment strategies. Today you will meet with several different people," Dr. Green explained. "First, you will meet with Dr. Cornelia Rathdrum, our genetic counselor. Cornelia will explain the test, what we can and can't determine, and the ramifications of what you might learn."

Bergen stiffened. "If you are still interested in proceeding with the sequencing, you will meet briefly with Isabella, the receptionist who greeted you upon your arrival. Isabella will go over our release forms and collect payment. The fee for the test is $2,500. I think you'll agree, a far cry from the three billion dollars it cost a little more than ten years ago," the doctor said, shaking his head affirmatively. "Come. Let's walk."

Dr. Green continued, "Once the paperwork is complete, Isabella will escort you to our laboratory. Although there are several ways to collect the DNA, we prefer taking a blood sample over buccal tissue. After it's drawn, you are free to go. In approximately three to five weeks, we should have your results back. At that time, Dr. Rathdrum and I will meet with you to discuss the findings. Any questions so far?"

"Sounds pretty simple," Bergen replied. "Let's get started." *Let's get this over with.*

Dr. Green looked to Hadley for her agreement to proceed. Hadley didn't care for hairy men, especially those with bushy backs and shoulders. She couldn't stop looking at the doctor's ears and desperately wanted to trim them. Bergen turned to face her. "Should we proceed?"

Hadley nodded and gestured with her hands that she was ready.

Dr. Green took them down the hall to talk to the genetics counselor. It was outfitted with a wooden desk, a black swivel desk chair, two blue fabric chairs, and a tall potted palm. More pictures of DNA strands hung from the walls, along with Dr. Rathdrum's diplomas.

"Bright woman," Bergen whispered to his wife. The two sat patiently examining the helices when Dr. Rathdrum entered the room and introduced herself.

Bergen stood to shake her hand. Hadley remained seated and offered a polite hello. She was surprised how large the doctor was. *How can a medical professional let herself get so big?*

"How much do you know about genetic sequencing?" Dr. Rathdrum asked.

"I did a little review of DNA and chromosomes, but I don't know much about sequencing, to be honest," Hadley replied.

"Ditto," said her husband.

Dr. Rathdrum pulled a laminated sheet of paper from her desk drawer. She turned it in their direction and pointed to the pictures. "Genes are located on small thread-like structures called chromosomes. Usually, we have forty-six chromosomes in most cells. We inherit one set of twenty-three from each biological parent. Whole genome sequencing is the most advanced and looks at over six billion letters—A, C, T, and G—in the genome. Our testing identifies changes in chromosomes, genes, or proteins. These changes are referred to as mutations and can cause genetic conditions such as Down syndrome or cystic fibrosis. We can also use the sequence to detect a variant that increases your risk of heart attack, for example."

Bergen winced, breathing deeply to prepare himself for the impending hornet's nest.

Dr. Rathdrum continued, "The results could achieve early disease detection. The genetic sequencing test could confirm or rule out a genetic condition or help determine your chance of developing or passing on a genetic disorder. This test does not replace the annual physical, but it would give your primary physician insights to better inform future tests and treatments based on the identified risks. Of course, there are also benefits to doing the test, but also limitations. Before we proceed, you are not looking to confirm or deny a suspected illness, correct?"

"Correct," Hadley nodded, wanting to get on with it.

"A negative result," the doctor continued, "can mean a few things. For example, if you don't carry the gene for Huntington's, you don't ever need to worry or get tested for it. On the other hand, if you receive a positive result, you can be proactive about monitoring and treatment options. Of course, a positive result does not guarantee that you will get the symptoms or disease. Are you still planning on having more children?" she asked.

"Glory no." Hadley laughed. "I'm almost forty-eight!"

"I ask because, for those considering children, a positive result may influence that decision. Understand so far?" Dr. Rathdrum paused. They nodded.

Dr. Rathdrum opened an orange folder and removed a form outlining the sequencing procedure, the risks, and the consequences if positive results were determined. "As you know, DNA testing can diagnose a genetic condition and the risk of developing certain diseases later in life. Some of these diseases also reveal other family members' genetic risk."

Bergen stole a quick glance at Hadley. *Why is she so calm when I'm a bundle of nerves?*

"If you are at risk for a disease, there may not yet be available treatment options. And if you have an inherited condition, it cannot predict whether you'll have symptoms, how severe those symptoms will be, or the progression of the disease," Dr. Rathdrum explained. "Part of my job is to be sure you understand that you may learn something you weren't expecting."

Bergen stared blankly. His mind filled with endless chatter. *What will our DNA reveal?*

"If that were to happen, I will be here to help you understand the ramifications and how to deal with them. Once you receive your report, there is no going back." Bergen swallowed.

"You make it sound scary," Hadley said.

"We just want you to know the risks and benefits. Is there any specific concern either of you have? Do you have a family history of cancer, Alzheimer's, or Crohn's disease?"

"I don't know," Hadley said. "My parents died in a car wreck when I was seventeen."

"I'm so sorry," Dr. Rathdrum said.

"My uncle on my dad's side had cancer, but I don't know what kind. That's really all I know of my family history," Hadley said. "My grandparents also died when I was quite young."

"I'm pretty much clean as a whistle," Bergen said, feeling a little better. "No cancer or Alzheimer's yet. My father died of a stroke at sixty-five, but my mom is alive and kicking."

Dr. Rathburn explained, "I will be available should you have further questions. Shall we proceed with the testing then?" Hadley and Bergen squeezed each other's hands and nodded. They followed the counselor back to the receptionist. Isabella was ready with the paperwork.

"Okay, *allora*, you can go in the waiting room and take your time to read and sign these papers. There are additional forms: one for a biobank in Boston to share research results with, one for insurance, and another releasing the results to your primary care doctors. You don't have to agree to any of them." She handed them pens and forms and returned to her desk.

Once she was out of earshot, Bergen moved closer to his wife and placed his hands on her shoulders. "Hadley, are you sure this is something you want to do?"

She cocked her head to the side. His face was drawn with a deep wrinkle knitted between his eyebrows. "Wait, you don't? Aren't you even a little curious?" she asked, surprised.

"Well, I'm not so sure I want to know if I'm going to die soon," he replied, tapping one foot on the floor. "What if they find out I have some incurable disease?"

"Bergen, darling," Hadley said softly, pulling his chin down, "we are the quintessential pictures of good health."

Bergen dropped his hands from her shoulders and turned to retrieve two bottles of water from the small fridge. He unscrewed the cap from one and took a big mouthful.

Hadley was disappointed and saddened by his apprehension, but not enough to call off the test. He could back out if he wanted, but she was going through with it. "And, if they find out one of us has or will get cancer, we can be proactive and treat it, before it gets us."

Bergen looked at his wife. This was his anniversary gift. He didn't want to be ungrateful. *Man up*, he told himself, then gave her a half smile. "Okay, honey. Happy wife, happy life," he said, hoping he wouldn't regret it.

CHAPTER 7

Rachel stepped out of the shower and plucked a light blue towel from the hook. She started drying off, put her robe on, and went to her room. Then, an unexpected shock halted her.

"Help!" She gasped, barely able to find her voice. The urgency in her cry echoed through the hallway. "Help! Help!" she hollered again. She ran out of her room, colliding with Mandy in the hallway. "Call the police, Mandy. Lock your door. Hurry," Rachel demanded, trembling as she rushed into Mandy's room. She could feel her heart racing, pounding loudly in her ears, as the adrenaline pumped through her veins. Mandy rushed in, slammed the bedroom door closed, and locked it. Both girls stood paralyzed until Mandy quietly asked what was going on. "Someone's in my room, in my closet," Rachel said, hyperventilating.

"Rachel, what?" Mandy narrowed her gaze. "How could someone be in your room?"

"I don't know, but someone is in my closet," Rachel whispered. "The pencil. It's down."

"The pencil?" Mandy asked, confused how a pencil connects to an intruder.

Rachel tried to slow her breathing. "Yes, I always have a pencil leaned up against my closet door. If the pencil is down, someone has opened the closet door. When I got back from the shower, the pencil was on the floor and not propped against it."

"Good lord," Mandy said, letting out a long breath. "I was in your room. I put your shirt back that I borrowed last week." It was another episode of panic and fear that Mandy helped extinguish. Rachel bursted into tears.

"I had no idea about your pencil trick," Mandy said. "I didn't mean to scare you."

"You didn't do anything wrong, Mand. I'm so sorry." Rachel pulled the sash on her robe tight. "I'm supposed to be at Mom's for dinner in an hour. Can you just go back in my room with me and check the closet?" she asked sheepishly, embarrassed.

Mandy opened the closet door, pushed the hanging clothes aside, then shut the door. "All clear," she said and gave Rachel a hug.

—

"CHILI SMELLS GOOD, Mom," Rachel announced, entering her mom and aunt Claudette's three-story brownstone. She took off her coat and placed it on the bench by the front door.

Rachel's mom turned from the stove to greet her daughter. She gave her a hug, put her hands on her daughter's shoulders, and said, "Are you feeling okay? You look a little pale."

Rachel rolled her eyes. *Here we go again.* She put the cornbread she brought on the counter and then joined Aunt Claudette at the kitchen table, greeting her with a knowing smile. The table was a comfortable, safe place for Rachel. Her mom had brought it with her when she moved, and it still had the same pale-yellow cloth that Rachel grew up with. Rachel began to recite her well-worn line, but her brain took a left turn. "No, I'm not actually. My day kinda sucked. Just before coming here, I had another panic attack and scared Mandy to death."

Sadness fell across Gloria's face. It was hard to see her daughter in so much pain.

"The closet again," Rachel replied, looking away.

"The hangers?" her mom asked in a sympathetic tone. Her stomach churned.

"No, it was my silly pencil security system."

"What's wrong with the hangers?" her aunt asked. Claudette knew most of the details of Rachel's rape and the sequela but wasn't sure if this was an approachable topic.

"Sometimes Rachel hears hangers clinking against each other, and it reminds—"

"Okay, I understand. Sorry I asked." Silence, and then, "Let's eat. I'm starving."

Rachel served the chili and piled each with grated cheese and sour cream. Besides her mom and dad, Aunt Claudette was Rachel's only living relative. Even though she looked older than her sister, Claudette was four years younger. In her late twenties, she became a partner at her law firm and married the job, which left little room for marrying anyone else. Claudette and Rachel were very close, especially after her mom moved in. It was meant to be temporary, but Claudette discovered how much she enjoyed having a roommate and convinced Gloria to stay.

Growing up, Gloria was protective of Claudette. Now the roles were reversed. Gloria relished the support and treasured the bond of their sisterhood. Rachel was pleased they had each other. *Family is important*, she thought, *especially women sticking together.*

"Rachel, honey," her mom started, "how's it going with your psychiatrist? Are you finding her helpful?" Rachel stirred her chili and sipped her beer. She was usually prepared for her mom's line of questioning, but after the pencil scare, she couldn't dig any deeper. "We don't have to talk about it, but I'm always here if you want." Rachel gave a weak smile.

"I know, Mom. Thanks," she interjected. She regretted her decision to come to dinner. *On bad days like this, I should just stay home.* Rachel's mom had changed after the rape. She was overprotective and in a constant state of anxiety over Rachel's mental health.

"Hey, I have an idea," Claudette piped in. "How about if you replace your hangers with those felt ones, and instead of a pencil that could fall over on its own, install a sliding bolt lock?"

Rachel winked at her aunt. "Now, why am I paying all this money for a shrink when I have *you* to solve my problems?" she said. Rachel took her bowl to the stove for another serving. "Anyone else?" They shook their heads. Rachel recognized the familiar frown on her mother's face. "I had a date last week," she said. Rachel knew her mom needed to hear positive news.

"A date?" Gloria asked, her tone overshadowed with concern.

"Yes, I met him through my dating app."

Gloria looked warily at Claudette. "Well, that's great, I guess. You checked him out, right? He's not a social media stalker or some creepy guy, is he?"

Rachel rolled her eyes. *Damned if I do, damned if I don't. I can't do anything right.*

Claudette could feel the mounting tension. "That's great! How did it go?"

"His name's Will. He's nice. Good-looking too. We went to a pizza place in the village."

"Will you be seeing him again?" her mom asked.

I shouldn't have come. It's too much work pretending, putting on a show that I'm okay. "I don't know, Mom. I just met him." Rachel cleared her dishes. She stood at the sink. *If I tell Mom about my panic attacks, she gets all wigged out. If I tell her good news, she wigs me out.*

Once again Claudette jumped in to soften the growing friction. "Dessert, anyone? I made a cheesecake. Who wants a slice?"

"I gotta go, but thanks for dinner," Rachel said. She pecked them on the cheek and put on her coat. Just before leaving, she looked back at Claudette and raised her arms and shoulders as if surrendering. Claudette winked and blew her a kiss before Rachel closed the door.

CHAPTER 8

Hadley sat at her desk and turned on her MacBook. After scanning through emails, she opened Facebook. Betsy McLaughlin had posted another picture of her dachshund, Bill Williams was ranting about the president, again, Susan Adler had uploaded her vacation pictures from Tahiti, and Karen Billows had shared a YouTube video of a ten-year-old girl singing opera. Hadley shook her head. Why do my friends want their lives to be so transparent? Then her phone lit up with a FaceTime call from Sydney. She smiled. It was their daily check-in. "Hi, Sydney," she greeted, feeling a rush of warmth. For a moment Hadley drifted back to a simpler time, seeing herself, a younger version, hurrying out of the office each day to pick up her daughter from school. But as quickly as the memory came, it faded away. Hadley longed for the day when their conversations were not confined to screens and schedules but unfolded organically in the shared moments of their everyday lives. "Remember when I used to pick you up from school every day?" Hadley mused, her voice tinged with nostalgia. "I miss those days."

"I miss them too, Mom, but I'm glad we have FaceTime. That way, at least we can see each other," Sydney said softly. Then her eyes brightened as she recounted her day, her classes, her friends, and her plans for the weekend. Hadley listened intently, soaking up every detail, her heart swelling with pride at the vibrant young woman her daughter had become.

"I have great news, Syd," Hadley said excitedly. "Brook was accepted early to NYU's Tisch School. Isn't that dope?"

"Yeah, Mom. You told me last night. And you can't use that word. It doesn't sound right coming from you."

"Hmm," Hadley replied quietly. "I've been so excited, I guess I don't remember who I've told so far. Anyway, when will you be coming home for Christmas?"

"Saturday, the twenty-first. You're picking me up from the airport, remember?"

Hadley opened her day-timer and paged to December twenty-first. There in red pen was *pick up Syd, 3:52 p.m., United, JFK.*

"Of course, United, JFK," Hadley said, recovering quickly. "Okay, dear, I'd better let you get back to your schoolwork. Good luck on your finals. Kisses. I love you."

Sydney said, "I love you too, Mom," and they hung up.

Why am I forgetting everything? Probably too much on my plate, she thought. Then she typed "why am I so forgetful" into Google. A list of possible causes populated the screen: alcohol, medications, lack of sleep, underactive thyroid, stress, perimenopause, depression, dementia. Perimenopause seemed to be the only one that fit her. Hadley typed "forgetfulness, perimenopause." She sighed a breath of relief after reading Healthline's description: "If you're in perimenopause, you may be worried about lapses in your memory. But mild memory problems and a general fogginess are very common. They happen because your body is making less estrogen." She vowed to call Dr. Glassman and schedule an appointment.

—

WITH THE SNOW coming down faster than the forecast predicted, Hadley decided it was time to go. She had errands to run before heading home. After gathering her things, she pulled on her coat and gloves and headed for the elevator. "My purse," she said and headed back to the office. *If I didn't have my head screwed on, I'd probably forget that too,* she teased herself.

The snow blew horizontally down the street, sticking to the sides of the blue mailboxes and graffiti-covered yellow fire hydrants. Hadley drew circles in the snow with the toe of her shoe as she attempted to hail a cab. Everyone in Manhattan had the same idea: leave work early and beat the impending snowstorm. *Oh, forget it. I'll walk and get there faster.* Hadley turned left onto Fifty-Seventh and stopped in front of Bergdorf's. She stared at the holiday window display, tilting her head to the side. Something niggled at her. *But what is it? Why do I need to go in the store? A birthday gift, more La Mer hand cream, a new dress?* "It will probably come to me at two in the morning," she said, continuing on her way. Turning into Margaret's Market, Hadley walked amid the aisles, trying to recall what she had come for. She texted her husband:

> Need anything at the store?

Then, out of habit, grabbed a bottle of wine, *The New York Times* evening edition, oranges, Greek yogurt, and a bouquet of white lilies, red tulips, and Douglas fir branches. *This is festive. Am I supposed to pick up Bergen's shirts?* She decided it could wait.

Hadley arrived at her building just as Bergen pulled up in a cab. *Uncanny.*

"Hi, honey," he yelled, "let me help you with the bags."

Before he could, the doorman scooped them up and took them to the elevators.

Bergen and Hadley kissed hello and rode to the fifteenth floor. Once inside the apartment, Bergen removed his overcoat and took the bags to the kitchen. He plucked *The New York Times* and nervously twisted it. "Dr. Green called today," he called out.

"What did he say?" she called from the living room. Hadley dropped fish cubes into the aquarium, watching them swim in circles, sucking in pieces drifting to the bottom of the tank.

Bergen joined Hadley. "The results are back, and we should schedule an appointment."

Hadley felt excited and nervous. Bergen turned toward the picture window and nervously tapped the paper against his thigh. "I've been thinking about it a lot. I know this is important to you, and I don't want to disappoint you, but I'm not sure I'm going to hear my results."

Hadley ran her fingers along the keys of the piano. She exhaled loudly. She was irritated by Bergen's reticence. *Why's he being such a wuss?* she wondered. "I've said it before, dear. We are pictures of great health. I understand we might find a health issue, but that's precisely why we're doing the test. To be proactive. It's your choice, though. I can't make you go." She dropped the keyboard cover closed.

—

TWO WEEKS LATER, a young woman in a GenSeq lab coat greeted the Stantons. Akiko was a technician in Dr. Green's lab. "Isabella is out sick today. Dr. Green asked me to take you to the conference room. He and Dr. Rathdrum are waiting for you there," she said. Her shiny black ponytail bobbed as she walked down the hall. "In here." She opened a door leading to a conference room.

Bergen swallowed. The room seemed deliberately impersonal, no warm fabrics or pictures. The bland blinds were partially closed. The smell of cleaning agents burned his nose. The doctors were seated next to each other at an oval table. He tried to read their expressions.

Dr. Green stood and greeted the Stantons. Dr. Rathdrum remained seated and nodded. Bergen pulled out a chair for Hadley. "I see on your consents that you both passed on having your doctors with you here today. This will prevent any untoward outcomes from becoming a part of your medical chart and disqualifying you for health and life insurance," Dr. Green said.

Bergen cringed "untoward outcomes."

"Well," Dr. Green continued, "Dr. Rathdrum and I will review the genome test results with you. Would you like us to present them privately to each of you?" he asked.

"I think we're fine hearing each other's report," Bergen said.

"Yes, together," Hadley replied, the first hint of trepidation on her face.

"Quick question first," Bergen said, "do *you* think we should hear our reports in private?"

Dr. Green held up his hands. "This is a personal choice. I have no conviction either way."

Dr. Rathdrum sat with her arms propped on the table. Her head jutted forward like a chicken. She was dressed in a black blouse and skirt. She reminded the couple that results may include issues related to paternity, adoption, and heritable diseases.

"I understand," said Bergen. "We're fine together. Let's proceed."

"Okay then." Dr. Green opened the top file. "All right if we start with you, Mr. Stanton?"

Bergen took a deep breath and squeezed Hadley's hand. For a moment he pictured himself standing on an ice-covered lake. He watched as a thin blue crack raced away from his feet, jigging and jagging its way toward shore. "Yes, of course," he said, releasing his breath.

"This is a blueprint of your DNA. We want to emphasize that any identifiable mutation does not predict when, how long, or the severity of the related symptoms," Dr. Green explained.

"Understood," Bergen replied, nervously chewing the inside of his right cheek.

In a clinical manner, Dr. Green said, "We mapped every A, T, C, and G that make up the three billion base pairs of DNA. Everyone has two copies of each gene, one from the mother, one from the father. A dominant mutation, where only one copy is needed, predisposes us to certain illnesses or conditions. A recessive mutation requires two copies of the defective gene."

Dr. Green smiled. "Mr. Stanton, I'm happy to say you have a fairly clean bill of health."

Bergen sighed. The enormous weight on his shoulders was lifted.

"We found very little, which is a good thing. These reports are extensive. Today I will review our major findings. You will take your reports home with you. Of course, we can meet again to answer any questions you might have."

Bergen's anxiety eased. He was ready to hear the details of his report.

"You carry a variant that prevents weight gain from high-fat diets."

"Lucky you. That's a good mutation," Hadley said.

Bergen smiled and shrugged. *This isn't too bad after all.*

"I'm sure not news to you," continued the doctor, "but you have color vision deficiency, color blindness. Eight percent of the male population, an estimated two-hundred-fifty million people worldwide, are color blind. "

"That's why you have so much trouble matching your socks," Hadley teased.

The doctor continued, "Last, you are a carrier for cystic fibrosis."

Hadley sat up in her chair and gripped Bergen's hand firmly.

"That means you carry the gene, but you, yourself, do not, and will not, have the disease. Mrs. Stanton is not a carrier, so there is no risk to your children." Hadley relaxed into her chair. "Mrs. Stanton, even if you were a carrier, you'd know by now if your children had it. Symptoms show in most cases by age two."

"Wow, that's really it?" Bergen said with more energy. He squeezed Hadley's hand. The deep furrows between his eyes had disappeared, and his pulsing temples had relaxed. This is why she'd arranged the tests—to be confident about their futures. He could thank her later.

Dr. Rathdrum reiterated that the full 400-page report contained information including allergies, ancestry, food intolerances, and clinical insights into medications. She encouraged Bergen to read the report at his leisure and call with questions.

This day of reckoning had finally come. Bergen had dreaded it, yet he received the best news of his life. He would live to a ripe old age. Pictures of babysitting the grandchildren, cruising down the Danube with Hadley, and golfing into the twilight hours with his buddies flashed in his mind. "Is that it? I don't have any fatal diseases. You're sure?" he asked, dumbfounded. Both doctors smiled and nodded. Bergen was giddy with relief. He wanted to jump from his seat, hug the doctors, and kiss his wife.

"Coffee or water break?" Dr. Green offered.

Is he stalling on purpose? Hadley wondered.

"Not for me," Bergen answered, "but maybe a glass of champagne to celebrate."

"I'll have a glass of water," Hadley requested. Dr. Rathdrum took a bottle of water from the small refrigerator in the credenza. *Has Dr. Rathdrum done the genome test for her obesity?*

"If there are no more questions from you, Mr. Stanton, let's proceed with Mrs. Stanton's report," Dr. Green said. He picked up the folder. "Your testing has yielded different results."

Bergen looked up questioningly. He drew in two quick breaths.

"You have a variant on the EIF4E2 gene," the doctor said.

"What does that tell?" she asked nervously.

"It's associated with a 2.38-fold decrease in survival outcome for patients treated with the drugs for non-small cell lung cancer," the doctor explained.

Hadley's eyes widened. "Am I going to get lung cancer?" she asked. "I don't smoke."

"No, no, it just points out the survival rate with a certain treatment if you did. But be assured, you do not." Hadley sat back in her chair, her shoulders relaxing.

"Mrs. Stanton," Dr. Green said in a softer tone. He looked briefly at her husband. "The results do show that you have the London mutation, which causes the formation of abnormal amyloid precursor protein." Dr. Green gave Hadley time to digest. Hadley looked at him blankly. "This protein is attributable to early-onset familial Alzheimer's," he said in a slow, soft voice.

Hadley dropped her arms down onto the table, her gold bracelets tinkling as they hit. "That can't be," she contested, face pale and mouth agape. "Wait, you said familial. Neither of my parents had Alzheimer's. So, I should be fine?"

Bergen's mouth was dry. This is not what he expected. His world had shifted.

Dr. Rathdrum pulled her chair closer to Hadley's and put her hand on her arm. "You told me your parents died when you were seventeen. How old were they when they passed?"

Hadley sat stunned, pulling at the fibers on her mohair jacket. The air suddenly felt thick. Hadley felt numb. The room blurred as fear and anxiety washed over her.

Bergen broke the silence. "That can't be. Hadley's a VP of marketing. She's raising three kids, running galas. Her mind is a fortress. Can we test again, Doctor?" Bergen was nauseous.

"My parents were thirty-nine and forty-one when they died," Hadley answered robotically. "We wouldn't have known by then, right?" Like a deer in headlights, she stared out the window, rubbing her palms up and down her thighs.

"That's correct," Dr. Green replied. "Familial Alzheimer's disease, or FAD, is quite rare. It accounts for only two to three percent of all Alzheimer's cases. People diagnosed with it have generally had one parent with the disease. Siblings and children each have a fifty percent chance of inheriting it. It would be extremely rare for it to make a first-time appearance in a family."

It's not menopause, she told herself, then asked, "How long do I have?"

Dr. Green pursed his lips and looked at his lap. "On average, people live three to eleven years after the onset of symptoms, but some survive twenty years or longer."

As the doctor explained the disease's progressive nature, Hadley's mind flickered with anger and frustration. *This is unfair. I feel helpless.*

"Do you have living siblings?" Dr. Rathdrum inquired.

"Yes, she has an older brother, Mark," Bergen jumped in. "He's been working overseas with Exxon for the last ten years. They don't really stay in touch that much."

"To your knowledge, is he well? Has he had any signs of memory impairment?"

"Is he at risk, too?" Hadley asked, panic rising in her chest.

Bergen stood from his chair and paced the room. "What does the 'familial' part of this Alzheimer's really mean? And tell us about the 'early.' How early? She's only forty-seven."

"This type of Alzheimer's can begin as early as thirty-five," Dr. Green explained. "One of your parents probably carried the same mutation."

"But there's no sign of it, so that's a good thing, right?" Bergen pressed. Except there were signs. Twice, she'd forgotten to pay HOA fees, resulting in hefty penalties. Last month, she missed Tucker's science fair, and she frequently misplaced her wallet, keys, and sunglasses.

"Mr. Stanton, this is certainly not the kind of news you and your wife expected or wanted to hear. I'm very sorry. I suggest you take some time together and come back in the next few days. There is information, referrals for neurologists, and counseling we can offer."

Bergen was speechless, trying to digest this. He pinched his lips together with one hand and rubbed his forehead with the other. He abruptly reached for their coats and helped his wife up from her chair. "Let's go, Hadley." Bergen put his arms around her trembling shoulders as they walked silently toward the elevator. Dr. Green followed behind them.

As the elevator opened, Hadley turned. "You said children have a fifty percent chance of inheriting it," she said through tears. "Are you saying my children have a fifty percent chance?"

Dr. Green nodded affirmatively. "Yes, Mrs. Stanton, I'm sorry."

Hadley's body went limp. *The earthquake's aftershock*, Bergen thought, catching her.

Entering the cab, Bergen placed his warm hand on Hadley's knee. "Sweetie, it's going to be okay. I'm going to get you the best neurologist in the world, and we'll beat this thing."

Hadley turned away from Bergen and shredded her tissue into little pieces as they rode home, deep in thought. The journey home, once routine, now marked an uncertain path. *How can my memories be taken away? They're all I have left of my parents.* As a young girl, Hadley watched her grandmother carefully preserve every letter and greeting card, saved between pages of her cookbooks. And in her childhood house, family photos offered glimpses into their lives. *But I can't lose the image of my mother's smile or the tobacco smell of my father's aftershave.*

She leaned her cheek against the window's cold glass. Her mind, once an invaluable treasure, was now her betrayer.

"6927 Lex," the cabby said, pushing the meter button. As they entered the apartment, Hadley realized their home would never be the same. She went straight to their bedroom.

Bergen called out to the kids, then went into his study and shut the door. He pulled a whiskey bottle from the bookshelf and poured a full glass. Bergen downed the entire glass. He filled it again and thought he might throw up. He wanted to expunge the vile news from his body. He pulled his phone out and dialed his office. "Karilynn, hi, it's Bergen. Listen, cancel the rest of my appointments and calls for today. Something's come up. I won't be coming back in."

"Yes sir," Karilynn replied, cracking a piece of gum loudly. "Everything okay, boss?"

"Yeah, yeah, just gotta take care of something here at home. See you Monday." He hung up. Bergen called Rodney Bingham.

"Hey, old buddy," Rodney answered. "What's up, man?"

Trying to sound chipper, Bergen replied, "Hey, Rod, glad I caught you. Can you chat?"

"On my way to rounds, but I've got a minute. You okay?" Rodney asked. When he unconvincingly said he was fine, Rodney asked,

"What's going on? Hadley and the kids okay?"

He stammered, choking back tears, "Rod, we did this genetic testing thing. I didn't want to, but I did it for Hadley." The comradery of an old friend became a lifeline in the storm.

Rodney was silent on the line. Only bad news could follow.

"We got the results today. It's Hadley. She carries a genetic mutation that indicates she will develop early-onset Alzheimer's. She's only forty-seven." Gulping air, Bergen looked around his study. It looked the same, yet his world had changed. Everything had. He took another mouthful of whiskey. Rodney was stunned. He didn't know what to say.

Bergen pushed through the burning bile in his throat. The ground beneath him roiled and buckled. "You're a doctor, Rod. You must know someone you can call to get the best treatment," Bergen pleaded. "We'll go anywhere, pay anything."

"I do, I do," Rodney answered. "Letty, my sister-in-law, is a neurologist at Johns Hopkins. I can call her and ask for info. How's Hadley? Did you tell the kids?"

"She hasn't said a word since we left the doctor's," Bergen explained. "This test," he said bitterly, "was meant to improve our lifestyle, not determine our destiny."

"Hang in there, man," Rodney said. "I'll call Letty and get back to you after I get some info. Listen, if you want, I can switch my schedule and be there tomorrow. It will be okay." He immediately felt guilty for promising that. He knew everything was not going to end up just fine.

Bergen replied, "Thank you. We just need to get through this bombshell together. I'll talk to you later. You're the best," he said, ended the call, and finished his drink.

What am I going to do? Images of a sick Hadley crowded his thoughts. "Holy fuck!"

The door to his study clicked open. Hadley stood in fresh makeup, a cotton-candy pink turtleneck, and black slacks. "Get the kids. We're going out to dinner," she said, forcing a smile.

Bergen looked up at her in surprise. "Out for dinner?" he asked. "Now, tonight?"

"Of course. You don't expect me to wallow in self-pity, do you?" Disease or not, she had a duty as a mother and wife. She would be the pillar of strength. Instead of succumbing to despair, she would draw on an inner well of courage and face this with grace and dignity. Hadley gave him an eerie Stepford smile. "Anyway, by the time symptoms appear, they'll have found a cure. One caveat, though. No telling the kids. I mean it, not a word. Losing a parent is the worst thing a child can endure. I won't have them suffer any more than they have to. It's not fair."

Where did this stoic acceptance come from? "Not a word." He kissed her on the cheek.

The family walked a few blocks to their favorite Italian restaurant on Sixty-Second. Hadley laced her arm through Bergen's. They were regulars and quickly seated.

"Two glasses of the house Chardonnay, please," Bergen told the waiter.

"Make mine a double martini, Grey Goose, straight up, with two olives," Hadley said.

"Same for me, actually. Thanks," Bergen corrected. Brook stared at her phone. "No phones at the table, Brook." She looked up sheepishly and put it on her lap. She was the spitting image of her mother, except for a lopsided smile that was the result of a forceps birth. "So, how was your day today?" Bergen tried to keep things normal.

"My day was great!" she said. "Robbie asked me to the winter formal, I got an A on my trig test, and our substitute English teacher is a babe."

"Brooklynn," her mother cautioned, "young ladies shouldn't be saying things like that."

Brook dismissed the comment, reminding her she was almost eighteen.

"And your day, Tuck?" Bergen asked.

Tucker looked down at his lap. Unlike Brooklynn and her mother, Tucker looked nothing like his dad. His face was pudgy and round, and he had a weak chin. He was thirteen, that awkward age with braces, pimples, and facial hair, the texture of fuzz, trying desperately to grow above his upper lip. "I don't want to talk about it."

"Sorry, son, some days just suck!" Bergen said, patting him on the shoulder.

"Bergen," Hadley chastised, "let's not use such vulgar words."

"Sorry." He looked at her in solidarity, then gave her hand a squeeze.

"In English, we learned about anadromes," Tucker said. "Anybody know what they are?"

Hadley shook her head. Engaging in the present conversation was a struggle.

"They're mirror words. When read backward, they spell an entirely different word. Like denim or mined," he said.

"Cool," Brook said, "let's have a contest and see who can name the most."

"I'll win," Tucker said. "We learned them today. I'll go. Dog—God. You're next, Mom."

"You two play," Hadley said, blanking. "I'm tired and just want to enjoy my cocktail."

"Avid—diva," shot Tucker.

"Edit—tide," offered Brook.

"Repel—leper," Tucker said. Between bites of pasta, the kids peeled off word after word.

Hadley pushed the croutons in her Caesar salad from one side to the other. She wasn't hungry. "Another round please." Bergen pointed at their martini glasses as the waiter walked by. Tucker and Brook shared suspicious glances. "So, what's on everyone's schedule tomorrow?"

"I want to go shopping for my winter formal dress," Brook answered excitedly. "Mom, can you come with me?" Hadley stared blankly ahead. "Mom? Did you hear me?"

Hadley shook her head to clear the intrusive thoughts, then turned to her daughter. "Oh dear, no, I can't," she answered. "I have book club." *I'm not myself. Not joining the game and saying no to my kids. Do the kids know something is wrong?* Even working full-time, her MO was always to fully participate; she was Room Mom in their elementary school years, a meticulous birthday planner, and a cheerleader at ballet, T-ball games, and plays.

Brook put on her *poor me* sad face and whined, "*Moooom.*"

"I have to go, honey. We're discussing *The Hundred Foot Journey* by Richard Morais. It's a great story about an Indian kitchen and a French restaurant. Mrs. Connor, our group leader, suggested we follow up next month and do a field trip to a cooking class at the CIA."

"The CIA is teaching cooking now?" Tucker asked incredulously.

Hadley laughed. "The Culinary Institute of America. Some of the most famous New York chefs graduated from there. I'll be back from book club in time for dinner, but not to shop."

Disappointment crossed Brook's face. She jutted her bottom lip out and pouted. Unable to resist Brook's emotional appeal, Hadley placed her napkin on the table and met Brook's gaze with affection and resignation. "Oh all right," she said, her voice softening, "we can go shopping tomorrow." Missing book club wasn't the end of the world.

Brook's eyes lit up with gratitude and excitement. She leaned from her chair to give her mom a tight hug. "Oh, that just reminded me that Bergdorf called again. They want to know if you're going to pick up that handbag you ordered."

"Oh darn, I keep forgetting," Hadley said and looked at Bergen with fear in her eyes.

Bergen summoned the check. "Wait, can I get dessert?" Brook asked.

"Honey, we really shouldn't leave Bear Bear alone that long," Hadley replied.

"Not funny, Mom!" Tucker said. His face reddened.

"What?" Hadley questioned, putting her hand on her chest.

"What did I do?"

"Let's just go," Bergen replied and offered the waiter his credit card.

It started raining, and no one brought an umbrella. The large droplets came in sheets. Bergen dodged puddles collecting on the sidewalk, raising his hand for a cab for four.

On the ride home, dozens of incidents of Hadley's forgetfulness popped into his mind. *How could I not have noticed?* He looked in the rear-view mirror at Hadley. Her wet hair stuck to her cheeks and forehead, but she was beautiful. *How could someone so vibrant have this disease? It isn't fair.* It hadn't even been two hours since he'd called Rodney, but he checked his phone in case he'd missed something. Nothing. Waiting was excruciating. *What am I in for? What are we all in for?*

CHAPTER 9

As Rachel returned home from her mom's, the weight of the day clung to her, turning bedtime into a dreaded ordeal. She double-checked the bolts on the door, then went to her room. It had been a long day. The haunting fear and dread that plagued her for six years was relentless, refusing to release its grip. Bedtime was the worst, a time when shadows whispered of unseen terrors. When will the fear stop? Isn't six years of torment enough?

Clink. Clink. The sound set Rachel's heart racing, and she bolted upright, a primal instinct. She heard it again. Clink. Clink. *Who's there?* She opened her mouth, but the words made no sound, and the closet door slid open. She smelled something sweet, like cloves. She scooted to the side of the bed, her back pressed up against the wall. Her bed felt wet, sticky. Tears streamed down her face. She tried to scoot off the side, to hide under her bed, but he grabbed her, his face hot and dark and pressed so close to hers. She gasped for air.

Suddenly, the sound roared out of her, and she thrashed free. She slumped to the floor, yelling, "Help!" The tiny hairs on her arms and neck stood up. Rachel shivered under her sweat.

"Rachel!" Mandy shook her as Rachel hit her.

"Don't touch me. Get off," Rachel screamed, trapped between dreams and reality.

"Rachel, look at me, it's Mandy. You're okay. You're in our

apartment. It's me, Mandy."

Rachel looked at her with excruciating panic. Her head jerked wildly, and her eyes scanned the room. "God, please stop this," Rachel begged, pounding her fists on the floor. "I can't take it anymore." Rachel sobbed, holding her knees to her chest. "I'm so scared to go to sleep. I'm going crazy. These fucking nightmares are just as bad as the rape. They're getting worse. They're reenactments." She gagged from the taste of blood in her mouth—she'd bitten her lip. Mandy reached for a Kleenex and pressed it to her mouth.

"Let's try one of the relaxation things you learned," Mandy suggested.

"It won't help. It never does," Rachel shot back. "Nothing helps. I wish I was dead!"

Mandy sat quietly. "I'll make you some tea," she finally said and left the room. Rachel knew this pattern all too well. Friends and family tried to help, but she pushed them away.

—

RACHEL ARRIVED A few minutes early for her weekly appointment with Monica. She hoped that the lady who came each week at the same time would be there again. Albeit brief, their waiting room conversations were enjoyable. There was something soothing about her, something refined and kind. Rachel entered the brownstone and smiled. "Hi, Hadley," she said. "We have to stop meeting like this." She chuckled.

Hadley put down her travel magazine. "Hi," she replied, oblivious.

"You know it's funny, but I look forward to seeing you," Rachel said. "It makes coming for my sessions a little more bearable."

Hadley looked at her watch. "Do you always come Tuesdays at four?" she asked.

Rachel nodded affirmatively and took a seat. Hadley acted like she'd never seen Rachel before. "I've been coming since the fall." She leaned closer. "Do you like your shrink?"

Hadley shrugged. "He's okay. I guess I'm not sure what I'm supposed to get out of these appointments, but he's nice and lets me talk about whatever I want. So, I come." Hadley took her lipstick from her handbag and put on a fresh coat.

Rachel noticed that the tip of her lipstick was rounded and smooth. She applied her lipstick that way too. She remembered reading in some fashion magazine that different lipstick tip shapes revealed one's personality. Rounded and smooth meant you loved taking care of friends, your family is the most important thing in your life, you take pride in artsy things like music and writing, and you've probably never gotten a speeding ticket. "You're very pretty," Rachel said. "You don't look like you could even have any problems."

Hadley laughed. "You too."

Monica opened her office door and motioned Rachel to join her.

"Bye." Rachel grabbed her backpack and walked into the office. She plopped down in her usual spot on the couch. Typically, Rachel started each session with an update, but today was different. Rachel didn't want to review her disastrous week.

"Rachel, you seem upset today," the doctor said. Rachel bit her nails and stared blankly.

"Rachel?" The two sat quietly for many seconds. "Did you have a difficult week?"

"Difficult would be putting it mildly. Horrendous or dreadful is more like it."

Monica had a warm, inviting smile. She never rushed or pressured Rachel. Rachel liked that about her. She felt safe with her.

"Three nights in a row of nightmares, another screwed-up first date, and then my phone fell in the toilet. Oh, and I saw my dad at the mall. The nightmares, though, take first prize."

"I know the nightmares must be disturbing," Monica commented. "Each person heals in their own way. There are no hard-and-fast rules, but we can work toward your recovery if you're willing. Recovery is a slow process, and as you're experiencing, it doesn't come easily or without pain." Rachel huffed. "Recovery isn't going to erase what happened, but it can help you move on and enjoy your life," the doctor assured her. "The physical pain has healed, but you need to continue working on the emotional pain. With the nightmares, I'm concerned you're not getting quality sleep."

Rachel nodded. "I get some sleep, but I could definitely use a little more."

"Keeping your bedroom cool and not watching television right before bed might help. I'd also suggest staying away from any caffeine after 3 p.m. and getting at least thirty minutes of exercise each day," Monica continued.

"You're right. I don't exercise, although I know I should, and I do watch TV in bed."

"Rachel, I'm sure this is preaching to the choir, but many people with PTSD feel they need to be on guard to protect themselves from danger. Since your rape occurred in your bedroom while sleeping, difficulty falling asleep or waking in the night, especially when you hear a noise, can occur. It becomes a vicious cycle; you worry about being able to fall asleep. The key will be to manage your anxiety. I can give you suggestions for habits and apps that may help. Let's try one now," Monica said. Rachel knew the key to recovery was through acceptance, but images, smells, and sounds were still difficult for her. *Relaxation exercises will bring up unwanted images.* Up until now, she fought the images and pushed them away. They controlled her, which meant *he* controlled her life. But she was ready to move on. She closed her eyes.

For five minutes, Monica led Rachel through a guided relaxation exercise. "Don't forget to breathe in and out slowly and stay focused on the beach I'm describing. I want you to smell the salt air and feel the sand between your toes. If other thoughts interfere, bring your awareness back to the beginning, and we can start again," the doctor said in a slow, rhythmic voice.

Rachel was in a relaxed state. Her breathing had slowed, and her hands rested lightly on her lap. "I want you to take your time coming back here to me in the office. When you're ready, you can walk slowly away from the beach and open your eyes. This is what relaxation feels like. Your ultimate goal is to be able to bring yourself back to this state of relaxation yourself."

With fifteen minutes left, the doctor wanted to address Rachel's latest failed date. "I don't think we need to spend time on that. I wasn't really into him anyway," she said. "It's kind of weird, but the whole time I was on the date, I kept thinking of Will, the guy I ran out on."

Monica encouraged, "Break down the aspects of your date with Will. Reframe the situation with the aftershave smell. Think about how you could have handled those thoughts."

"Since it was the first date, I wasn't going to tell him why his aftershave bothered me. I should have just excused myself to regroup. Practice mindfulness instead of picturing that asshole. Then," Rachel thought, "I could try the grounding exercises you taught me."

"Great job, Rachel. You are right on track. What grounding techniques would you use?"

"I would try to ground myself using my senses," Rachel answered. "Since the aftershave triggered me, I could inhale the smell of pizza coming from the kitchen. You also taught me to hold or chew on a piece of ice, so I guess, when I got back to my seat, I could do that. I could focus on visuals, like tablecloths and flowers—and maybe how cute Will is. Man, I wish I could go back to that night and redo it."

"We only have a few minutes left, but I don't want to ignore your comment about seeing your father. What happened?"

Rachel sat up straight. "I went to the food court on my break for lunch. I was about to order my usual at the Chinese place when I saw him at the burger stand. I froze, literally. I mean, I couldn't move. He picked up his order and sat down at a table. I don't think he saw me." Monica remained silent. "What? Why are you looking at me like that?" Rachel asked.

"Do you feel like I'm looking at you differently than I usually do?" the doctor asked.

Rachel rolled her eyes. "Let's not add paranoia to my list of problems."

Monica glanced at the clock, removing her glasses. "Our time is up. I think we should talk more about your father next week. Practice the relaxation exercises and try to incorporate healthy sleep habits into your lifestyle. I'll see you next Tuesday at four."

Rachel and Hadley exited their sessions at the same time. They smiled in solidarity. Rachel was curious why this woman, who outwardly appeared so put together, needed to see a psychiatrist.

It was rush hour, and it would be difficult to hail a cab. A half dozen rushed by with their lights off, all occupied. Hadley stepped off the curb and extended her arm. A green Prius slowed and pulled up beside her. The man inside put his passenger window down and offered them a ride. It was a gypsy cab. Hadley took Rachel's arm and walked in the opposite direction of the car. Across the street was a legitimate cab with its light on. "I'm going downtown," Hadley said. "Do you want to share a cab?" Rachel nodded, and they climbed into the back seat.

Rachel was nervous, quiet. She had never met anyone like Hadley before. "Are you in school, or do you work?" Hadley asked Rachel.

"I'm taking a break from school and working in retail. It's temporary, and I plan to go back to school," Rachel added, in case Hadley was judgmental. "And do you work?"

"I'm in marketing," Hadley answered. "I did an internship in business school and have been at the same company ever since." Hadley laughed. "I'm the chief marketing officer for a large, international law firm in Manhattan. "Wow. It's been twenty-five years. Tempus fugit."

"You married?" Rachel asked, glancing at her emerald and diamond ring.

"I am, to the love of my life. We've been married twenty-two years and have three wonderful children." She showed Rachel photos on her phone.

It's nice she's so proud of her family. Round, smooth lipstick, she reminded herself.

The usual fifteen-minute ride from the doctor's office was longer due to traffic. Rachel didn't mind. Hadley was interesting. With her nerves abated, she felt comfortable. Hadley discussed her charity work, rooftop garden, and dog-rescue volunteer work. Rachel perked up. "I love dogs. I wish I could have one, but my apartment is small. Do you have one?" she asked.

Hadley showed a photo. "This is Bear Bear," she said. "He's gone over the rainbow bridge. We miss him terribly. Someone dumped a bag of puppies into a dumpster. A kind soul heard them whimpering and took them to a rescue. That's where we got him. They have so many wonderful dogs looking for their forever home. Maybe you could get a small dog?"

Rachel imagined life with a dog. "It's a great idea, but I don't make a lot of money. I don't think I can afford it."

Hadley patted Rachel on the thigh. "My dear, I have just the answer. Pooch Rescue, where I volunteer, has a special program for senior dogs. They'll pay the vet bills for life." Rachel crinkled her nose. She really didn't want an *old* dog. Hadley could see the aversion. "A senior is any dog six and over."

Rachel nodded. *Six isn't too bad.*

"That's only forty-two in people years. Almost my age," Hadley said and winked. "Why don't you come with me sometime? I go every other Saturday. No pressure to adopt, just look."

"I'd like that," Rachel said. It felt good to think about something other than her problems. "Do you want to meet for coffee before next week's doctor's appointment to plan our field trip?"

The cab pulled up to Hadley's building. "Yes, let's. Here's my info."

They exchanged numbers. "Can I help pay?"

"No dear, that's sweet of you. I'll see you next week." Rachel exited the cab.

Hadley waved goodbye to her new friend. She inserted her credit card in the terminal. "It's sad, don't you think?" she said, "That a woman that young needs to see a psychiatrist?"

Rachel climbed the stairs two at a time. On the couch, she searched Pooch Rescue. On the *ADOPT ME* tab were questions: Who is the primary caregiver? How much time can you spend? Dog-friendly neighborhood? Energy level? Rachel clicked *I Agree* and *Adopt a Senior*. Rachel read the list. "'Princess, eight years old, spayed female. Sweet and friendly, loves to snuggle.' She's the one!"

CHAPTER 10

"I'm going to ask you a series of questions. Do your best and try not to get flustered. If you're ready, we'll begin. What is your name?" Dr. Boswell asked.

"Hadley Beaman Stanton." She hated numbskull questions. *Like I don't know my name?*

Dr. Boswell continued, "What is your birth date?"

"April fifteenth, 1967, a tax return baby."

"The last four numbers of your social security number?"

"4536."

"Can you tell me your mother's birth date?" Dr. Boswell asked.

"Of course," Hadley replied, "April tenth, 1938."

"What is the date today?"

"It's, um, December fifteenth or fourteenth. Well, it's Wednesday," she answered.

"And the year?" the doctor asked.

"2014," Hadley said somewhat testily.

"Can you tell me what you had for dinner last night?"

Hadley hesitated. "Grilled salmon and a salad," she lied. *This is something I would eat.*

"Okay, now I'm going to tell you three things, Mrs. Stanton," Dr. Boswell said. "I want you to remember them. I'm going to ask you to repeat them in five minutes."

"Okay," said Hadley.

"Ball, pine tree, crib. Now repeat them please."

"Ball, pine tree, crib." *Ball, pine tree, crib. Ball, pine tree, crib.*

Dr. Boswell instructed Hadley to draw a clock at 9:00. Hadley drew a circle and labeled the numbers. "Put hands on the clock," the doctor asked. Twitching her leg, Hadley did so.

The interview continued for forty-five minutes. Dr. Boswell asked Hadley to name the three items, list the last four presidents, and do math computations. When she finished, Hadley asked to invite her husband in to join them. Dr. Boswell went to grab him.

Do I remember the three items? she wondered. She looked around at the furnishings for clues. It reminded her of doctors' offices from the sixties: apricot-colored curtains, brown-and-orange upholstered chairs, a simple pine desk set, and a New York City poster. Dr. Boswell and Bergen entered the room and took their seats. Bergen smiled at Hadley, quelling her angst.

"Mr. and Mrs. Stanton, I completed the mental status exam," Dr. Boswell said. Hadley squeezed Bergen's hand. "The maximum score is thirty. You did quite well with a twenty-three."

"What does that indicate?" Bergen asked. *Sixty-five percent? Doesn't sound "quite well."*

"A twenty-three suggests mild impairment," she said.

"I don't know if I should be relieved or not. What did I get wrong? Was it the math?"

Dr. Boswell opened her folder and pushed the drawing across the desk. Hadley and Bergen looked curiously. The hands did not join in the center and were instead placed haphazardly across the face of the clock. "I drew that?" Hadley asked incredulously.

"Yes," the doctor replied.

"But I know how to draw a clock," Hadley protested. "Let me do it again. I was distracted before, trying to remember the three items."

"Mrs. Stanton, I understand how difficult this must be for you. Your genetic testing has already told us you do have FAD. Our chief goals are to monitor and manage your symptoms, slow its progression, and offer resources and support. Cognitive abilities can be slowly lost over time. The clock drawing is just one example. It looks at spatial orientation."

Hadley clutched the folds in her skirt, then buried her face in Bergen's shoulder. "I'm so scared," she said, tears running with mascara. She looked up beseechingly. "How can I not be able to draw a clock? Did I at least remember the three items correctly?" she asked the neurologist.

Dr. Boswell closed her eyes and shook her head. "We'll do some more tests that our manager will help you schedule. Here is the prescription for the medicines we discussed earlier."

"But everyone forgets things," Hadley protested. "If I told you three objects, do you think you would remember them five minutes later?" she asked, looking sadly at her husband.

Bergen looked away. Dr. Boswell loved her job, but rarely did she have good news for patients. "Have you contacted the Alzheimer's Association? You may find them quite helpful."

Bergen shifted in his chair, feeling guilty that he hadn't reached out to them. "We've been a little overwhelmed," he said. "And we haven't told the children yet."

"Have you seen the psychiatrist the team recommended?" she asked Hadley.

"Yes, I've seen him a few traits. Trimes, I mean times," Hadley answered, flustered. "But I'm not sure what he can do to help me." She was independent, self-reliant, a fighter, not one to curl up in a ball and give up. "I don't think the psychiatrist can answer the questions I have."

Dr. Boswell tilted her head. Hadley looked away, uncomfortable. The air felt heavy. Bergen knew what questions she had. He had them too. "Go on, honey. She's here to help."

"Well, pardon my French, but shit. I want to know things like how long I'll live, when I'll forget who I am, or how to bathe myself." Hadley's face reddened. "I'm sorry. I'm tired. I guess we should go," she said, standing up and pushing her chair away.

Dr. Boswell put her hand on Hadley's arm. "Mrs. Stanton, you are a brave woman. No one will deny what a terrible hand you've been dealt. We all want to help you. I hope Dr. Kopple will help you manage your feelings. If you're scared or worried, share that with him. As your neurologist, I will try to answer clinical questions, but I don't know the exact timeline of the disease. Each patient is unique and progresses differently."

Wide-eyed, Bergen shook his head. "I don't know the value in discussing average life expectancy. I read many people live beyond twenty years from diagnosis, so let's use that as our gauge," he said, desperate not to hear a death sentence. "I also read that women and people without complicating health factors live longer than the average person. It seems to me, since we caught this early and she's on the medicine, she'll beat the twenty-year mark. Hadley's always been top of her game."

Hadley looked into Bergen's eyes. *My cheerleader.*

"I think it's a good approach to be positive, but I also want you both to be properly prepared should symptoms progress more rapidly. Have you thought about cutting back or leaving your job?" the doctor asked. "Maybe spend more time with the family?"

Hadley knew it was time. She wanted to go out a successful businesswoman, not peter out as a failure. Hadley nodded sadly, acknowledging that the doctor was right.

"We will continue to assess your symptoms and add support as needed. For now, continue the medications. These will help slow or delay the symptoms. And I suggest you get in contact with the Alzheimer's Association," Dr. Boswell instructed. "I'll see you in three months. If you have concerns or notice changes with your memory or mood, feel free to call me."

—

HADLEY AND BERGEN arrived home to find Mariah, their longtime housekeeper, scrubbing the kitchen floor. The sharp, chemical smell of ammonia took Hadley back to summer camp. Deep-seated memories came easily to her. It was the more recent ones that quickly slipped away.

"Christ, Mariah, can't you use a different cleaning solution?" Hadley said.

Mariah jerked upward. It was unusual for Hadley to use such an offensive tone with her. "I'm sorry, Mrs. Hadley," Mariah replied. "I'll get a different one." Hadley thanked her, then abruptly left the kitchen. Mariah looked at Bergen. Hadley had frightened her. *Is she okay?*

"I'm sorry. She's got a lot on her mind right now," Bergen said.

"It's okay, it was just so unlike her. Can I share something?" Bergen nodded. "Today when I was putting away the laundry, I found Mrs. Hadley's phone in her underwear drawer. Last week she kept asking me the same questions repeatedly about my husband, and come to think of it, she's actually the one who bought that cleaner. Is everything okay, Mr. Bergen?"

"Have a seat, Mariah," Bergen said. "There's something you should know."

While Bergen was in the kitchen, Hadley tiptoed to Bergen's briefcase. Looking around like a kid sneaking cookies before dinner, she took his computer into the office and closed the door. *What's that damn password?* She punched in Bergen's birthday, her birthday, and their anniversary. None worked. Feeling urgency, Hadley opened the door slightly and hollered into the hall, "Bergen, I need to renew my library books online. What's your password, honey?"

"Why don't you use your computer?" he shouted from the kitchen.

Hadley lied, "I left it at work." Truthfully, she'd forgotten where she left it.

"It's Hadley4ever," he called to her. "The four is a number, not a word."

She shut the door and returned to her desk. Fearful she would forget, she wrote it down and typed it in. The computer came to life.

Hadley searched *assisted suicide* and clicked on a heading about dying with dignity. She read about the current legislation and states that legalized it. Several links for Dr. Jack Kevorkian interviews popped up. Hadley scrolled through the choices and chose one titled "Dr. Death." Worried that her husband or Mariah might hear the video, she used headphones. She pressed play.

She knew about Kevorkian and his activist work with the terminally ill but was surprised to learn he was an accomplished composer, instrumentalist, author, and painter. She was glued to the screen. In one interview, the host challenged the doctor: Are you playing God?

Hadley shook her head. *They don't understand. I may need this kind of help in the end.*

As Bergen left Mariah, he cursed the genome procedure. The outcome would be the same, but months of ignorance would have been bliss. He was angry that his wife opened Pandora's box, changing their lives forever. Bergen pushed the ugly thoughts away and decided to focus on work. He went to retrieve his computer.

Bergen opened the office. Hadley sat with her back to the door. He glanced at the screen, recognizing the anchor. "What are you watching?" Hadley jumped and slammed the laptop closed. She pulled the headphones out of her ears and turned to face him.

"You scared me," she exclaimed, panning the room and hallway for signs of the kids or Mariah. "Bergen, we need to talk," Hadley said in a subdued tone. "Can you shut the door?"

Bergen felt shackled. *We need to talk? This is never good.*

"I'm scared, Bergen." She took his hand. "It's been a month, and we haven't really talked about what's going to happen."

Bergen closed the door and pulled up a chair. She rubbed her hand on his cheek. His stubble was rough but comforting. Hadley preferred his sexy morning shadow to clean-shaven.

"I know, my love," he said. "I never quite know where to begin." His face got hot as guilt and incompetence flowed through him.

Bergen glanced out the large picture window. It was easier to talk if he didn't look into Hadley's eyes. "I talked to Frank Grisby about our will. He said it all looks in order. If I die before you—"

Hadley laughed. "We both know that's not going to happen."

"Hadley, sweetheart, please," Bergen implored, "if I die before you, everything is left to you. If you go before me, I manage our estate. If we both pass together, everything is left to the kids. Everything is taken care of." Hadley's heart ached.

"Not quite everything," she said. "The life expectancy for my kind of Alzheimer's is less than five years. It's more rapidly progressive than other dementias." She pictured Bergen at Brook's graduation, his arm around his new wife. She imagined Tucker giving his new mommy a kiss goodnight. And she saw the mantle embellished with family photos of the grandchildren sitting on the new Mrs. Stanton's lap. Hadley shuddered, biting down hard on her lower lip. She was firm in her resolve: she would not be an albatross to her family. "I want the remaining years to be quality," she said. "I don't want to become a burden. It's not about the will, Bergen. It's about having a plan before I lack decision-making capabilities. It's important to me. Please."

"Hadley, you will never, ever be a burden," Bergen replied, wiping his eyes. He felt desperate. Talking just aggravated his feelings of helplessness. He wanted to fix it.

"I will, Bergen, and you know it. I refuse to become a feeble vessel, being spoon-fed. I don't want that for me, or for you and the kids. That's not the memory I want to leave you with."

Bergen practically fell from his chair and knelt in front of his wife. He took both her hands in his and buried his face amid the silky folds of her dress. Hadley stroked his hair softly, then lifted his face up to meet her eyes. "My darling, I've been reading about assisted suicide."

Bergen jerked his head away, his eyebrows knitting deeply together. "Are you serious? We are *not* doing that," he insisted. He couldn't breathe.

"I am, Bergen," Hadley answered softly but resolutely, "and I'll need your help." She closed her eyes. "If I had a different terminal disease, like cancer, I'd know when enough was enough and could do it myself. The problem with dementia is, by the time enough comes around, I won't know it, and I won't be able to do anything about it. I need you, Bergen, to help me die with dignity. It's going to happen faster than you think. It already is."

"In sickness and in health," he said, his tone mixed with anger and grief. "I don't think it's something I can do," he continued, his voice barely audible. "Besides, it's illegal. And if I got caught, what about the kids? They'd lose both their parents."

"It's legal in D.C.. When you think the time is right, we could go there, just you and me. Our last adventure," Hadley said quietly, reaching out to her husband.

Twisting his wedding band around on his finger, Bergen slowly shook his head. "Even if I morally agreed to it, I don't think I could, physically, Hads. I love you too much," he said. Bergen felt broken; his arms hung limply by his side.

"Then love me in sickness too and help me die with some self-respect," Hadley pleaded.

They were so young. Their family was so young. They should be planning their next dinner party or where to go on their family vacation. Not Hadley's death. "I'll think about it," he said, but he knew in his heart that he would never agree to it.

CHAPTER 11

Rachel dressed quickly. It was Saturday, and their visit to the shelter had finally come. She swallowed her last few sips of coffee and left the apartment.

Rachel stood on the corner and blew warm air into her hands. Thick, low clouds hung overhead. At precisely 9:30 a.m., Hadley pulled up. She tooted the horn and waved to Rachel.

"Good morning. Looks like snow," Rachel said as she climbed into the old Volvo.

"Yes, I heard the forecast. We're supposed to get two or three inches. That's why I brought this old clunker. My husband has a sport's car. I don't trust it in the snow."

"Tell me more about the Rescue," Rachel said. "Where do they get most of their dogs?"

"Pooch Rescue is on a call list for dogs that land in kill shelters. If we can't get that breed's rescue organization to go, we'll pick up the dog," Hadley explained.

"Kill shelter?" Rachel asked, wincing. "Sounds terrible."

Hadley explained, "Shelters are where stray, lost, abandoned, or surrendered animals end up, and some have a policy or law that prohibits euthanizing the animal. Kill shelters, though, have a time limit on the animal's stay and will euthanize them to make space for new ones."

Rachel put her hand to her mouth. "Oh my gosh. That's so sad," she said, shocked.

"Some dogs come from puppy mills, where dogs are bred for profit. When females can no longer breed, they are turned in. Sometimes a tearful owner brings a beloved pet to a shelter because they are moving. Others can no longer care for an animal."

Hadley knows her stuff, Rachel thought.

Twenty minutes later they drove through a large stone arch and entered the Pooch Rescue. Four-foot-high metal crates with long runs lined the yard. In each were water and food bowls, a bed, and doggie toys. The enclosures were empty. Rachel looked around for someone who might be in charge. "It looks like a dog ghost town," Rachel said.

Suddenly, a pack of fifteen or more dogs appeared on a hill and sprinted toward the guests. The deafening sound of barking was music to Rachel's ears.

"Milo, Cassidy, Lucky, *come*," the handler commanded. A young woman dressed in jeans, a puffer jacket, and rubber boots rounded the bend. "Milo may jump, but they're friendly."

The German shepherd won the race to greet his new friends. "This is Sergeant," Hadley said, reaching to pat the dog. The dog wagged his bushy brown tail and wiggled his large ears.

The trainer caught up. "Milo, get down," she scolded as the black Lab jumped on Hadley.

"It's okay, Meghan. Milo just missed me. But who do we have here?" Hadley pointed at the small Yorkshire terrier sniffing her shoes.

"That's Pudding. An owner turned her in last week. She has seizures."

Rachel was surprised and saddened. She looked from one to the next. *Maybe Princess has been adopted. Who wouldn't want to take her home?*

Meghan recognized Rachel's face. "Hadley told us you are interested in Princess, so we have her in the grooming room for a bath." Rachel relaxed. "Allow me to introduce them. The Chihuahua is Taco, this one is Jack, and this shaggy one is Lucky. We don't know what mixture of breeds he is. We found him stuck on a highway and named him Lucky."

They passed through the play yard, complete with a big truck tire, stuffed animals, balls, an empty plastic wading pool, and a rope toy suspended from an oak tree. "This is where they stay most of the day," Hadley explained. "They eat in their crates then come to play. Many of these dogs, like Biscuit here, have been abused and are shy or aggressive. Part of my work is to help them socialize." Hadley closed the gate behind her after the last pup entered the yard.

Rachel felt fluttering in her stomach. It sickened her to think Princess might have been abused. *Humans are cruel enough to each other. Why do we need to treat animals that way too?*

"An elderly couple dropped Princess off. They moved to a residential facility. If you do take her, I'm sure they'd enjoy a visit every now and then—if you're open to it," Meghan said.

Rachel gently stroked Biscuit's head. "Of course," she said, "I'd be happy to."

"And here's one of my boys," Meghan exclaimed, patting an elderly Dalmatian on the back. "Hero lived at a firehouse in upstate New York. He's almost one-hundred-percent blind now, so they couldn't keep him. I saw him on Craigslist and nabbed him. And this," she continued, "is Bella, a Portuguese water dog, formerly a stray, Penny, a mutt who was found in a Walmart parking lot, and Dufus, a bloodhound from a shelter. They're my family," Meghan said, beaming with pride. "Hey, what do you say we go meet Princess?"

The grooming room resembled a large bathroom. In it were three big porcelain tubs with attached spray and heat hoses, a few four-foot-high tables, hooks with a dozen or so assorted colored leashes, and two brown dog beds in the corner. A musty smell permeated the air. Princess was tethered to one of the tables in the grooming room. Her coat was silky and shimmering. Her hazelnut eyes, angular muzzle, and large hairy paws made her look like a show dog. "This is Rachel. She came to meet Princess," Meghan said to the handler. The volunteer unclipped the leash and placed the squirming spaniel on the floor.

Rachel knelt and slowly put out her hand. "Hi there, Princess," she said in a gentle voice. Princess wagged her tail and came to sniff Rachel's hand. "Oh, she's perfect."

Hadley smiled. It felt good to introduce Rachel to the Rescue. Perhaps a dog could help with whatever has her visiting a psychiatrist. Meghan described, "English cocker spaniels are cheerful, affectionate, and highly educable, and they love to swim and retrieve. Princess is a little overweight because her previous owners didn't walk her as much as they should have. Princess is eight. Most cockers live to be twelve to fifteen, so you'll have plenty of years ahead together. At Pooch Rescue, we are very supportive of older dogs. Most people tend to adopt the younger ones. To offer encouragement, we guarantee all medical bills are paid throughout her life. You don't need our approval to get care. Just submit the invoices, and we'll reimburse you."

Rachel nodded. "Yes, that's what Hadley told me. It's so generous of you." Rachel looked from Meghan to Hadley and then down at Princess. Suddenly, she thought, *Will I be a good fit? My apartment is small, I have no yard, and she'd be home all alone while I work.*

Hadley noticed Rachel picking at her nails, and the smile had disappeared from her face. Hadley wanted to help. "Rachel, it would make me happy if you would accept Princess as my gift to you. I can get you set up with all the things you'll need." Rachel's face brightened. She reached in her coat pocket and pulled out the new pink collar she bought for Princess. After the paperwork, Princess and Rachel spent the next hour getting to know each other while Hadley went about her volunteer duties.

Paw prints of all sizes and shapes decorated the fresh layer of powder on the ground. It was comforting to know the once abandoned dogs were now loved and having fun in the snow. When it was time to go, Rachel handed Meghan an envelope. "A small donation," she said. "You do such good work here." Just as Rachel, Hadley, and Princess got to their car, a little white fluffy dog ran over to kiss Princess goodbye.

CHAPTER 12

The intercom buzzed, alerting Hadley that Steve, the man who came every Thursday to clean the saltwater aquarium, had arrived. The fish tank was Tucker's tenth birthday gift. Architects had expertly crafted the frame of the tank to match the wooden walls in the den. The room offered so many places to sit and relax, whether looking out at Central Park, playing the piano, or gazing at the spectacular aquarium's colorful reef fish and vibrant coral.

Tucker had always been a lover of nature. In his younger years, he was often late to school because he had to stop to rescue an injured pigeon or move stranded worms from the concrete to the grass. Tucker always requested an animal-themed party. Zoo animals at five, pony rides at six, a reptile show with a banana boa constrictor at eight, and a party with lizards, frogs, and tortoises at nine. Hadley thought, *He will become a veterinarian.*

Steve entered the apartment with his equipment. He set everything on a towel on the floor and lifted the aquarium lid. Hadley watched with fascination as the fish zipped about, evading the intrusive vacuum that cleaned the gray pebbles. Then Steve took out a plastic bag from a cooler. "I've brought you two new fish today," he said, carefully spilling the yellow fish into the aquarium. "This here's a One Spot Foxface." He pointed to the black spot on its back. He took out another bag. "This is one of my favorites.

The lionfish." Steve carefully emptied the bag into the tank. The brown-and-white banded fish dove to the bottom of the tank and took cover among the coral. "When he's swimming, he has beautiful showy pectoral fins and spikey fin rays. The lionfish is also known as the Devil Firefish, and for good reason. His fins are extremely venomous and will cause quite a bit of pain if touched. Since only I clean the aquarium, this shouldn't be a problem, but I did want to caution you. Continue feeding as usual, but add two more cubes in the evening," he said and packed up his equipment.

"I'll be sure to tell the kids, Thanks, Steve." She showed him to the door.

Hadley watched the two new fish, imagining what living under the sea would be like. A pang of panic grabbed her. *Have I been scuba diving before?*

Bergen soon joined his wife and watched her. "New fish?" he said.

"Oh, hi dear," Hadley answered. "Yes, a bear and a lion, or something like that."

Bergen recognized the striped one. "It's poisonous, isn't it?" he asked with hesitation.

"I'm not really sure," she answered, "but they're both awfully pretty." Bergen noticed how hypnotized Hadley was by the fish and their back-and-forth movement; it was calming her.

"Is it this afternoon that you're going with your book group to the CIA?" Bergen asked.

"Yes, we're all meeting at one o'clock," Hadley replied.

"Do you want me to go with you?"

"No, why? It's a girl thing?"

"I dunno. Do you think you should drive there alone?" he asked sheepishly.

"Are you kidding me? Bergen, do not go there. I'm not an invalid yet!"

Bergen stepped back, stunned by her hostility. "I'm sorry, honey, I didn't . . . mean it that way. I'm just worried. What if you get lost?" he asked.

"So, what if?" she replied. "I'll check Google Maps or ask someone."

She was not going down easily, Alzheimer's or not. If she could carry on without crumbling, he would too. He pulled her into his arms and kissed her cheek.

—

TEN HOURS LATER, Bergen paced in the kitchen, anxiety gnawing at him. His eighth call to his wife went straight to voicemail. It was almost eight o'clock. She should be home by now. Frustrated, he considered who else he could call. Then it hit him: Babs Connor, the book club leader. Bergen opened the kitchen drawer and riffled through packages of batteries, a ball of twine, a hammer, and boxes of picture hooks until he found Hadley's old-school brown leather directory. He slid its silver tab to C. The directory popped open, showing a dozen or so names. Bergen scanned the page for Connor and punched her number into the phone.

"Pick up," he muttered. She answered on the fourth ring. "Bergen Stanton here. Are you at Hyde Park?"

"No, no, I've been home since six. We all left around four-thirty. Why?" she asked.

"Well, probably nothing to worry about, but Hadley isn't home yet."

Then Brook ran into the kitchen. "Dad, I found mom's cell under her coat in the office."

Bergen explained, "Oh, we just found her phone here. Please call if you hear anything."

"Hadley left at the same time as me," Babs said. "I'll call the others and get back to you."

"Nine-one-one, may I help you?" came the voice on the other end.

"Yes, I'd like to report a missing person," Bergen barked.

"Sir, what is your name?"

"This is Bergen Stanton. My wife, Hadley Stanton, is missing. Please, you must get the police out looking for her." His fear spread like a malignant tumor. "She was at a cooking class at the Culinary Institute in Hyde Park," he said with pressured speech.

"Sir, sir," the voice interrupted, "how long has she been missing for?"

"Two hours," Bergen replied.

"I'm sorry, sir, but we don't file a missing person report until the person is missing for twenty-four hours or more. Is there foul play suspected?" she asked.

"No," he yelled. "But she has . . . Alzheimer's! She is lost somewhere in upstate New York, and I have no idea where to look." He dug his nails into his palm.

"Sir, please calm down. In that case, we can initiate a Silver Alert. If she hasn't been found by tomorrow afternoon, we'll send an officer out to you."

"Tomorrow?" he asked incredulously. "There's a huge snowstorm. She could freeze."

"I'm sorry, sir. Perhaps call her friends and see if they know her whereabouts."

Bergen slammed down the phone and marched to his office. His mind raced. *Should I drive to New Hampshire? Backtrack her route? Should I wait for her late arrival or a call from the police? She should've been home by now.* He poured himself a shot of whiskey, hoping to quell the spreading panic. He loosened his tie and slumped down in the leather chair by the window. Looking down, he saw children throwing snowballs.

Bergen dozed off throughout the night. Each time he woke, he checked his watch. Three a.m., and still not home. *Where the hell is she?* At 7 a.m., he went to the kitchen to make coffee.

"Mom home yet?" a sleepy Brook asked, walking up to rest her cheek against his chest.

"No, sweetie," he replied. "Go back to bed. I promise to wake you when she gets home."

Bergen watched as Brook shuffled back to her bedroom. His little girl was growing up. Time was moving too quickly. Everything was changing. Bergen turned on the TV. He switched to the local news: the Queens Bridge was closing, a dog was rescued from an icy pond, and there was a pileup on the Saw Mill Parkway. Then, it hit him. An accident. *Oh, dear God.*

Bergen ran back to his study and opened his computer. He searched hospitals in Westchester County. "Siri, call New York Presbyterian Hospital."

"Calling New York Presbyterian Hospital," she answered robotically. On the third ring, Hadley walked in the front door, her perfect hair now unkempt, her mascara smeared.

"Thank God!" Bergen exclaimed, rushing to her side. "What happened? Are you okay?"

Limp with exhaustion, Hadley dropped into his arms and sobbed. He held her tightly and shepherded her to the sofa. "Honey, tell me what happened." He handed her a tissue.

Hadley choked out, "We left the CIA at four. It was snowing, and I missed my exit. I got on some back roads and had no idea where I was. I guess I left my phone at home so I couldn't check maps." She took a deep breath and sobbed louder. "Oh, Bergen, I was so frightened. I didn't know what to do. Somehow, I ended up in Greenville. I stopped at a motel for directions, but the storm was getting worse. The clerk talked me into not going back out and offered me a room. I tried to call with his phone, but I—I couldn't remember anybody's number."

It unsettled Bergen to admit so soon that the time had come for them to speak more directly about her increasing episodes of memory loss and disorientation. She could have had someone look up their home number. Anything. *She isn't capable.*

"Mom, you're home," said Brook, running into the room and practically tripping over the rug. She jumped onto the couch and hugged her mom tightly. Brook gave Bergen a worried glance and then looked again at the stranger sitting next to her. Her mom had always been perfect, without defects or blemishes. *Who, then, is this disheveled, defeated woman?*

"What's going on? Is anybody going to say something?" Brook asked, tears forming.

Hadley pulled Brook's head to her chest and stroked her hair. "Everything is okay, my dear child. I got lost and didn't have my phone. I'm sorry I scared you all," she said, wiping her own tears away. Hadley assured her she was safe and had stayed in a motel until the morning and the roads were cleared. Hadley glared at Bergen, giving the unmistakable message that he had promised not to tell the children about her diagnosis. Fearful his tormented look might give away their secret, Bergen went to the kitchen to make more coffee.

"Weren't you scared, Mom?" Brook asked. "I mean, being in a sketchy motel by yourself? The desk guy could have raped you, or, God, murdered you."

Hadley took Brook's head in her hands. "You've watched too many scary movies, my dear," she said, tousling Brook's hair. "I guess I was a little scared, but not because of the motel clerk. What really upset me was not being able to reach you and Dad. From now on, I'm never going out again without my phone. Let that be a lesson for all."

Bergen stood in the doorway with two cups of coffee. *We should tell the kids.*

Brook climbed off the sofa and gave Hadley another hug. "I'm glad you're home safely, Mom." She started to leave but stopped. "Why didn't you just ask the motel clerk to call the front desk? They could have gotten Dad."

Hadley's brow furrowed. She tilted her head. "I didn't think of it, my dear. I guess I was too rattled by getting lost and the storm. It won't happen again. I'm sorry I worried everyone."

Bergen looked at the floor. The lie was causing him distress. He had never lied to his children. *Hadley is being selfish*, he thought.

Hadley padded toward Bergen. "Remember, you never break your promises," she said with a steely undercurrent. She tapped him lightly on the shoulder. "I'm going to shower."

CHAPTER 13

Rachel's phone lit up; Mom showed on the screen. "Hi, honey," her mom said. "I thought maybe we could go Christmas shopping and have lunch."

Rachel's heart sank at the mention of Christmas. She despised the holiday season. Navigating through crowded malls, bodies pressing against hers, amplified her vulnerability. "Mom, I'd love to, but you know, I hate the whole holiday thing. And I've been listening to 'Jingle Bells' at work since October. Can we just get lunch somewhere outside of the mall?"

They met at The Garden restaurant. "I'm sorry," her mom started, "this time of year is difficult for you. It was not very sensitive of me."

It wasn't just the crowds that bothered Rachel; it was the entire facade of jolliness while she felt emptiness. *It's as if they're rubbing it in my face.*

Not in a chatty mood, Rachel stared blankly at a television in the corner of the restaurant. Two commentators bantered about the likelihood of the Knicks winning the NBA playoffs. A meteorologist pointed at a map depicting storms coming their way.

A jewelry store on Forty-Sixth Street in the diamond district had been robbed. Video footage showed a man in a black ski mask running from the building. Rachel held onto her chair as she felt the room whirl. Beads of sweat broke out on her forehead, her skin clammy. She tried to use the relaxation technique Monica had taught her, but the panic had come on too quickly.

"We have to leave now, Mom, right now," Rachel said, trying to slow her breathing. "I have to get out of here." *Why am I still like this? Why does it keep happening?*

Rachel pushed past the other customers by the host's stand. She burst through the door and stood shivering on the sidewalk. A young couple by the door stared. Gloria put forty dollars on the table, grabbed their coats, and rushed out to join her daughter.

"Should I call an ambulance?" a woman asked. "I think she's having a heart attack."

Gloria felt like she'd been punched in the gut. *Another panic attack.*

Rachel panted while Gloria draped Rachel's coat over her shoulders and rubbed her back.

A middle-aged man came out from the restaurant and handed Gloria a paper bag. "Have her blow into this," he said. "It will help her stop hyperventilating." Gloria held it to Rachel's mouth. It felt good to be able to help. Rachel's breathing slowed, and she pushed the bag away.

"Thank you. I'm sorry for the bother," she said, looking up at the man.

"No problem. My son has panic attacks too. I'm always prepared. I hope you feel better." He patted her on the shoulder and returned to the restaurant.

Once home, Rachel sat on the floor with her back against the wall. She was wearing her long flannel nightgown, fluffy blue robe, and thick black ski socks. She wanted to cover her whole body. She wanted to be invisible. Princess rested her silky head on Rachel's lap.

Gloria had made a pot of tea. Neither of them spoke. Gloria couldn't find the words to bring her daughter any peace. *How could I have let this happen? I have failed as a mother.*

Rachel woke early the next morning. The dim light seeping through the bathroom window cast a solemn atmosphere over the room. She stared at the antidepressants on her bedside table, its mere presence intensifying the weight of her struggles. *What's the sense? It's never going to get better.* The allure of the pills became a haunting temptation, promising an escape. She took the pills into the bathroom, the cool tiles beneath her feet. Her reflection stared back, eyes clouded with despair and resignation. She questioned whether the six remaining tablets were enough to put her to sleep forever. As if looking for an anchor, Rachel rummaged through the medicine cabinet, the metallic clinks of bottles echoing in the confined space.

Rachel's hands shook as she sifted through the vials, hoping to find an unfinished one that could provide the illusion of the path forward. The room seemed to constrict around her.

Gloria appeared at the bathroom door, the creaking hinges breaking the silence. She froze, tears running down her face. "Rachel! No, please! What are you doing?" she shouted, knocking the pills out of her hand. "Did you already take them? Should I call an ambulance?"

Rachel buried her face in her hands. She felt exposed and ashamed. "I wasn't really going to take them. I promise. I'm sorry, Mom, but this shit just keeps getting worse." Deep down, Rachel felt a longing for her mother's support, but she was overwhelmed by the pain she caused.

"You're going to get through this." Gloria hugged her daughter as tightly as she could. "You will get through this. We're not going to give him the power to rob you of your life."

Rachel took a washcloth from the towel rack and dabbed the tears from her mother's face, then her own. "Why do you think he chose me?"

Gloria took Rachel by the hand and led her out of the bathroom. Her heart ached. "He didn't choose you, honey, and you did nothing to encourage him. You were just in the wrong place at the wrong time." Gloria felt inadequate, not knowing how to stop Rachel's guilt, pain, and fear. "Let's do something fun today," she said. "Do you have to work?"

Rachel shook her head. "I took the day off for my shrink

appointment, and I'm supposed to meet a lady for coffee before."

"Who?" Gloria asked, curious who the mystery woman could be.

"Her name's Hadley. Our therapy appointments are at the same time, so we meet for coffee beforehand. She introduced me to Pooch Rescue and bought Princess for me. I like her," Rachel said, shrugging. "She's really nice, someone I can talk to."

Gloria kissed her daughter on the forehead and smiled.

CHAPTER 14

Rachel sat by herself in the corner booth at the café. She checked her watch for the tenth time. "I guess she's not coming," she said. *Maybe she is too busy to care about a college-dropout random therapy girl.* She tipped a dollar, gathered her backpack, and left.

Rachel burst into the waiting room. Dorothy looked up from her computer with one eyebrow raised and gestured for Rachel to go in for her session. "Geez, I'm only a few minutes late," she said under her breath as she entered the office.

Rachel tried to focus on what the doctor was asking but found herself consumed with thoughts of Hadley. *Did Hadley come to her own appointment? Will I intercept her?* Rachel tapped the rubber toes of her sneakers against the coffee table and stared at the glass-domed clock, willing the hands to move faster.

"You seem far away," Monica said. "What's on your mind?"

Rachel sighed. "I had another panic attack. My mom was there. I hate causing her pain." She left out the part about the pills. After relaxation techniques and discussing possible triggers, Rachel pointed to her watch. "Oh, I think our time is up," she announced. "It's four-fifty."

Monica looked over her glasses and raised a quizzical eyebrow. "Are you in a hurry?"

"I'm hoping to catch a new friend before she leaves. Excuse me," she said. "Bye."

Then she saw Hadley. *She's here! Good.* She felt good around Hadley. Embarrassed by her girl crush, Rachel stood sheepishly to the side while Hadley paid her bill.

"Hi, my dear," Hadley said. "I didn't see you in the waiting room earlier."

Rachel cocked her head. "We were supposed to meet at Mika's today. Did you forget?"

"Oh, I am *so* sorry. I guess I did. Come with me." She took Rachel to the park and found an empty bench. "Rachel, I'm sorry about missing our coffee. I have Alzheimer's disease."

Rachel felt paralyzed. "You have what? But, but you're so young," Rachel stammered.

"It's why I go to therapy. Do you have time for coffee now?"

As Rachel and Hadley walked to the café, the streetlights came alive, flooding the sidewalks and streets. Twinkling white and multicolor Christmas lights glistened. Hadley seemed lost in thought as she admired the festive decorations. She was surprised when she passed by a green, furry Christmas tree and it wiggled and sang "Rockin' Around the Christmas Tree." Hadley jumped back, but then she laughed. *Tucker would like this.*

They ordered coffees and sat at the same table Rachel had before. The comforting aromas of rich coffee, velvety cocoa beans, and sweet cream permeated the small shop.

"Your Alzheimer's, I mean, does the shrink help? Does he help you remember?" Rachel played with the salt and pepper shakers. "My Grandpa had Alzheimer's, but he was seventy."

Hadley extended her slender hand, with perfectly manicured nails, and gently took the shakers out of her hand. "I have a rare type of dementia that starts early in life. The doctor doesn't really help me with my memory—no one can stop its decline, not even medicine. I talk about how scared I am to leave my children." Hadley paused and closed her eyes. "My parents died when I was seventeen. They were killed by a drunk driver. I swore I'd always be there for my family. I'd take care of myself, stay on top of things. Not get sick. It's why I got my genome sequenced, to stay on top of it." She let out a long breath. "I was so young when they died. It was a week before senior prom and looming finals. I had to pretend everything was all right. I didn't stop to grieve. I couldn't afford to."

Just listen. That's what a friend does, Rachel thought.

"My brother and I had to see a grief counselor for a year. She cautioned us that children whose parents die suddenly are at further risk for anxiety, depression, or substance abuse. She was kind of right, but it wasn't drugs. Food was my crutch. Pizza, McDonald's fries, milkshakes, candy bars, and everything crunchy and salty. Food was a reliable source of comfort. Eating offered momentary escapes; it gave me a feeling of control." Hadley stirred her coffee. Then she laughed. "I gained over twenty-five pounds my freshman year, and with that came rejection from boys and judgment. I vowed to lose all that weight and never let myself lose control like that again. To this day, I'm embarrassed, I have little empathy for anyone who is overweight. To me, it's a sign of weakness, and weakness has no place in my life."

She continued, "Losing both parents was torture, but I couldn't live without my mom. No one else got me. She was with me every day, and then she got ripped away. I became obsessed with the fear that I might lose all of her—my memories. Forget what she looked like, forget how she smelled, how she talked. I dyed my hair blond. I wore her clothes and perfume. I listened to her voice on our phone machine. I wanted to be like her, look like her so I wouldn't forget.

"It wasn't until I met my husband that I felt safe enough to truly process her death. He helped me see that people can have really bad things happen and still go on to live positive, happy lives. Whenever I felt overwhelmed, Bergen was there to listen without judgment. He would hold me close and let me cry, reassuring me that it was okay to feel the pain.

"He encouraged me to pursue activities that brought me joy, like my rooftop garden and volunteer work, reminding me that there's still beauty and happiness in the world.

"He was right. I'm a survivor. I didn't turn to drugs or suffer from depression. And now, I'm going to lose my memory. I'm actually going to forget my mother. I'm going to forget my children, Bergen, my friends. I'm going to forget you." She paused. "Well, enough about me. Tell me, how's Princess getting along?"

Rachel's mind raced. "Hadley, I'm so very sorry. You've been dealt a rotten hand." After a long silence, Rachel said, "She's great. She has such a patient and gentle temperament. I'm so thankful for you bringing her into my life. She helps me with my anxiety, so I'm working to get her certified as a therapy dog. We'll visit people in hospitals. It will be a win-win."

Hadley smiled. "That's wonderful. Tell me about you. Why do you go to therapy?"

It's ironic, Rachel thought. "I'm going to get rid of my memories."

Hadley squinted, confused. *Why would anyone choose such a thing?*

"Hadley," a voice yelled from behind the counter.

Hadley swiveled and looked questioningly at the girl who had called her name. "Yes?"

"Our coffees are ready," Rachel said. "Don't worry. I'll get them."

Hadley stirred cinnamon into the white foam of her cappuccino. Rachel thought she had lost Hadley's attention. Then Hadley said, "What kind of memories are you trying to get rid of?"

"Just the bad ones." She hesitated. "I have flashbacks from when I was raped in college. My official diagnosis is PTSD." Rachel could feel her stomach churn.

"Oh you poor, sweet girl, Do your parents know?" *What would I do if Brook or Sydney were raped?*

Rachel explained her assault, her parents' separation, and the work she was doing. "Sometimes I think I'm getting better, and then, *wham*, the nightmare grabs hold and hits me like a ton of bricks, and I don't even want to live. Then this voice tells me there's no point in trying."

"I know what you mean," Hadley responded flatly, apathetic.

"You do?" Rachel asked. "I mean, do you sometimes think of suicide too?" *Maybe I'm not alone in my pain. Hadley is my soulmate.*

"I do. I think about it a lot, especially when I picture myself at the end. Being slumped over a wheelchair, unable to walk or feed myself, my husband at my bedside, succumbed to sorrow." She wondered if he would also pray for it all to be over. She reminded herself to ask Dr. Kopple for sleeping pills. She'd tell him her sleep was interrupted. If he pressed her, she'd detail her worry for her family's future. She always avoided discussing her suicidal thoughts with him.

"Hadley, I'm so sorry. Such a shitty disease. Have you told your husband?"

Hadley nodded slowly. "I've tried to talk to him about it, but he doesn't like to think about what's going to happen," Hadley said, her lips puckered. "No one does. Sometimes I'm planning my final exit, and then just like that, I'm dreaming of spending the remaining good years traveling. Then I realize that would be a waste. I'm only going to forget. I've always wanted to learn how to play bridge, but what's the point?" Hadley looked away. "Most of the time, I just want to cuddle up with my kids and Bergen and never leave the house. Dr. Kopple says living with Alzheimer's is a process. I guess I'm still working through it."

Rachel finished her coffee. "My mom sorta knows how I'm feeling," Rachel said. "A few weeks ago, after I had one of the worst panic attacks ever, I decided it was time to end it. I thought it would release my mom from anguish. I don't know about you, Hadley, but I get tired of living sometimes. It's such a fight to go on from day to day." Rachel started fiddling with the salt and pepper shakers again. "I get so angry about what happened, and then I feel guilty and worthless. It's one big never-ending circle of pain. The morning after the panic attack, I was in my bathroom holding a bunch of pills when my mom walked in. The look on her face was torture and pain. When I looked at her, something snapped. I realized I couldn't do that to her."

Hadley stared blankly at the bare wall in front of her. She was confused by her friend's confession of not wanting to live. After all, Rachel was so young, with so much life ahead of her. Hadley drew in a deep breath. *Is it fair to judge Rachel? Is assisted suicide even the right thing to do?* "For me," Hadley said in a drawn-out voice, "I just don't want to be a burden."

The door to the café opened abruptly, letting in a burst of cold air and snow. Hadley shook her head and pulled her coat around her shoulders. "Goodness me," she said, glancing at her watch, "it's past six. I really should be getting home. We can share a cab again if you like."

Rachel wanted to continue their conversation, but she had errands to run. Hadley was so comforting, like the big sister she never had. "Let's meet again next week," she offered.

Hadley agreed and promised to set her phone alarm to remind her. She hugged Rachel tightly, glad to have found someone outside of her family to be herself with. Being able to share these kinds of things with Rachel made her feel less isolated.

Hadley flagged a passing cab, and before sliding into the back seat, called to Rachel, "Promise me you'll be here, next week and the week after that."

"I promise," Rachel said and smiled.

CHAPTER 15

Hadley's thoughts went wild. Rachel was going to take pills. Is that the best way to go? Will my medications be enough? Will I need something more lethal? Stronger? How will I choose a date, outfit? What do I need to do before I die? A school bus dropped off a dozen or so elementary school children, bundled up in ski jackets, mittens, and hats. "I'm getting out here," she told the cabbie. "I'm going to walk." Hadley handed the driver a ten. "Keep the change."

Not the summer. It'll ruin it for the kids. May is bad; my parents died in May. It was colder, and her hands felt numb. A group of construction workers leaving a bar on the corner interrupted Hadley's thoughts. She glanced at her watch, 7 p.m. She looked around. She texted Bergen,

> I have an unexpected client. Be home after dinner. Order takeout.

Hadley put the phone in her coat pocket and walked directly to the bar. It was dark inside, and it took a few moments for her eyes to adjust. *Well, here's one thing you've never done*, she admitted as she pulled out a chair at the bar and took a seat. "What kind of Chardonnay do you have?" she asked the bartender.

"Lady, we only have one white wine. Galloping Stallion. You want that?" he asked.

Hadley raised her eyebrows. "Yes, thank you. That will be fine."

Hadley looked around. She had never been in a bar like this before. A half dozen or so men dressed in blue jeans, flannel shirts, and work boots stood around two pool tables. Several tattooed men congregated at the other end of the bar, chatting up the waitress. "Mind if I sit here?" a man said to her left. She pulled her dress down over her knees. "You with someone?"

Hadley scratched behind her ear. "Are you speaking to me?" she asked, flustered. It wasn't that other men hadn't ever flirted with her, but this was different. She was in a pub, by herself. It was exciting but also wrong. "Oh, I was just leaving," she said, gathering her purse.

"Tab or pay now?" the bartender asked as he put the wineglass down in front of Hadley.

What am I doing? "How much do I owe you?"

"I've got it," the man said and reached for his wallet.

Hadley smiled. *That was sweet*, she thought.

"Why not stay a while, drink your wine?" the man said. "I don't bite."

Is he trying to pick me up? It was exciting, thrilling even. *Would he still try if he knew I was losing my mind?* Hadley settled into her chair. She took a small, timid sip of the wine. Hadley crinkled her nose and swallowed hard.

"Not used to that kind of wine, eh?" the man asked. Hadley laughed. "Ma name's Chance," he said, extending his hand. Hadley's mind swirled. Chance was handsome, untamed. Strong-jawed, with deep, dark blue eyes. Short, wavy black hair, tinged with gray. He reminded her of Dr. McDreamy from *Grey's Anatomy*.

"Um, well, hi, nice to meet you," Hadley said, extending her hand to shake. "My name's Suzette. Suzette, uh, Kopple." She briefly imagined what Dr. Kopple's real wife might look like.

"Nice to meet ya, Suzette Kopple." He glanced at her ring. "What brings you to The 99?"

"I should go, really. My kids are waiting for me." Her nerves were tingly, a good feeling.

Chance looked at Hadley, his gaze steady and familiar. Hadley took a long sip of her wine. Her knee brushed against his thigh, and she felt a warmth envelop her body. She looked coyly at Chance, her mind wandering to erotic thoughts. *Is this a sign? Should I take a chance?*

The two chatted for an hour. He treated her like a fully cognitive, functioning woman. He flattered her with his attention but made no moves to touch her or invite her back to his place. After a second glass of Galloping Stallion, Hadley felt more than just tipsy. It was fun, but she was unsure how it would end if she didn't leave soon. Hadley went to the restroom. When she returned, she said, "I must go. It was nice speaking with you. Thank you for the wine."

"Maybe I'll see you here again, Mrs. Suzette Kopple," Chance said and gave her a wink.

Hadley blushed and turned to the door. "Maybe," she said and left. The secrecy of their meeting made her feel exhilarated, and after all, she hadn't done anything wrong. She had just stopped in a bar to get out of the cold and gather her thoughts. If it ever came up—and why would it—that's what she'd tell Bergen.

CHAPTER 16

The red plastic poinsettias in the planters by the entrance seemed starkly out of place in front of the massive gray concrete building. Rachel pulled open the huge glass door.

Dressed in a white tee and navy sweatpants, the man at the front rolled out in a wheelchair and extended a gloved hand. "I'm Bomber Bob. Is this your first time at the VA?" he asked. "I don't think I've seen you here before."

"Yes," Rachel replied. "My dog, Princess, just graduated from therapy dog certification, and we're here to volunteer." Princess seemed to beam with pride in her orange dog vest.

"Well, welcome, little lady. Let me show you around and introduce ya to the guys."

Bob rolled down the hall and pointed out various meeting rooms. He stopped outside a large common area. "Vets gather here when not in treatment or therapy," he said. Rachel and Princess followed Bob into the room. It was depressingly plain, with beige walls, an old TV, and a scantily decorated Christmas tree. A large American flag stood prominently next to a picture of the commander in chief. Plaques and slogans from military branches hung on the walls.

Rachel read them all silently. "Which branch were you in?"

"Aim high, fly, fight, win," he said, pointing to the Air Force plaque. "This is Dixie Fox."

Dixie seemed too young to have been at war. He had blue-green eyes, tousled blond hair, and a long scar down his right cheek. She could see tattoos on his neck and a large one of an eagle standing on top of the world on his left arm. Rachel tried not to look at his missing leg.

Dixie sensed her discomfort and said, "Lost it in Afghanistan, but I still have another."

Rachel looked down. "I'm sorry," she said, blushing. Princess moved closer and nudged her leg. "Would you like to meet Princess?" Rachel pulled plastic chairs from the corner and placed them together. While Dixie and Bob patted Princess, several men came into the room.

"Who do we have here?" asked an older man, pushing a walker.

"Dan, get in here. Meet Princess," Bob yelled. "This is Dan the man Ia Drang. Dan fought in Nam in '65. He's a hero, awarded both the Medal of Honor and the Purple Heart," he said, pointing to Dan's cap.

"I'm honored to meet you," Rachel said to the war hero.

Dan did not wear his age well. His face was covered with coarse gray stubble, his hair thinning and unkempt. He wore a plaid flannel shirt, jean overalls, and a dark green baseball cap covered with patches and medals. *Vietnam Veteran* was embroidered in stars and stripes in the center. Wearing hospital slippers, he shuffled toward her with his walker, extending his hand.

"Don't let him fool ya," Dan joked. "I stole these medals from the guy in the next bed."

Rachel laughed and introduced Princess to each of the vets as they entered the room.

"I used to have a service dog," one commented, "but she died of old age. Need to get another."

"What kind of service did your dog perform?" Rachel politely asked.

"She was a German shepherd. Kingston was her name," he replied. "I don't do well around loud noises, so I got Kingston to help calm me. She was great, would come sit by me and put her paw in ma lap whenever there were loud noises. Didn't matter if it was a lawnmower backfiring, a door slamming, or—worst of all—fireworks." He squeezed his eyes tight. "She would sit by me and not leave ma side." The man pet Princess. He looked at her with sad eyes.

"Mind me askin' why you have a service dog?" he asked.

Rachel gulped; she wasn't expecting to have to divulge her own story, but then again, she had started it. Rachel pulled Princess closer and flipped her fingers back and forth through the leash. Lines of stress formed on her forehead. "Well." She hesitated. "Princess comforts me, like Kingston did for you." She fidgeted, trying to muster the courage to share. Princess looked up at her, sensing her growing anxiety. *Pet me. Focus on me*, she seemed to be saying.

The man stammered, not knowing if he should press her. "I'm Auckland Joe," he said and pulled up a chair next to Rachel. His clothes smelled musty, like they hadn't been laundered in a while, and his breath had a sweet, metallic smell, but it wasn't offensive. Musty and sweet were far better than the clove and leather scents she had come to abhor.

The three sat while Rachel told her story. "She has a calming effect on me, in my apartment and especially in crowds. My doctor wrote a letter so she can be with me all the time. It's called an emotional support pet." Rachel looked at the men: some missing limbs, some in wheelchairs, and two paralyzed. Her trauma felt insignificant. *Maybe this is part of my recovery? Sharing my story?*

"Joe, I was raped in college," she blurted. "It was horrific and violent, so now I—"

Joe held his hands up. "I'm so sorry, Rachel. I didn't mean to violate your privacy."

"You didn't. I have been holding on to this ticking bomb for years, and it's time I deal with it head-on. I have a hard time with smells, tastes, sounds, intrusions on my five senses."

"Wow, looks like World War III was just announced," Dan said, shuffling over to rejoin the group. "Why the tormented faces?"

Joe gave Rachel an encouraging look that it was okay to share with Dan.

"Who is this asshole? We'll kill him," Dan said, spit flying from his lips.

"Calm down, la Drang. This ain't Nam. I'm sure the guy's somebody's prison bitch."

Rachel's throat tightened. She hugged and kissed Princess. *Breathe.* "Actually, they never caught him."

"Shit," exploded Dan, "that fu—"

Although Rachel felt safe, the escalating conversation triggered more discomfort. "It's okay," Rachel said. "I'm really okay, especially now with Princess. Hey, I gotta go anyway. I have to cover an evening shift at work. I'll be back on Thursdays, and sooner if I can."

Joe smiled. He liked Rachel and her little dog. He had something to look forward to.

Once outside, Rachel threw her arms toward the sun and smiled. "We're not in this alone," she said to Princess. Rachel sat on the bench outside the VA waiting for the bus to arrive. She pictured each of the men she'd met in the hospital and realized they all had their own stories of trauma. She leaned down to pat Princess and told her that if those guys could manage their nonstop battle fatigue, she certainly should be able to conquer her one isolated incident.

CHAPTER 17

Hadley busied herself with Christmas decorations. She placed Douglas fir branches tied with red ribbons on the living room mantle. There, she nestled silver votive candles amid the branches and, in the middle, carefully placed a German antique Santa figure, a family heirloom. Bergen wrapped his arm around her tiny waist. He pecked her on the cheek. "I love Christmas," Hadley remarked, her voice tinged with sadness.

"The tree is up," Bergen said. "Shall we call the kids to decorate?"

Bing Crosby belted holiday tunes while the Stantons placed ornaments on the tree. Each one held a special significance, representing cherished memories: a ceramic baby bottle with June 10, 1998, for Sydney's birth, a glass lemon they got in Capri, a wooden sailboat representing Brook's time at camp on Martha's Vineyard, and several hearts for various anniversaries. But the most precious were the kids' kindergarten macaroni and ribbons.

"I remember this one," Tucker announced. He held up a figurine of a wrestler. "You got me this the year I joined the team," he said.

"How 'bout this one?" Hadley asked, holding up a glass koala bear ornament.

"I sure do," said Bergen.

"Oh, not this story again," Sydney, home from college, interjected with playful protest.

Brook cringed, while Bergen described how Sydney was the result of a romantic trip he and Hadley took to Australia. "We decided not to find out if you were a boy or girl, so we chose a unisex name. Sidney with an I for a boy, and with a Y for a girl."

"Dad," Sydney moaned, "get on with it. We've heard this so many times already."

Rather enjoying the kids' embarrassment, Hadley laughed and mentioned their townhouse in Brooklyn Heights. "It was small but cozy," Hadley said and winked at Bergen.

"Okay, enough, that's just gross." Brook rolled her eyes and fake vomited.

Dr. Boswell had explained the short- versus long-term memory loss Hadley would experience, but Bergen thought, *How can she remember thirteen years ago and not last week?*

"And then, you, Tucker, conceived the summer we rented that Nantucket beach house."

Tucker shook his head. "I will name my children Leia, Vader, and Chewbacca."

The kids took turns hanging the remaining ornaments. Hadley opened a box of foil tinsel and placed a few strands on the branches. She stood back and admired the tree. The fresh, woody fragrance brought back childhood memories of cookies, gingerbread houses, and caroling. Christmas was her favorite holiday. "Let me get the gifts," she said and left the room.

When all the gifts were strategically placed around the tree, Tucker urged everyone to start his favorite Christmas Eve tradition of opening one gift.

"Age before beauty," Sydney said and picked up a small box and unwrapped it quickly. "Mom, really, you got me the Apple watch? I love it. Is this the Hermes version?" she asked.

"It is," Hadley replied, beaming. "I thought you'd like that better than the plastic strap."

Sydney placed it on her wrist. "Thanks, Mom, I love it."

After gifts, Hadley instructed, "Get ready for church, the children's evening service, my favorite. And dress nicely, please, kids. We're going to dinner at Quince on Fifth after."

—

THE 6 A.M. alarm startled Bergen. He crawled out of bed, put on his red, plaid robe, and retrieved a large bag from his closet. Stealthily, he snuck into the living room and filled the stockings, looking over his shoulder every minute to be sure the kids weren't awake. He took a bite of the snowflake cookie on the plate and joined his wife in the kitchen. He put his arms around her. "Merry Christmas, my dear," he whispered. Hadley faced him and gently kissed him.

"Merry Christmas, sweetheart," she said. *How many more Christmases do I have? How many will I remember?* "OJ?" She popped a halved orange into the press.

Tucker was, as always, the first one up. "Finally, you're awake," he said. "Let's get everyone up so we can get started!"

"You know the drill," Hadley said. *Christmas brings out the child in my thirteen-year-old boy.* "Everyone has to have breakfast and be dressed before we start, but you can open your stocking." Tucker slid on the hardwood floor to the living room and grabbed his stocking.

Bergen encouraged, "Wait until I get my camera." He joined them in the living room.

Tucker began. "Oh, just what I needed, Mom, I mean Santa," he said with a wink. "Underwear, socks, toothpaste, and a toothbrush." He dug deeper, retrieving a chocolate orange, marshmallow snowmen, dental floss, ChapStick, and holiday thank-you notes. *Same as last year.* "Thanks," he said and shoved everything back in. "Now can I wake Brook and Sydney?" Brook stumbled into the room in flannel PJs decorated with skiing bunnies and raccoons.

"I'm up," she announced.

"Syd Neeeee," Tucker shouted down the hall, "it's Christmas. Get up!"

Sydney buried her head under the pillow and moaned, "Kids."

A few minutes later, everyone was gathered in the kitchen. Hadley took a round cake pan of fragrant cinnamon buns out of the oven. She spread white cream cheese icing over each roll and sprinkled chopped dried fruit on top. Working with two spatulas, Hadley carefully lifted the wreath of buns out of the cake tin and placed them on a Christmas platter. Red paper napkins rested in a holder in the center of the table next to the holly decorated salt and pepper shakers.

Bergen started a second pot of coffee and brought the orange juice in their heirloom holiday pitcher to the table. "Who wants cocoa?" Hadley asked. She brought over the Santa mugs the kids had since birth. Except for a small chip on the lip of Tucker's and the missing blue stone of Santa's eye on Sydney's, they were still perfect. Hadley poured steaming hot chocolate and plopped a dollop of Marshmallow Fluff into each of the mugs.

By 8 a.m., everyone was fed, dressed, and in the den. Bergen grabbed the scissors and a few trash bags and took his chair by the window.

"Who's gonna be Santa first?" Tucker asked.

Bergen reminded, "Mom is always first." Hadley stood by the tree. Dressed in a red wool suit and wearing a pearl necklace and earrings Bergen gave her earlier that year, she surveyed the pile of gifts. Now that the children were older, there were fewer gifts under the tree.

"Me first, me first," Tucker begged.

"Cool your jets," Brook warned. "If you think you're getting that Xbox, you're wrong."

"How do you know? If I'm not getting the Xbox, you're not getting new skis."

"Okay, Tuck," Hadley said, "you can go first. Here's one for you."

Tucker jumped up and took the rectangular box. He ripped the paper and threw it on the ground. "New wrestling shoes, cool. Thanks, Mom and Dad."

Sydney pointed to a thin square package covered in green foil paper. "Give it to Brook." Brook removed the wrapping and squealed over the Rihanna CD she had asked for.

Bergen got up from his armchair and handed his wife a wine gift bag.

"Gee, what could this be?" she joked. Hadley lifted the Peter Michael Belle Cote Chardonnay out of the bag. "I have one for you too." She handed him a bag with a bottle of wine.

"How about one for me?" Sydney said. Hadley chose a square box wrapped in silver and blue paper. Sydney graciously took the gift, slowly removed the tape, and pulled out the box. "More Apple?" she asked. Sydney stared at the watch. "Another Apple watch?" she asked.

Hadley stood up straight and put her index finger to her mouth. "Another?" she asked.

"Yes, Mom," Sydney said, "you gave me one last night. The one with the Hermes strap."

Hadley looked at Bergen in despair and ran out of the room.

"Dad, what's going on?" Sydney asked, scared.

"Daddy, is Mom okay?" Brook asked.

"Kids," he said slowly, "let me check on your mother. I'll be right back." He saw Hadley slip into the powder room. He knocked gingerly and tried the knob. It was locked. He knocked again. "Darling," he said, "please open the door." Hadley turned the lock, and he entered. Shaking her head, tears running down her face, Hadley clung for dear life to her husband.

"It's time, honey," he said. "You need to tell them."

"No," Hadley whispered, "I can't." Her throat felt tight. Her heart skipped beats, and she felt faint. Hadley sat on the closed toilet seat. Her hands and legs trembled. She felt profound vulnerability—no amount of strength or control could shield her from the inevitability of her own mortality. It was crashing down.

Bergen took a towel and wet it under cold water. He knelt on one knee in front of her and handed her the cloth. "They know something's wrong, honey. Keeping it a secret isn't helping; it's hurting them. We need to tell them." He knew the urgency to share was from his inability to keep it in any longer. Besides, he selfishly wanted to have someone to talk to about her illness.

Hadley put the cool cloth on the back of her neck and wiped her smeared mascara. Bergen's deep blue eyes pleaded. "Come, it's time." He guided her back to the den.

The girls sat straight up on the couch. Tucker looked at the floor. Bergen stood by Hadley's side, holding her hand tightly in his.

"Mom," Sydney said, "are you okay?"

She swallowed. It was humbling to reveal her weaknesses to the children, those she was meant to safeguard and support. "I have something I need to tell you." She wiped the tears on her chin and bit down on her lower lip. *It wasn't supposed to come out this way.*

"Mom, what?" Brook said, frightened. "Do you have cancer? Are you dying?"

"No, no dear." She feigned a smile. "I wanted to talk to you about this at the right time, certainly not today. I'm sorry. I've ruined Christmas." Bergen squeezed her hand. "I have a rare form of Alzheimer's disease," Hadley said in a hushed voice.

"You have what?" Sydney blurted out, shocked. "You're only forty-seven."

"It's called early-onset Alzheimer's." The bomb had been dropped; it was out in the open.

Sydney looked from Hadley to Bergen, her eyes darting as if watching a tennis match. "And?" she asked with urgency. "What does that mean?"

"It's a type of illness that affects memory. Your dad and I had our genes tested last fall, and that's how we found out," Hadley continued. "I have the type that can start early in life." Tucker ran to his bedroom and slammed the door. Hadley started to follow, but Bergen went.

"Hey, buddy," Bergen said, tapping on the door. Tucker was sobbing into his pillow. Bergen sat on the edge of the bed. There was a

Darth Vader lamp on his bedside table, wrestling trophies and medals cluttering his shelves, and a Lego castle blocking the closet door. But the sultry Taylor Swift posters on his door surprised him. His son was no longer a little boy.

"It's gonna be okay, buddy," Bergen said. "Your mom is a warrior. We'll get through this." He patted his son on the back. "Your mom needs you to be strong."

Tucker turned his head, snot running from his nose. "Is she going to die?"

Bergen closed his eyes. How could he tell this thirteen-year-old boy that his mom would most likely not be around to see him graduate from high school? "We're all going to die one day," he finally responded, unsure how much of her prognosis he should share. "You can talk to me about this anytime. I'll let you be for a bit. Then come back and be with us. It's Christmas."

Bergen joined his wife and daughters in the living room. Sydney and Brook sat on the sofa holding hands. "Mom, Dad," Sydney started, "how long have you known?"

"We wanted to understand all the information ourselves," Hadley said softly. "I'm sorry. We were trying to protect you."

Tucker rejoined them, leaning in the doorway, his eyes puffy and red. "Come sit, buddy."

"So, Alzheimer's?" Brook said matter-of-factly. "It's what Ronald Reagan had, right?" Hadley nodded. "Is that why you got lost coming home from your cooking class?"

"Yes, I think so," she said, admitting it not only to Brook but also to herself.

Bergen pursed his lips. "You're all adults, or nearly so," he said, winking at Tucker. "We want to be sensitive about how much information we share, how much you want to know, but who your mother is and her deep love for you will never change."

"Are you going to forget who we are?" Tucker asked timidly.

Hadley knelt in front of him. She took his hands in hers. "I think some people forget the names of family members, but they never forget how much they love them."

"Plus, we're going to get your mom the best care possible," Bergen said, staying positive.

"So, can I give you my gift?" A small smile returned to Tucker's face.

"Sure, honey," she answered sweetly, glad that the attention was off her disease.

"Jeez," Sydney barked. "How can you think of presents when Mom is dying?"

Hadley and Bergen jerked their heads in Sydney's direction. "Sydney, that is not called for," Bergen said sternly. "I'm sure you're upset about this news, but we are going to go on with our lives as best we can. It won't be easy, but we have to stick together as a family and carry on normally as much as we can. We can talk about this whenever you want. You can be involved as much or as little as you want."

"Let's try to have a merry Christmas. Tuck was right to go for that," Hadley said.

Sydney rolled her eyes. "Yeah, right, ho ho ho," she muttered.

Hadley plucked three envelopes from the tree's branches. "These all say *From Santa*."

Tucker ripped his open first, practically tearing the hundred-dollar bill as he pulled it out. "Wow, I can get two Xbox games with this. Thanks, Santa." He hugged his mom tightly.

Brook and Sydney sat quietly, holding their unopened envelopes. "I'm not really in the mood to open gifts. Can we get out of here and do something else?" Sydney asked. "Then maybe later we can come back in and start Christmas again."

Hadley looked to Bergen, hoping he knew what to do. *If I hadn't purchased two of the same gifts for Sydney, we wouldn't be here right now.* The mood was yet again solemn and heavy. "I think that's a great idea. Let's bundle up and take a walk through Central Park. When we come back, we can start again." Bergen put his arm around Hadley's shoulders and ushered the kids into the hallway to fetch their coats.

CHAPTER 18

The alarm sounded on Hadley's phone at 2 p.m, her reminder to meet Rachel for their weekly coffee and go to her psychiatrist appointment. Hadley combed her hair and brushed pale-pink powder across her cheeks. She cherished the special times she had with Rachel. Dr. Kopple was another matter. Hadley didn't see the use in talking about what was inevitable. *Am I supposed to feel ease for my future—or lack of one? I'm not in denial, angry. . . . So what is left to do? She would die in three years or so. Period. Talking about feelings wouldn't change that.* Hadley sighed. She'd keep going to make Bergen and Dr. Boswell happy. For them, not herself.

But today was different. She was looking forward to today's outing. She and Rachel would have their friendly coffee, she'd see Dr. Kopple, and she'd pass The 99. Maybe she'd see Chance again. Hadley couldn't stop thinking about him. *What will I do if I see him again?* But it was fun to fantasize, more fun than worrying about her family and processing her disease.

Once, she thought she saw Chance at a bus stop. She barked at the cabbie to stop but quickly realized she'd been mistaken. She was embarrassed and felt like a foolish schoolgirl. "Sorry," she said to Rachel and the cab driver, "I thought I saw my brother." Hadley wasn't sure why she hadn't shared her secret with Rachel. After all, it was the perfect fodder for girl talk.

Hadley walked from her dresser to the walk-in closet. She pulled two silk blouses from the top rod and held each one in front of herself. Hadley chose the leopard shirt—perfect with the black cigarette pants she was wearing. She pulled her sweater off. Glancing briefly at her bra, she changed to a black lace one. Hadley smiled as she scolded herself for having lascivious thoughts and pulled the blouse over her head. She tucked it in and added a black leather belt.

Hadley walked to the elevator. Fantasies of Chance filled her thoughts. It had been a month since they met. *Was he only in town for the holidays? Will he come back?*

Hadley stood on the sidewalk and waited while the doorman whistled to summon a cab. She rubbed her hands together. It was cold, and she'd forgotten gloves. A Yellow Cab pulled up, and the doorman gave the address to the driver. Once in the back seat, Hadley leaned toward the plexiglass partition and asked the cabbie to take a route that would pass by The 99.

Rachel was already inside. She faced the door at their regular table, blowing at the whipped cream that covered her hot chocolate. Hadley approached and removed her overcoat.

"Hi, Mrs. Stanton," the waitress said. Rachel and Hadley were regulars. "Your usual?" Hadley bobbed her head and reminded the server to put extra cinnamon on her cappuccino.

"By chance, do you have any more scones?" Rachel asked. "I'm famished." Hadley sat up straight. She looked away dreamily as a wide smile spread across her face.

Rachel tilted her head. "Hadley, what's up? You look like the cat that ate the canary." Hadley was quietly immersed in her fantasies. "Do you have a secret?"

Hadley rapidly fluttered her eyelashes. Her smug grin telegraphed her mischievous intent. The waitress placed the coffee and scone on the table and left.

Hadley poured a packet of sweetener into the cappuccino, swirling the cinnamon. She was stalling. She wanted desperately to tell her friend about Chance but worried what Rachel would think. "Come on, tell me," Rachel demanded a bit louder and stronger than she had meant.

Hadley put her coffee cup down, dabbed the corners of her mouth, and told Rachel, "I met a man, Chance, at The 99. Nothing happened, I swear. It was innocent, just drinks, but I can't stop thinking about him." She paused, the wide smile returning. "Don't you think it's strange that I can remember every detail of his face, hands, accent, but I can't remember what the weather was like yesterday or Tucker's grades?"

The perfect, beautiful, mannerly Hadley, devoted wife, loving mother, quintessential picture of good breeding, a confidant, trusted friend . . . I guess she has needs too, desires. "What does he look like? Is he handsome?" Rachel tried to shove judgment aside.

Hadley breathed in deeply. "He has deep bedroom eyes, a strong jaw, and an enchanting smile." A rosy color spread across her cheeks and neck. "The 99 isn't the fanciest of bars. Most guys are dressed in jeans and work clothes, but Chance, well, Chance was dressed nicer. Not in a Manhattan way, sophisticatedly rugged. He had on a leather vest and snakeskin cowboy boots with turquoise studs." *Does he think about me like this?* "Rachel," Hadley said, her voice dropping an octave, "I feel young again. I feel attractive, sexy. I haven't felt this giddy in years. I'm seventeen with my first crush. Is that wrong?"

Rachel squeezed Hadley's hand and gave a warm smile. "I think we all like to feel pretty. Needed and loved. You're lucky. You have Bergen, and he loves you. It's okay to have fantasies about Chance. He's obviously touched something in you. It's written all over your face."

Hadley blushed. "I've gone back several times, but he hasn't been there."

A young woman in her late twenties pulled up a chair at a nearby table. She removed her knit ski cap and unzipped her jacket. She checked her face on her phone and combed her fingers through her blond hair. An older man approached the neighboring table. He reached out to the young woman and brought her into an embrace. After a long time, he released her and cupped her face in his hands. The two stared into each other's eyes and kissed tenderly. Hadley wondered if this was a clandestine moment between secret lovers or an established couple.

Rachel looked at her watch. "It's time to go," she said, rising from her seat. Hadley finished her cappuccino and stood.

"The 99?" asked Rachel, "or Kopple and Blanzaco?" Hadley's face lit up.

The cab pulled up to the neighborhood bar. An old woman wearing a torn gray trench coat and mismatched sneakers pushed a grocery cart filled with cardboard, plastic bottles, and cans. Hadley paid the driver and opened the door. "This is it. I told you it wasn't swanky."

Rachel pressed her lips together. "You can say that again."

The 99 was small, unglamorous, with outdated Western-style decor. Rachel pulled the collar of her coat tight around her neck and thanked herself for wearing pants. Hadley seemed less concerned and walked to the bar. "Two Galloping Stallions," she instructed the bartender.

"Your daughter?" he asked. "You got ID?"

Hadley ignored him, and Rachel pulled her license out. He nodded and left. Rachel crinkled her nose at the strong smell of yeast and peanuts. It reminded her of college bars.

Hadley looked around for Chance. *Playing pool? In the restroom? Does he care about me?* Embarrassment and fear came over her. "We should go," she said. "He's not here."

The bartender returned with wine. "Not my business, but are you looking for someone? This is the third time I've seen you in a month. This joint doesn't look like your kinda place."

Hadley's eyes widened, and her skin flushed. "No, no," she stuttered, mortified.

Rachel leaned forward. "Yes, actually, we are looking for someone. We're looking for a guy named Chance. Hadley thinks he may be a long-lost cousin."

"Is that so? Well, I do know Chance. He's the brother of the owner. He lives in Wyoming but drops in when he comes to New York. Is your cousin's last name Collins?"

Hadley was embarrassed. *Caught in a lie and now a stalker. Great.* Hadley reached for her handbag, plucked a twenty from her wallet, placed it on the bar, and stood to leave.

"He'll be back in two weeks. His niece is getting married on Valentine's weekend," the bartender said, curling his upper lip as if he had a bad taste in his mouth.

Her eyes relaxed. "Thank you." The bartender wrote *Hadley* on a cocktail napkin and said he would tell Chance she stopped by. Too bad she gave Chance an alias before and forgot.

CHAPTER 19

Hadley checked the calendar Sydney hung on the kitchen wall. In the designated box, she saw MADD Gala Meeting, 1 p.m., scrawled in bold red ink. Painful as it was, Hadley knew it was time to step down as the gala's chair. The weight of her decision was compounded by another painful reality: she had just stepped down from her job at the law firm. Once highly respected for her intellect and dedication, Hadley struggled to keep up with the demands of her profession. Once simple tasks now left her frustrated and inadequate. The constant pressure and failure gnawed at her confidence. It was better to resign than be forced to leave.

However, stepping down from the gala chair was even more agonizing. Mothers Against Drunk Drivers, MADD, held a profound significance in her life. It wasn't just about organizing an event; it was about honoring the memory of her parents. MADD had provided her with purpose and community, allowing her to channel her grief into meaningful action. Every gala was a tribute to her parents' legacy and a beacon of hope for others affected by similar tragedies.

For years she poured her heart and soul into organizing the gala, overseeing details with precision and dedication. Understanding the intricacies of the budget, coordinating the vendors, and keeping the committee members' names straight were once second nature to her. But not anymore. Picking up the phone to tender her resignation,

Hadley reflected on the past three galas she had chaired; they felt distant and fragmented. She couldn't recall the themes or impressive fundraising, but she held onto the undeniable truth: they were successful under her leadership.

It all began when Hadley met Linda Brewster, the executive director for Manhattan's chapter, at a dinner party years before. Like Hadley, she had lost a loved one to a drunk driver. Linda's daughter was returning from a ski trip when a thirty-seven-year-old man with a blood alcohol level of 0.2 crossed the median strip and hit her head-on. She was killed instantly. As much as Hadley enjoyed Linda's company, the constant reminder of her parents' death was too hard to deal with. The driver who had killed her parents was a local dentist who had mixed drugs and alcohol and had a blood alcohol level of 0.144—eight drinks for someone 180 pounds.

Hadley picked up the phone. After social pleasantries, she explained, "Listen, Linda, I hate to do this, but I'm stepping down from chairing the ball. I'll be traveling quite a bit this year," Hadley fibbed. "I'm happy to help you find a replacement. In fact, Lori, eh, Lori, what is her last name?" she asked without expecting an answer. "You know, Lori with the red hair?"

"Benson," Linda replied.

"Yes," said Hadley, "Lori Benson said something about helping." Hadley laughed. "You'll be better off with her when it comes to asking; she won't take no for an answer."

"I completely understand," Linda replied. She was relieved. The committee had noticed Hadley's organizational skills slipping. It would have been messy to replace Hadley midseason. "We are so appreciative of the amazing creativity you brought to our fundraiser. It certainly raised the bar and made our galas one of the best in the city. All of us here at MADD are grateful for your time and energy. This year you'll actually get to relax and enjoy the fete." Linda chuckled. "Thank you, Hadley. Let's stay in touch and grab a cup of coffee soon."

Hadley agreed, "Sounds good. Bye, Linda." *What will I have to give up next?*

Without her job and philanthropy, Hadley filled her days with Pilates, Pooch Rescue, and memory boxes. She had purchased three decorative storage boxes to house important memories for the children. From the office file drawer, she took their birth certificates, pictures of footprints taken at birth, and original social security cards. Next, she visited her bedroom closet to retrieve a bin filled with memorabilia. Tears blurred her vision. *I'll never see my children marry. Never meet their babies.* Her throat tightened. *I wanted their lives to be better than mine.*

Before she could wallow in her misery, her phone rang. Hadley walked from the closet to the bedroom. It was Rachel. "I'm coming over. I have a surprise. What's your address?"

Hadley dug deep into her memory. "It's Lex," she said with a sigh, "Thirtieth and Lex."

"What number?" Rachel asked, trying not to pressure her.

Numbers jumbled together. Phone numbers, addresses, measurements, and bills—none made sense anymore. "I don't know," Hadley answered, "we're on the Upper East Side."

Rachel Googled *apartments Lexington and Thirtieth* and breathed a sigh of relief when only one option appeared. "You're in Lexington EastParc. Does that ring a bell?" she asked. Hadley said it did, although she wasn't one-hundred-percent certain.

An hour later, Rachel reached the lobby of Lexington Parc East. The man at the front desk called Hadley for clearance and pointed to the elevator. Rachel rode in silence, wondering what Hadley's reaction would be. She tapped on the front door. Hadley met her in the foyer. Rachel cradled her laptop and held a cardboard tray with two paper cups. Hadley took the steaming cups and gave Rachel a hug. Hadley was happy for the diversion from filling boxes.

"Holy shit, this is a nice place," Rachel said. *Wow, a crystal chandelier in the foyer.*

Hadley smiled. "Glad you like it. We call it home," she said, guiding Rachel to the kitchen. She had been to nice apartments on the Upper East Side, but this one took the cake.

"These were my parents' rugs," Hadley said, looking at the brick-red and beige Persian carpet in the hallway between the foyer and kitchen.

"That's nice you kept them," Rachel said. "They had good taste."

Rachel plugged her computer into a socket on the kitchen island. Hadley thought, *Why did she bring her laptop?*

The computer came to life, showing a beautiful backdrop of a snowy mountain resplendent with tall pines and fluffy clouds. "I thought we'd do a little recon," she said. Hadley wasn't following. Rachel typed in Chance Collins. Newspaper headlines filled the page. "Wyoming Millionaire Acquires Another Ranch," "*Forbes* Adds Collins to Billionaire Ranchers List," and "Collins Buys $725M Ranch."

Hadley was speechless. Rachel clicked on the images tab. The photos were mostly of a young boy who proclaimed to be a warlock. Hadley let out a long sigh. "I thought maybe you found him," she said, disappointment in her voice. Rachel ignored her. This time she typed in Chance Collins Wyoming Rancher. Once again, the screen was populated with a plethora of photos. Some in color, some black-and-white, but in almost all the shots, the man in the pictures wore a cowboy hat and a leather vest. "It's him." Hadley gasped. She moved closer to the screen.

Rachel was equally surprised. "That's your bar friend? He's gorgeous!"

Hadley nodded and continued scrolling. She stopped suddenly. Dressed in gala attire, Chance stood with his arm around an attractive woman. Hadley clicked the photo. "Wrangler's Ball," it said. "2006. Chance & Gwendolyn Collins." Hadley's heart sank. "He's married."

Rachel read the caption. She put her hand on Hadley's shoulder. "So are you," she reminded. Rachel tapped the back arrow. She clicked on Wikipedia. Chance's bio came up.

He was born in Brooklyn, New York, in 1965, son of Wall Street banker Walter A. Collins, and his mother Juliette Collins, a prominent interior designer whose clientele included Gloria Vanderbilt, Martha Stewart, and Ron Howard. Chance has a younger sibling, Melanie. He attended one year at Princeton University but dropped out to pursue his dream as a cattleman.

He had fallen in love with horses and ranch life after he spent several summers vacationing at dude ranches in the Midwest. Chance married Gwendolyn, a ranch hand, at twenty-two. They had two girls: Shiloh and Sierra. Chance and his wife divorced in 2009.

Hadley stopped reading. *He's divorced.*

"Now what?" Rachel asked.

Hadley wasn't sure. She wasn't going to comb the ranches in Wyoming and Montana for him. She had given up hope of running into him again and was conflicted about her interest. *It's purely innocent. Nothing happened. But I do have a teenage crush on this gorgeous man.*

But still, it niggled at her. He was so attentive that day. Did he find her attractive, witty, and fun to be with—or could there be something more? She had to know. *Am I more than an old woman with a wasting mind?* That's how she felt around Bergen. His attention was focused on her dementia. If Chance wasn't interested, she'd drop it and move on. If he was, she'd thank him for the compliment, remind him that she is married, and never see him again. Or would she?

Rachel and Hadley sat in silence. The air was palpably thick with guilt and condemnation. *What is today? Has Valentine's Day come?* She couldn't remember. Hadley closed the Wikipedia page. She clicked on the calendar icon. February 12, 2015, it read. Hadley closed her eyes and tried to think of the date for Valentine's Day. *I know it's February, but when?* "When is Valentine's Day?" she asked Rachel.

Rachel answered, "February fourteen, and you and Bergen are going to your favorite Italian restaurant." Even though Rachel had witnessed these lapses many times before, it always surprised her. *How can she remember a man she recently met and not an annually recurring date?*

Two days from now, Hadley thought. She had an idea. "I'll see Chance one more time. The *last* time. After, there will be no more stops at bars, internet searches, or teenage obsessing." She would get her one question answered, and that would be that. She promised.

Reluctantly, Rachel agreed. *It's harmless, just a fantasy. Who am I to deny a dying woman her wishes?* Rachel typed in "Luxury NYC Hotels." The Four Seasons, Baccarat, The Pierre, Ritz-Carlton, and Mandarin Oriental filled the page. Rachel jotted names and numbers.

Rachel typed in "Melanie Collins New York." Several links popped up, but only one read Melanie Browning, nee Collins. "Bingo," Rachel announced, "We've got the bride's maiden name. This is fun." The two women started their investigation. They called the catering department at each hotel and asked for the details of the Browning wedding. Dead ends everywhere. No Browning wedding in NYC for the upcoming weekend. Hadley was tired and about to give up when she had an idea. "There's a club on Fifth Avenue, near Central Park. I can't remember the name of it," she said, frustrated. "It's very prestigious. We should try there."

Rachel shook her head; she didn't know of a country club on Fifth.

As Rachel Googled clubs in the city, Hadley spurted out words that came to mind. It was like they were playing charades. "It's an opera," she said, the name just out of reach. "Only men, a social club." Just as Rachel tapped on a link for The Metropolitan Club New York, Hadley shouted, "That's it, the Met. It's the Metropolitan!" She was as excited to remember as she was to find the club. One step closer to finding Chance.

Rachel made the call. After being transferred, the wedding coordinator confirmed that the Browning-Goldstein wedding was on Saturday, February 14, starting at 6 p.m. It was to take place in the President's Ballroom, and the attire was black tie. Hadley wrote down the details.

"What now?" Rachel asked, shaking her head. "I mean, you can't just show up at the wedding. And what about your dinner with

Bergen?" If Hadley canceled her dinner with Bergen, she'd have to lie. If she lied, she'd just be digging the hole deeper. If she didn't go to the club and see Chance, her insatiable curiosity wouldn't be fulfilled, and she'd continue obsessing over a man she couldn't or shouldn't have. This was a no-win. Not for Hadley, Bergen, or Chance. Rachel wrote Hadley's options on a piece of paper, something her father taught her. Write the pros and cons for each, and then make an educated decision. "Let's play it out," she told Hadley. "To see Chance, you have to wait in the club where you'd see him coming or going. Because you don't know how late he'd stay, your best bet would be to get there a half an hour before and catch him when he's arriving. If you wanted to wait outside, you'd need to be appropriately dressed so you wouldn't seem out of place. Wait in the lobby by the main entrance."

The look on Hadley's face was deep in thought and sheer joy. "How would you get away from Bergen? What would you tell him? What if he followed you? What if Chance comes in a different entrance? What if you see him? What if he doesn't remember you? Or kisses you?"

Hadley was confused. *Too much information.* The room spun. *One thing at a time.* She rubbed her index finger across her teeth. *This isn't fun anymore.* She hadn't thought of the outcomes. "What would you do?" Hadley asked, her face suddenly troubled.

Rachel raised her eyebrows. *Damn it, Rachel. You created a hornet's nest.* She was torn between loyalty and ethical concerns. She wanted to see Hadley happy. Maybe her crush was a sign of longing for something more in life, but betraying Bergen didn't feel right. "It's like you have a bee in your bonnet, Hads. This desire to get the attention of another man is not like you. I feel bad encouraging it. I shouldn't have come today. Many people never find their soulmate. With Bergen, you have that. He loves you, and you love him. Flirting with Chance is dangerous. Is that really the memory you want to leave your husband and kids?"

Hadley covered her face. She was embarrassed, disgusted and felt like a traitor. "Can you go?" she politely asked. "I want to be alone."

Rachel hugged her friend. "I'm not judging you for this," she said. "You are my very dear friend. I can't imagine what you're going through. I think Chance added a spark to a dismal situation. It's okay to dream, fantasize, but leave it there. Let it be your little secret. You can go there anytime you want, but keep it in there," Rachel said, lightly tapping Hadley's head. Hadley looked up and pushed her hair away from her eyes. Rachel was right. She had a wonderful husband and a loving and supportive family. She would take a chance and tell Dr. Kopple about this. She would ask him to help her with her feelings of inadequacy that would only intensify as she got sicker.

Hadley picked up the Styrofoam coffee cup. Her coffee was cold, the frothy milk flattened. She needed something stronger. She poured it down the sink and turned to retrieve two wineglasses. Rachel smiled. "That a girl," she said and helped her friend uncork a bottle of rosé. Rachel was impressed with how resilient Hadley was. She always seemed to bounce back, take control. *Note to self,* she told herself, *a good lesson to live by.* They clinked glasses and discussed what Hadley might wear to dinner on Valentine's Day.

CHAPTER 20

Hadley stretched her legs on the sofa. It was time for her "memory boost," as she called it. With Bergen's help, Hadley set up a series of daily activities to help with her memory. She finished reading The New York Times and attempted the spelling bee and crossword puzzle. Even the online mini puzzle was more difficult. She picked up her iPad and tapped on the Brain Train app. A picture with five colorful butterflies appeared. The instructions were simple enough: on the next screen, click on the locations of the matching butterflies. "A kindergartener could get this one," Hadley said. The second screen popped up. Hadley was gobsmacked. She had no idea where the three blue-and-white matching ones were. She clicked randomly, producing a large X.

The front door opened, and in pranced Sydney. "Mom? You here?" she called out.

Why is she home? Is it still winter break? Hadley cursed herself for not remembering the date. Water dripped off Sydney's blue raincoat. She placed her suitcase and backpack on the floor and removed her coat, then hugged her mother. The weather in April was highly variable, fluctuating from freezing to temperate, but one thing residents could count on was plenty of rain. "I have an A in French, so I didn't have to take the midterm. I found a ride, and here I am!"

It was comforting to have her oldest daughter home. Hadley was pleased. She picked up her iPad and considered asking Sydney to try the butterfly test, but it slipped from her mind quickly. "Come, tell me about school." She steered Sydney toward the kitchen. "Care to join me for a cup of tea? You can unpack later." Sydney took two teacups from the china cupboard and sat at the kitchen table as her mom boiled the water. "Peppermint, chamomile, or green? Supposedly green tea helps with memory, performance, and focus."

Sydney smiled. "Green."

Hadley put a spoonful of sugar in her daughter's and sweetener in hers. She joined Sydney at the table, the look on her face suddenly sad and tortured. "Syd, I have something important I need to talk to you about." Sydney looked up from her tea. "It's about my Alzheimer's," she continued. "You're old enough to understand and make your own decisions."

Sydney wanted to change the subject but anticipated "the talk" and wanted to get it over with. "Mom, I've been reading about dementia. You know, some people never fully lose all their memory and can live with it for twenty years." *We'll be together for a long time.*

"Syd, honey," her mom replied, "I have what they call familial Alzheimer's disease."

"Familial?" Sydney asked, putting the pieces together.

Hadley let out a long-hitched breath. She wished she didn't have to deliver this part of her diagnosis. "This type, the risk"—Hadley made a guttural sound and swallowed hard—"is passed down from generation to generation. The risk of getting it . . . is fifty percent."

"Wait. What? Are you telling me I have a fifty-fifty chance of getting what you have?"

"I'm sorry. I'm so very sorry," Hadley answered, shaking her head.

I want to go back to school. Start over. "Have you told Brook and Tucker?"

"Not yet. We will once they're old enough to make an educated decision."

"Decision about what?" Sydney asked. "Jesus, is there more?"

"Well, you can learn the way I did. Gene sequencing. This is important, not something to decide overnight. To help, I could introduce you to the genetic counselor we spoke to."

"I come home early from school to see everyone, and this is what you dump on me? That's so unfair, Mom. Look what this stupid test has done to our family. I don't want to know, ever." Sydney stormed out of the room.

Hadley put her head down and felt unbearably sad. *It is unfair, so very unfair. How can I allow this dreadful disease to be passed on? If only my parents were still alive. I'd have known the risk of having children.*

The smoke alarm startled her. "Shit, sugar, the kettle," she said, jumping from her chair. Hadley grabbed a potholder and pulled the smoking kettle from the burner. The copper bottom was black. Hadley dropped it into the sink and took the smoke alarm battery out.

THE NIGHT BEFORE going back to school, Sydney said, "I have an announcement to make."

"You're pregnant," teased Brook.

"Very funny. No, and this is serious," Sydney shot back.

Hadley gave Brook a look of disapproval and gestured for Sydney to continue.

Sydney squared her shoulders and looked to Bergen for support. "I wanted to let you know I am going to take next semester off," she stated.

"Do you mean semester abroad?" Hadley asked, confused.

Bergen sighed and explained, "No, dear. Sydney and I have been talking. We think it's a good idea for her to take a little time off from school and stay here to help out."

"Absolutely not," Hadley said, her voice rising. "And what do you mean *we*? What about what *I* think?"

Tucker grimaced. "I forgot, I was supposed to meet Charlie to work on our history project. Excuse me."

"Uh, excuse me too, uh bathroom," Brook lied.

"Bergen, I will not hear of this. Sydney has a bright, promising business career ahead *if* she continues her studies."

"I will continue my studies," interrupted Sydney, "after a short hiatus. I want to be here; I want to help. You said I was old enough to make my own decisions, and this is one of them."

"Help how?" Hadley asked. "I'm not an invalid. I can take care of myself."

Bergen reached across the table to touch Hadley's arm. She shoved his hand away.

"I know you want to help, and the time will come when I need it," Hadley said, hesitating. Her nostrils flared. "But not now. Leave me with some dignity. Please. I can take care of myself."

Sydney rose and hugged her mom from behind. "I love you, Mom. We all do, and we want to help. Maybe you don't see what we see."

"What do you mean?" Hadley demanded. "What do you see?" *Is this me against them?*

"Sweetheart," Bergen said tenderly, "let's not do this. We have noticed changes. I know this is hard, and I can't imagine how frightening it must be for you."

Hadley shook her head. "I appreciate you wanting to help, Sydney, and it would be nice to have you here. I wish my mother was around when I was in college." As if suddenly in deep mental absorption, Hadley started to tell a story. Her voice was flat, almost robotic. "It was a Thursday night. Mom and Dad went to see a play. Mark was away at school. I was watching *Hill Street Blues*. At 9:45, the doorbell rang. I remember because Mom and Dad weren't due home until eleven. Mrs. Kapshaw, our neighbor, was at the door, with two policemen. She was crying. I didn't know why. I thought she was sick, or her dog had died.

"She took my hand and led me to the couch. She asked me to sit. The policemen just stood there with their hands clasped. Mrs.

Kapshaw was wearing her robe and slippers. She sat on the couch, her knees touching mine, and then . . ."

Bergen reached for her hand. *Why is she doing this to herself?*

"And then, she told me. She came right out and said it. Mom and Dad had been killed in a car accident. They died instantly and didn't suffer. I remember thinking about how weird it was that she said they didn't suffer. What did that matter if they were gone?" Bergen stood behind Hadley's chair, wrapping his arms around her shoulders and chest.

"Mom, I'm so sorry," Sydney said. She had known there was a car accident but never heard the details. *What will I tell my kids about their grandmother?*

"I wish this was just a dreadful nightmare," Hadley said, her voice less mechanical. "If you say I need help, then I guess I do," she said with resignation. Time with her family would be short-lived. She'd have to give up stubbornness and dogged independence to be with them more. It wouldn't mean she was defeated, just adjusting her early-adopted coping skills.

"It'll be okay, Mom. I'll work on my research project and only help when you ask. I want to be with you while you are still as good as you are. I'll add trackers to the keys, leave Post-it notes, and update the calendar. We can also do girl things together, mother-daughter time. Have fun."

It was difficult to hear. "I'll surrender to your offer to help, but I'm not giving up yet."

Bergen smiled. "You're a fighter, sweetie, but we are all in this together, forever."

Forever. The word echoed. *Forever never ends. I don't want endless suffering.*

Bergen and Sydney washed the dinner dishes. Hadley excused herself. Inside her bathroom, she locked the door and ran the water. Competing images of Bergen cocooning her like a child and Chance staring dreamily into her eyes vied for her attention. Bergen made her feel safe, but Chance, or at least fantasies of him, made her feel exhilarated and alive.

This is all too much. She rifled through the various medicine bottles in her cabinet. There was nothing useful. Then she remembered, *The closet.* She removed an old quilt from the top shelf and retrieved a small, blue plastic bin. In earlier years, it was hidden to keep the children safe: their unfinished prescriptions, antibiotics, and muscle relaxants.

She took an old makeup case and dropped several bottles in. Then she found the pain killers. One half-used vial was prescribed when Sydney had her wisdom teeth out, one for Tucker after his appendectomy, and another after Bergen's ACL repair. It was full. Narcotics made Bergen nauseated, so he used over-the-counter analgesics instead. All the pain killers had expired. In fact, most of the pills in the bin had. Hadley shrugged and dropped them in. She zipped the makeup case closed. She would check the internet to see how much would be lethal.

Then the sadness washed over her. Now that she'd gathered the pills, it frightened her. *What if one of the children finds me? Like Rachel's mom? What if the expired pills don't work and I become a vegetable?*

Bergen's knock on the door startled her. She shoved the bin and quilt back onto the shelf. She closed the closet and turned off the water. Still holding the makeup bag, Hadley unlocked the door and walked past Bergen and into the bedroom. She pulled out the top dresser drawer and shoved the bag toward the back of her socks and underwear.

Bergen stood behind her and put his arms around her waist. He looked at the reflection of her face in the mirror over the dresser. "All good from our discussion?" he asked.

Hadley turned to face him. "Sure," she answered, not certain what discussion he was talking about.

Bergen smiled and gave her a peck on the cheek.

CHAPTER 21

"Hey, you're becoming a regular 'round here," Bomber Bob called from behind the desk.

Rachel waved. "This is Meghan Rady. She owns Pooch Rescue, where I got Princess."

"Nice to meet ya," Bob replied. "And who do we have here with little Miss Princess?"

"Bob, meet Casanova. Cassie for short. Meghan and I came to talk about the adoption program we started at the Rescue. We've been looking for a German shepherd for Joe and came upon this guy. He's six, neutered, and looking for a forever home. If Auckland Joe will have him, he will be our gift to him. It's a surprise."

Bob's wide grin said it all. "And a fine-looking dog he is. I won't say a word."

The five of them went back to the common room, where the men were gathered for Princess and Rachel's weekly visit.

"Hey, Princess, come here, girl," one of the men called. Rachel let go of the leash.

Meghan stopped to look around. *This is the same look as the puppies at the kill shelters. Forlorn, lost, anguished.* Meghan rubbed Cassie's ears. *What a perfect match. Second chances and new beginnings—for the dogs and veterans.* She smiled, excited to announce the program.

Auckland Joe came over to Casanova and bent down. "This dog

looks just like my Kingston," he said. "Is he your dog?" he asked. Meghan looked to Rachel for guidance.

Just then, a man started to play the piano as vets came to pet and socialize with the dogs.

"Ten-hut," Bob belted over the chatter. In an instant, all men came to attention. "Well, that worked." He laughed. "Rachel has brought Ms. Rady here today to tell you about her new program at the Pooch Rescue. So, let's give her and Casanova here a warm welcome."

The men clapped and took their seats. "Thank you, Bob. I work with Pooch Rescue, a nonprofit dog rescue located just outside the city on the Jersey side. Rachel got Princess from us." The men looked at Princess and smiled. Meghan described her rescue operation, fostering between ten and fifteen dogs. She explained, "They come to the Rescue from different means, but they are all looking for their forever home. Because we have a soft spot for seniors, the majority of our rescues are six or older. Cassie, for instance, is six and a half. His owners moved to North Carolina and left him behind. A neighbor called about a week later. Poor thing hadn't had any food. The good news is, Cassie is now happy and healthy, full of energy and love."

Auckland Joe looked over at Rachel. She returned his glance with a wink and a smile.

Meghan continued, "We have some exciting news and want you all to be the first to know. Rachel, do you want to tell them?"

Some of the men cocked their heads expectantly at Rachel. "Sure, I'd be happy to," she replied. Rachel explained the veteran's program and credited Meghan for the grant that funds it.

"So, what exactly is it?" Da Nang Dan asked.

"The vet program, which we're calling The Auckland Project"— Joe looked up quizzically—"is an adoption program for veterans. Pooch Rescue will work with interested vets to find the right match and then provide the funding for necessary dog training. To sweeten the pot, Pooch Rescue will also provide full medical care for the life of the dog."

The men erupted in wows and awes. "Is Casanova available?" one asked.

"The answer to that is up to Joe," Rachel said, looking over at him.

"Moi?" he said, eyebrows raised, pointing a finger at himself.

Meghan jumped in. "Lieutenant Auckland Joe, it would be our great pleasure if you would be the first recipient in our program and keep Casanova for yourself."

Joe buried his face in his hands, using all his inner strength not to break down. A moment later, he called, "Come here, boy. Come, Casanova." Cassie perked his large, soft ears and looked at Joe with warm, intelligent eyes. He padded over to Joe and nuzzled his wet nose into Joe's chest. Joe knew immediately: he would be a devoted companion. The men exploded with applause.

Over the next hour, the men lined up, talking to Rachel and Meghan about their needs and the kind of dog they'd someday like to have. The men wanted companionship, a reason to get up in the morning, motivation to leave the house, and to reduce stress. Some needed more than emotional support. For those vets with serious memory loss, panic attacks, or sleep disturbances, a service dog would be the better match. She would help coordinate that too.

Joe held tight to his new companion. "We're going to be best friends," he said. Cassie licked his face. "I guess I am going to have to work on getting better so I can take you home."

Princess and Cassie have already impacted our lives—both mine and Joe's. Dogs, unlike some people I know, offer unconditional love. They never judge. This is how I want to spend my life, around animals. Rachel briefly pictured herself working in a veterinarian's office.

After an hour of visitation, Rachel, Meghan, and the dogs said their goodbyes. Joe held Cassie around the neck and kissed his muzzle several times before releasing him. Cassie leaned into Joe's body and wagged his tail. He was naturally attentive to Joe's emotional state. Rachel looked on and smiled. She knew the support would be life-changing.

CHAPTER 22

Rachel woke to find Princess sprawled out by her side. Her legs extended outward and paws twitched in a dream-induced dance. The rise and fall of her chest was steady and serene. Rachel kissed her soft muzzle.

Rachel raised her arms and stretched. She felt rested. A good night without nightmares. She wanted to linger in the blanket's warmth a little longer, but the day beckoned. "Time for breakfast, then our morning walk," Rachel announced. Princess wagged her tail.

It was Saturday, 7 a.m. Having Princess established a grounded routine amid unpredictable PTSD. Rachel felt stability and control, fostering security and peace.

Rachel filled Princess's bowl with kibble and refreshed her water bowl. Then, a walk.

The sidewalks were busy with early morning joggers and moms with strollers. Princess walked dutifully by Rachel's side, their steps synchronized with the city's pulses. Amid the hustle and bustle, Princess remained unfazed, eagerly anticipating the adventure ahead.

Then, the cacophony of the city streets halted. An elderly lady cried out in pain, her raspy voice echoing against the concrete. Rachel froze. Behind her, an old woman lay sprawled on the sidewalk, her walker toppled over. There was blood and crying. Princess leaned against Rachel's leg, her warm fur comforting. With each deep breath,

Rachel felt grounded, steady. Frantic footsteps closed in as Good Samaritans rushed to the old woman's aid. Someone was calling 911, while others lifted the woman to her feet and on a nearby bench. *She is in good hands.*

Princess and Rachel navigated the streets back home. Rachel watched Princess frolic in the park, her mood contagious, lightening Rachel's mood. *I can sit and watch the chaotic city life unfold, anxiety no longer lurking, and it's all thanks to Princess, my loyal canine companion.*

CHAPTER 23

Hadley stretched her arms overhead and let one drop behind her onto the sheets. Bergen was gone. Hadley glanced at the clock on her bedside table: 8:17. She pulled the sheet and comforter off and swung her legs to the side of the bed. She glanced at her naked body and then looked around the room. Her panties and nightgown lay on the floor next to the bed. Hadley was pleasantly surprised. Since her diagnosis, Bergen's overtures had become less frequent. The same had happened when she was pregnant. As if he was afraid she'd break. Hadley scooped up her clothes. There on the vanity was a note from Bergen: Didn't want to wake you from your beauty sleep. Took the kids out for breakfast. Join us at The Penrose if you wake in time. ILU, B.

After she showered, dressed, and made the bed, she headed to the kitchen. Warm yellow rays shone through the window revealed tiny silver flecks dancing in the air. It was a nice day for a walk. Hadley went to the hall closet and took out her Uggs and puffy jacket. She pulled a scarf and gloves from the pockets and headed for the elevator.

Outside, Hadley took in her surroundings. The sun was cheerful and bright. The shoveled sidewalks were dimpled with pock marks left by the salt scattered earlier that morning. Hadley looked at The Penrose. She checked her watch. She wasn't in the mood for avocado toast or blueberry pancakes. A simple croissant or muffin would be fine, but she just wanted to walk. Hadley turned left and walked down

Lexington Avenue, admiring the store windows' Easter displays. Then she turned right on Fifty-Ninth toward Columbus Circle. At 10 a.m., Hadley was hungry. She rode the escalator down to Whole Foods, where a display of Easter lilies, tulips, and bright pink hyacinths greeted her. She got a green juice and ahi poke. Then she grabbed some chicken and sweet potatoes for dinner and took her place in the queue to check out.

Hadley stood in line, paging through a magazine. She pushed her basket with her foot.

"Suzette Kopple," the man behind her said again. "Mrs. Suzette Kopple?"

Hadley turned her head slightly, looking for the familiar voice.

"Is that you?" the voice said again. There was Chance, standing behind her.

"It's Hadley, Hadley Stanton," she said, a smile blossoming. "I was afraid I'd never see you again."

"Hello, Hadley. I'd hug you, but my arms are kind of full," he said warmly, motioning with his chin to the bags of chips, avocados, salsa, and beer he was balancing in his arms.

"Oh my lord, I'm so sorry," Hadley said and lifted her basket off the ground. "Here, put them in here." Chance held the six-pack in one hand and slowly moved the others to her basket.

"It's your turn," an elderly woman behind them urged. Hadley divided the items on the checkout counter. After she checked out, she stood to the side to wait for Chance. Her mind was spinning. *Is it presumptuous to wait for him?* She cursed herself for wearing her puffy coat. It made her look fat. She licked her lips, sucked on her front teeth, and blew a puff of air into cupped hands, hoping she didn't have coffee breath. Chance joined her, placing his hand on her shoulder. She shivered. Her body felt as if electricity was coursing through her veins. Hadley took in a long breath, trying to calm her nerves.

"Hadley, are you okay?" Chance asked, his warm smile sending shivers down her spine. "Do you have time to chat?" He motioned toward the small dining area. Hadley nodded. She removed a plastic fork from the cutlery dispenser, scanning the room for familiar faces. Chance pulled out her chair and gently slid his hand across her back. Her stomach turned to mush.

Hadley fiddled with her groceries and pulled out the poke. With her stomach doing flip-flops, raw fish was the last thing she wanted to eat. She took the lid off and pushed it toward Chance. "Would you like some?"

"No, thank you. Sorry, I don't have anything to share. I'm just in for the weekend and leave late tomorrow. I've been back a few times since we met and hoped I'd run into you again," he said.

God, he's handsome. "I went back to The 99 once or twice too," she told him.

Chance reached across the table and placed his thumb over her wedding band.

Hadley pulled her hand free. Her throat tightened. "I've been married for over twenty years and have three children." She packed up her lunch quickly. "I should go."

Chance smiled. He did not insist she stay. Instead, he helped Hadley with her coat. "I won't lie to you, Hadley. I find you extremely attractive. I'd like to see you again."

Hadley zipped her coat. She tucked her hair behind her ears, then, without hesitation, leaned forward and kissed him on the cheek. A warm feeling flooded her body. Chance cupped her face with his hands and tenderly kissed her mouth, first the top lip, then the lower. Blood rushed to her inner thighs. She felt out of control, but in a good way.

"I can't. I shouldn't," she said. "I really must go."

Chance released his hands. "I'm staying next door at the Mandarin. It's where I always stay. I'll be back in two weeks. I hope you'll come see me."

Hadley looked around the alcove, filled with tourists and kids with their cardboard salad boxes and juices, and she felt confused, disoriented. *Why am I in Whole Foods with Chance? Did I arrange to meet him? Why a public place?* She looked into his brown eyes and slowly nodded.

"I have to go. I'm sorry," she said and swallowed hard. She lifted her hand and trailed her fingers lightly over his arm. "I really have to go." She looped her grocery bag over her arm and turned to leave. "Goodbye, Chance," she said. Chance watched as Hadley exited the store.

Outside, Hadley took a seat on a bench. *What just happened? I'm married. I kissed—was kissed by—a sexy cowboy I met only once.* Her face felt warm, and her fingers tingled. Her mouth was dry, and she could taste metal. It was nearing noon, and she still hadn't eaten. Hadley reached into the paper bag. She pulled out a plastic container and was surprised to find salsa and not poke. It wasn't hers; she didn't even like it. Chance. It was Chance's. *Is he still nearby? I should return it.* Hadley rose quickly and wobbled forward, grabbing the bench to steady herself. She was dizzy. Hadley pulled out the green juice and unscrewed the cap. She sat back down and downed the drink. Within a few minutes, Hadley felt better.

Hadley looked at the buildings on Columbus Circle. *Where did Chance say he stayed?* Hadley crossed the street and walked to the stairs of the Trump International. One of several doormen outside greeted her and opened the door to the lobby. Hadley approached the desk. "I'm dropping off something for Mr. Chance Collins," Hadley told the woman. The woman punched the name into her computer. No guest by that name.

"Perhaps he's registered under another name," the clerk offered. Hadley shook her head, thanked her, and left the building. There was the Mandarin Oriental, Park Central East, and The Plaza, although it was a few blocks away. Hadley turned right and walked toward the Mandarin.

Am I returning this because he'll need it, or is it an excuse to see him again? She looked at her watch. Bergen and the kids would be worried. *Four texts and two missed calls from Bergen. I hate how he's always reminding me I'm diseased.* Hadley turned the ringtone back on and called Bergen. She shook her head in disgust and rolled her eyes, explaining, "I was just picking up a few things at Whole Foods. I'll be home soon."

As she approached the next hotel, the doorman leaned his shovel against the wall and opened a large glass door. "Welcome to The Mandarin Oriental," he said, tipping his hat. Hadley entered the lobby and rode the express elevator to the thirty-fifth floor, the reception area. The grandeur of the staircase, Lalique-inspired ceiling, and commanding city views amazed her, but the blown glass sculpture rising out of a moss garden took her breath away.

"It was commissioned by Dale Chihuly," the front desk clerk said. "It was designed to follow the feng shui principles that embrace unity, harmony, and a constant flow of energy." Hadley nodded. Although she could not recall being at the hotel before, she was familiar with the Chihuly sculptures, Chinese textiles, and art in the grand marble and granite lobby.

"I'm here to drop something off for Mr. Collins, Chance Collins," Hadley told the clerk. The clerk smiled. She acknowledged that Mr. Collins was a guest and lifted the phone receiver to call him. Before she could ask Hadley her name, Hadley quickly interjected "I can just leave it here. You needn't bother him." It was too late. The clerk told him he had a guest.

"Who may I tell him is here?" she asked Hadley. Hadley's face flushed. There was still time to put the salsa on the desk and leave. "Ma'am, your name?" the agent repeated.

"It's Hadley Stanton. Can I just leave the item here with you?" she asked. She was flustered, embarrassed. *A guest who can afford to stay in one of New York's five-star hotels can afford the room service to get more salsa.*

The clerk raised her hand. "He'll be right down. He asked if you could please wait."

Hadley gave the agent a half smile and nodded politely. She combed her fingers through her hair and took out her phone to check the time. *Twenty minutes since I called Bergen. I should be home by now.* She quickly typed a short text,

> Ran into an old friend in the park.
> B home soon.

Chance stepped off the elevator. Hadley's heart skipped. "I was hoping you'd come." Hadley was prepared to hand him the salsa and leave, but Chance motioned for her to get in the elevator. Without hesitation, Hadley stepped in. The doors closed. Chance stood in front of her, his hands on her shoulders, and lifted her chin to his gaze. They looked into each other's eyes.

Before Chance could place his mouth on hers, Hadley reached into the bag for his salsa. Chance stepped back and blinked. "I, I, I, just came back to return your salsa. It was in my bag. I thought you'd want it." Chance closed his eyes and took a deep breath.

The elevator stopped, and the doors opened. A middle-aged woman in a gold tweed suit entered, her mink coat draped over her arm. She pushed sixty-three and turned. "Hadley, my dear, hello." Her diamond earrings reflected in the mirrored wall. "What a pleasant surprise to see you. It's been ages. My dad lives here in one of the residences. You visiting anyone I know?"

Chance pretended to place a call. Hadley hesitated. The elevator came to another stop. "My floor," Chance said and exited without looking up.

"No, no one you'd know. I'm visiting a college friend who's in for the weekend," Hadley said but quickly realized there was no other button illuminated except sixty-three. "I think I got her floor wrong. I'll have to go back down and check with reception again. Silly me." Once again, the elevator stopped, and the woman stepped out.

"Let's get together for lunch soon." Hadley nodded and smiled awkwardly.

Outside, Hadley threw the salsa in a trash can. "Fucking salsa."

Why did I really go to the hotel? Why did I get in the elevator? The shame suffocated her. *Bergen doesn't deserve this.*

She stared at her reflection in a storefront window. She saw her mother wagging an index finger at her. What she was doing was wrong. This is not who Hadley was or how she'd been raised. *That is it. Final. I'll never see Chance again.* The reflection of her mother moved her hand and placed it over her heart. Hadley dropped to her knees. Then a feeling of calm enveloped her. *I'll be okay. We all will.*

CHAPTER 24

As the midday sun filtered in, Hadley noticed how dirty the master bedroom window was. She retrieved her notebook and jotted a reminder to ask the building super to have them washed. "Whatcha looking at?" Bergen asked as he rounded the corner from the bathroom.

"Oh, nothing in particular," she answered, having already forgotten. "Have you seen my, oh goodness me, the word is on the tip of my tongue. My, oh that thing I carry my money in?"

"Your pocketbook?" he asked.

"No, no, the coin thing. My willy, I mean my wardrobe. Shit," Hadley said, exasperated. "My wallet," she finally said, both pleased and frightened.

She's doing it more frequently, he told himself, *not being able to recall words—and the swearing*. It surprised him. This was certainly not the Hadley he knew. "Your wallet? No, sorry, honey, I haven't, but I'll keep an eye out for it. Do you need cash?"

Hadley shook her head. *Why do I need my wallet anyway?*

Bergen went into the closet and started dressing for work. Hadley stood in front of her dresser. It had been her mother's and her mother's mother before that. Its dark mahogany and block shape was not stylish, but it was still in good shape, a daily reminder of her mom. On the top of the dresser, Hadley kept her box collection. Her mother introduced the small boxes to her when she was a little girl. Every year, on her birthday, Hadley's mother gave her a small trinket box, each one with a special meaning. Even as an adult, she had collected them. Now she had two dozen boxes of varying shapes and sizes. She picked up the Mother-of-Pearl one with its golden clasp and rubbed her thumb and forefinger over its smooth surface. "My first box."

"What?" Bergen called from the closet. "Are you talking to me?"

"No, dear," she answered, "I'm just looking at my boxes." A wave of anxiety filled her chest. *What if I forget what each one means?* Hadley retrieved a notecard, tape, and pen from her bedside table. On the bottom of each, she put a piece of tape and numbered them one to twenty. She started with the shell: one, Florida, she wrote, recollecting her first family trip to Daytona Beach. She cataloged as many as she could remember. *What else do I need to label?* The day would come when she wouldn't know what a lamp is or how to make the bed. *Can Sydney help?*

Bergen interrupted, "My dad collected coins, and I collected stamps as a kid."

"I didn't know that. Do you still have your collection?" she asked.

"No," he said, "it was just a passing phase, like Tuck and his Pokémon cards."

"Everyone in my family collected things," Hadley said. "My mother collected silver spoons, my dad collected old toy trains, and Mark started to collect rare coins. I'm not sure if he still does or not," she said, shrugging. "I'll never forget, though," she said, stopping mid-sentence, saddened that one day she likely would. "My grandpa collected—or, in truth, stole—ashtrays from hotels all over the world," she said, laughing.

Bergen came out of the closet dressed in a navy suit, pale-yellow shirt, and a blue and yellow paisley tie. "You look handsome," Hadley commented.

"I'd hope you'd think so," he replied. "You picked out this suit."

Hadley silently questioned who would be choosing his next

wardrobe. "If not for this, you'd be perfect." She ran her finger across his left eyebrow, a small patch void of hair.

"Hey, you once told me scars are manly and make us even more perfect," he said. He held her in his arms and kissed her forehead, then placed his hands on her bottom. *She still has a perfect ass*, he thought. "Love to stay and show you more of my perfection, but I've got a meeting with Feldman and his team. Sydney went to the library but will be back for dinner."

Hadley went to her desk. Pen in hand, she took a piece of cream-colored stationary from the drawer. On the desk sat a framed photograph of her mother and father. "Why is this happening to me?" she said softly. "You left me when I was so young, and now, I'm going to do the same to my kids." Hadley dropped her head and arms on the desk and cried. When there were no more tears, she raised her head and scolded herself for the self-pity. At least Bergen hadn't been there to see her break down. She retrieved the pen and started to write.

> *Dearest Bergen, the love and light of my life,*
>
> *Who would have thought I would one day be writing a letter saying goodbye to you? My hopes and dreams for us extended well into our eighties, if not our nineties.*
>
> *I'm not exactly sure how to say goodbye, but I want you to know you are the love of my life, my inspiration, and my compass. You have brought out the best in me and always been there. You have given me the most precious gift of all: our three beautiful children.*
>
> *I am sorry for bringing so much pain to our family and hope that the children can come to terms with this horrible disease and their own destiny.*
>
> *Oh, my dear, my dear, what dreams I had for the children and us. I'm hoping in Heaven I won't have any memory loss so I can hold on to all the treasured time we spent together.*

You are still vibrant, young, handsome (and so sexy). I want you to find another partner and marry again. You mustn't be a martyr. You need someone to love and share your life with, and the children will need a mother, especially Tucker.

Please be sure that Sydney goes back to school and completes her degree.

Every month during the full moon, look up, and I will smile back at you, sending kisses from above. I hope your pain and sadness disappear, and you will think of me with a smile.

With ALL My Love, Hadley

Hadley read the letter to herself three times before placing it in an envelope and sealing it. She held it in her hands and looked around the room, wondering where to put it so Bergen would find it after her death and not before. She wrote, "For when I am gone" on the front and placed the letter in the desk drawer. Also in the drawer was the daily checklist Dr. Boswell gave her. Hadley retrieved the questionnaire, vaguely remembering she had promised she'd quiz herself daily. "Question one: What day is today?" she started. "Today is . . . Yesterday was Sunday. Bergen was home all day," she reminded herself. "Today is Monday. Good. Number two: Who is the president? Fuck, shit, how can I not know this?" she said, furious. "Number three: What is your address? It's three, hmmm, three-something Lexington, New York. C'mon, Hadley, these are simple questions," she scolded. "What season is it? Spring," she answered, quickly smiling. "Count backward from one hundred by sevens," she instructed. Hadley held out her right hand and tapped each finger in the air. "One hundred, ninety-nine, ninety-eight, ninety-three, ninety-two, ninety-three. Damn it," she shouted. She rolled the exam into a ball and threw it across the room. *I could answer these last time.*

Hadley sat on the end of her bed and pulled her knees to her chest.

She wrapped her slender arms around her thighs and gently rocked herself back. "God, why me?" Hadley pressed her fingers and palms together in prayer. "Whatever it is you want me to do, I promise, I swear, I will," she said desperately. "Please save me. Let this diagnosis be a mistake, please!" she yelled, wailing convulsively. "I'll start going to church. I'll stop drinking. I'll give up chocolate. I'll do anything, please," she pleaded. She was bargaining again. She was regressing in the stages of grief too. "Are you even there?" she yelled. *A real God wouldn't let people suffer and die.*

When there were no more tears or bargains left to make, Hadley crawled under the comforter and hid. She dozed off. An hour later her phone reminder dinged. She woke, surprised to find herself in bed. Hadley read the message: "3 p.m., meet Rachel at Mika's." Wondering if it really mattered or if she even had the energy, Hadley decided against going and pulled the covers up to her chin. Then her iPhone rang. Rachel. Hadley put the call on speaker.

"Hey, it's me, your backup reminder for our coffee date today," Rachel said cheerfully.

"I'm going to skip today. I'm not feeling so well."

"You okay?" Rachel asked. "You sound a little low."

It took every ounce of energy for Hadley not to break down. She wanted the companionship so much, especially right now, but it wasn't fair to keep placing her burden on Rachel. *I don't want to drag her down. She's better because of Princess and therapy.*

"Hadley, I'm coming over. Stay put." She hung up.

Rachel ran to the Christopher Street subway station. She jumped onto the train just as the doors were closing. She looked down at her shoes. The floor was grimy, brown gunk, crushed food items, and sticky liquids. Crowds in malls and concerts were one thing, but being crammed together with no escape unless the train stopped was another. She only rode the subway when she was broke or late or the weather was unbearable. Or if there was an emergency like today.

The smell of cheap perfume, sweat, and cigarettes attacked her nose, causing her eyes to water and saliva to accumulate in her mouth. She took a piece of chewing gum from her coat pocket and popped it in her mouth, swallowing the bile creeping up her throat. Rachel stared at the map over the filthy window and counted the stops on her seven-minute ride to Times Square. There, she changed to the N and exited at Forty-Ninth Street. "Excuse me," she said politely but urgently. Outside, Rachel zipped her jacket to her neck and ran to Hadley's building.

She couldn't lose Hadley. She needed her. Mindy was supportive and trustworthy, but it was different with Hadley. Hadley normalized Rachel's experiences. They were soulmates.

Rachel dashed past the doorman and pushed the revolving door.

"Excuse me," she said, half out of breath, "I'm here to see Hadley Stanton."

"And you are?" the skinny man behind the desk said. The fluorescent light above reflected off his shiny, bald head. He was new and didn't know the regular visitors yet.

"I'm Rachel Weissman. Hadley's, um, Ms. Stanton's friend." Rachel pulled her phone out of her pocket. She touched the phone icon. "Here," she said. "I was just talking to her."

The scrawny man glanced briefly at the phone. "Is she expecting you?"

"Call her, please. Tell her Rachel is here to see her. Please, it's urgent," Rachel pleaded.

Given how little energy she had, Hadley would have ignored the front desk's call, but she knew it was Rachel in the lobby. She folded back the crisp white comforter and swung her legs over the side of the bed. The single landline was in the hall on the lowboy and quite frankly only used to communicate with the reception desk and as a backup for their security system.

After giving approval, Hadley stopped in the powder room to splash cold water on her puffy eyelids. She combed her fingers through her hair and smiled at her reflection. It was a good feeling to have a friend who understood and cared so much.

Hadley opened the door. Rachel hugged Hadley tightly.

"Thank God you're okay," she said with relief. "I was, well, worried you might have done something."

Hadley gently separated their bodies and took Rachel's face in her hands. "Dear child, we made a promise. I never break promises. Come inside. We'll have some tea and talk. Then we have doctor appointments to get to." She winked and led Rachel into the apartment.

Hadley stood against the large granite kitchen island. Her gaze had taken on that distant look Rachel was beginning to recognize. She was lost. Not physically but mentally.

Rachel glanced at the microwave clock; it was past three. They barely had time for tea before their appointments. Hadley made no motions to put the kettle on or get mugs, so Rachel decided to skip it all together. Rachel had been so panicked before, thinking Hadley had succumbed to her death wish. *What would life without Hadley be like? I don't want to know. But is suicide ever the right answer? Besides Mom and Aunt Claudette, would anyone really miss me? Is this safe to discuss in therapy?* The clock said it was time to go. Looking out the kitchen window at the thick, dark gray clouds, she suggested, "We should bring an umbrella."

Hadley shook her head and looked up from her gaze. "Why? Where are we going?"

"Our psychiatrist appointments," Rachel answered. "We go every Tuesday at four."

Hadley cocked her head. There was a mischievous twinkle in her eye. "Let's play hooky. My husband won't be home until seven, so we'll have girl time. Stay for dinner and meet him."

Rachel wanted to be spontaneous but knew it would mean another no-show charge that insurance wouldn't cover. "I, well, I would love to stay, but," Rachel stammered. She liked the idea of meeting her husband. "What about the cancellation policy? They'll charge us again." Rachel didn't want to disappoint Monica.

"Just one more time," Hadley said, her eyes round and soft like a puppy dog. "I'm really not up to sitting and staring at Dr. Kopple for an hour today. I'll pay your charge."

Rachel couldn't resist. She loved this impulsivity. She needed it. She had forgotten how to give into herself. "I'd love to stay." Rachel grabbed her phone. She quickly called the office and said she wasn't feeling well. Rachel pictured Dorothy, the secretary, rolling her eyes.

Hadley had forgotten about her offer of tea and led Rachel to the den. Rachel flitted her eyes around the room at the oil paintings flanking the fireplace, the Chinese vases on the bookshelves, and the perfectly coordinated upholstered chairs. She had never been in this room.

Hadley walked to the aquarium and put her hand on the glass. "I love these fish."

Rachel smiled. She could see the stress melting away from Hadley's face. "They're beautiful. Do they have names?" She immediately regretted it, setting up Hadley's memory loss.

Hadley turned without answering and sat down in one of the big, tufted chairs piled with decorative pillows. She pulled her legs up and tucked her feet beneath her.

"It's so nice to have you visit me today," Hadley said rather formally.

"Hadley, I came over because I was afraid you were going to do something to yourself."

Hadley shrugged and knitted her soft eyebrows together. "Do something?"

Rachel considered dropping it but decided instead it was important, one that shouldn't be brushed under the rug. "Hadley, you may have forgotten, but several weeks ago, we told each other our thoughts about suicide."

Hadley nodded slowly, her eyes darting around the room as if searching for the clues to a puzzle. She unfolded her legs and walked to the bookshelves. "More things are escaping my memory. It's why I've asked my husband to help me with a plan. I'll need him to know when it's time. Have you ever rented a movie and then realized you'd already seen it? Or worse, had watched it the evening before?"

Rachel nodded but couldn't get past Hadley's comment about asking her husband to partake in her death. *Who would do that? It is selfish, even cowardly.*

Hadley plucked a silver picture from the shelf. "These are my children," she said and walked back to the sofa next to Rachel. "This is Sydney, my oldest, and Brooklynn and Tucker." "I'm not exactly sure, but I think this photo was taken a few years ago." Rachel already knew about the children and had seen similar photos.

Hadley rubbed her fingers over a gold angel on her charm bracelet, a wave of sadness enveloping her. "I had another child," she said. "My fourth baby, dear sweet Angelica. She was stillborn."

Rachel closed her eyes. *This poor woman has suffered so much loss.*

After this tragedy, she learned another side of Bergen: his inability to cope with sadness and grief. She had carried and delivered the child, and she, in all her grief, supported the family through the pain and heartache. *Funny how I suddenly remember all that so well*, she thought.

Bergen had refused to go to grief or couples' counseling. He busied himself by dismantling the crib and turned the whimsical nursery into a stoic office. Hadley told the children about their sister and funeral. After the burial, Bergen never spoke of Angelica again. Hadley looked to the ceiling and blew a kiss into the air. "I'm sorry about your baby, Hadley," Rachel said. "You have a beautiful family, just like you."

"Tucker just turned fourteen." She tilted her head and smiled at the picture. "He's such a sweet boy. I worry about my children, but I think Tucker is having the toughest time with my memory loss. It's a tough age, caught somewhere between wanting to be a man and not wanting to let go of being a kid who needs his mom. I worry about how he'll do when. . . . What would you do, Rachel? If you were in my shoes, what would you do?"

Rachel took Hadley's hands in hers. Rachel knew what she meant. "Sometimes, when I have a really bad flashback or just can't take another trigger, I think about ending it. I've thought about a zillion ways to do it, but then, what if I get better? What if my life turns out okay?" Rachel dropped Hadley's hands by her side. "Mostly I worry about Mom. If I killed myself, she'd be alone. My dad left her because of me. It wouldn't be fair. I couldn't do that."

"My situation is different," Hadley said, staring at the approaching storm. An easterly wind splatted large drops of rain against the glass. Rachel nodded. She was right.

Rachel wished she had the right answer. She gazed at the fish darting around in the tank, hoping for their calming effect to be directed her way. "Your situation is different, but you can't give up. Maybe you'll be the exception and live twenty more years."

Hadley leaned against the bookcase and slid onto the floor. A crack of thunder startled her, and she dug her nails into the light blue carpet. Rachel lowered herself and sat cross-legged.

"Soon after I first learned of this death sentence, I researched assisted suicide. I couldn't imagine withering away as my family watched—and waited. You know, they call it the long goodbye." Hadley picked at the hem of her sweater. The rain pelted harder, then turned into chunks of ice creating a white blanket on the skylight. Hadley shivered.

"When I was growing up, we had this neighbor, Mrs. Statkis," Rachel began. "She had multiple sclerosis. Her kids were older than me. I was twelve. After she was diagnosed, her husband had an in-ground pool installed. Every day, he would take his wife to the pool for water therapy. It was supposed to help give her greater range of motion and muscle relaxation. One day after camp, my mom was in the kitchen, crying. Mrs. Statkis had drowned." Hadley's eyes widened and her mouth dropped. "My mom later told me that after the water therapy session, Mr. Statkis put his wife on her inflatable raft and went to the store for ice cream. When he returned, she was at the bottom of the pool." Hadley put her hand to her mouth.

"Everyone in the neighborhood believed it was an assisted suicide.

I mean, who would leave their wife, unable to swim, on a raft? The saddest part, and the reason I'm telling you this, is that her children also believed that their father had participated in their mother's death. My mother stays in touch with Mr. Statkis. He remarried and moved to Connecticut, but two of the four kids never forgave him and stopped talking to him altogether."

Hadley pushed her hair off her face. "How could I do that to my kids?" The hail turned to freezing rain and battered the windows. Hadley hugged herself tightly.

Rachel shimmied across the carpet and sidled up next to Hadley. This crumbled, desperate woman was not the Hadley Rachel knew.

Muffled sounds coming from the hall broke their private moment. Hadley jolted upright and fluffed her hair. Rachel bounced to a standing position, feeling guilty for the tender moment.

"Mom, did you see the hail?" Tucker yelled. "It was so cool; you could make snowballs."

Tucker, Brook, and Bergen emerged with wide smiles and dripping hair. Hadley laughed and used her sweater to tousle dry Tucker's hair. Bergen kissed her cheek, then noticed Rachel. "Hello." After introductions and pleasantries, Hadley reiterated her dinner offer to Rachel.

"Thank you for your offer. I hope I can get a rain check, no pun intended, but I really should get back to Princess. I need to let her out and feed her," she said.

"Is Princess your pet? Tucker asked. "We used to have a dog. Bear Bear was his name."

"She was a gift from your mom. You should come meet her. She's the best dog ever."

Bergen walked her out. "It was a pleasure meeting you. Hadley talks a lot about you."

"She has? Ditto. She beams talking about you all. Maybe someday I'll meet Sydney."

"You're welcome here anytime, Rachel. Can I ask you a question?"

Rachel nodded. "Do you have time to visit her more often? She needs caring, supportive friends like you."

"It would be my pleasure. I feel the same way about her."

Rachel hugged Bergen goodbye. *Maybe we can go to museums, volunteer together, or take a class together. It will be fun. Something to look forward to.*

CHAPTER 25

Hadley stood on the deck and admired her planted flowers from the previous fall. Majestic purple crocuses poked their heads up from the soil. Hadley plucked the dead leaves that covered the emerging daffodils and tulips. It was a perfect spring day, a rapture-blue sky, not a single cloud. Hadley removed the green tarp from the chaise lounge. She stretched out on the chair and unfastened the top three buttons of her shirt, exposing her chest and décolleté to the warm sunrays. A fat honeybee buzzed overhead and then landed on a flowering vine that surrounded the deck. Out of nowhere, a fleeting memory of being stung by yellow jackets emerged. She was ten and fell off her bike. Her right leg went into a ground nest. The bike fell on top of her and trapped her while swarms of bees attacked her skin. The yellow-and-black wasps stung repeatedly, causing sharp blasts of pain and burning. She covered her face while screaming for help. Within a minute, her mother pulled the bike off and carried her inside. Hadley remembered the red swollen blotches. And just like that, the memory was gone.

Hadley rummaged in her tote bag for sunglasses and a book. She opened it to page one and began, not remembering if she had started it already. Forty-five minutes later, Hadley was startled awake by her phone. Rachel. "I'm downstairs in your lobby. The desk clerk called your apartment, but no one answered. Are you home?"

Hadley instructed, "Come to the roof." She buttoned her shirt, noticing her chest was tender and hot to the touch. She moved her chair into the shade.

"Happy birthday," Rachel called out as she pushed open the door to the roof.

Hadley stood and hugged her friend. "Birthday?" she asked, astounded. "Did I tell you?"

"Bergen did." Rachel reached into her backpack. "Here, I have something for you."

"How sweet of you, Rachel. You didn't have to get me anything."

"I made it. Open it," Rachel encouraged.

Hadley slowly removed the ribbon and paper, keeping it intact. As she unwrapped it, she said, "My mother saved all the used wrapping paper from gifts and even ironed it." She slid the framed collage out and stared at the pictures. Hadley frowned. "Where did you get this?"

"I made it," Rachel replied. "You do it online."

They sat on the chaise lounges and talked about the photos. Rachel noticed that each picture elicited a different look from Hadley. Joy, happiness, confusion, and anguish.

"Where did you get these?" Hadley asked when they finished.

"I made it," Rachel reminded her. "It's your birthday present."

"It's my birthday?" Hadley asked.

"Yes," Rachel said, rolling her eyes. *It's not Hadley's fault, but it's frustrating!* "Come, we're going out to lunch to celebrate." She noticed the book. "Is it good?"

Hadley laughed. "I don't know. I keep restarting it. I guess that's one advantage of my memory lapses. I never have to buy a new book." The two left the deck and stopped at Hadley's apartment, where she changed her shoes and scribbled a note that she was out with Rachel.

"As a birthday treat, I thought about taking one of those carriages to the restaurant, but I don't like how they treat the poor horses," Rachel said. "They stand out there in all kinds of weather, on hard concrete, from sunup to sundown. It's cruel."

Carriages? Hadley thought. She smiled. "Look at the blooming forsythia on the bushes."

A short ride away, they arrived at the retro Lobster Club. "Have you been here before?"

"I'm not sure," Hadley answered, "but it looks very interesting."

They decided to share the miso soup and Hadley's favorite, teppanyaki scallops.

"This is so sweet of you, Rachel. It's hard to talk to my family about my illness. They try to be so strong and don't want to acknowledge the inevitable. Bergen has his head in the sand."

"Do you have other girlfriends you can talk to?" Rachel asked.

Hadley explained, "My diagnosis has tested my relationships. Some adamantly refuse to believe I have Alzheimer's so young, and some offer to hang out but never call. They've withdrawn from my life. I guess they don't know what to say or do around me. You know, I can't remember when it was, but Bergen and I were at a party with friends. A girlfriend asked Bergen how I was doing. I was right there! She could have asked me directly."

"It sounds very lonely," Rachel said. "I won't abandon you." Rachel blew on her soup. "It's funny how we are alike in so many ways but opposite in others."

Hadley tilted her head, curious. She lifted her fork and pierced a perfectly grilled scallop. "Oh, these are divine. If I had to live on a desert island with only one thing to eat, it would be scallops." Hadley took another bite. "Tell me, other than me wanting my memories, and you wanting to forget, what have you noticed?"

Rachel put her bowl down. She didn't want to frighten Hadley away with mushy talk. "Well, I was thinking how we're alike because we've both become kind of invisible. You can't talk about your Alzheimer's with your family, and I couldn't even say 'rape' in front of my dad."

Hadley felt for her friend. It didn't bother her that there were twenty years between them; they were like sisters. "I consider you one of my best friends. You say it like it is. I like that."

Rachel's cheeks flushed. She felt the same way. "Can I tell you something? I often wonder if the man saw me through the window that night in my underwear. And that maybe, if I had a nightgown on or if I'd drawn the curtains, it wouldn't have happened."

"I can't even fathom what you went through, but I have heard that rape is not about sex; it's about power. And it's a terrible lie that you did anything that brought it on or invited it."

I heard the same thing from my rape counselor. Didn't believe it then. Don't now.

"Rachel, it wasn't your fault. It didn't happen because you did anything wrong. That guy is a sick pervert. I care deeply about you. If you ever want to talk, I will listen. I want to be someone you can trust. And don't wait too long if you want an intelligent answer."

Rachel smiled. *She's so cogent.* No sudden lapses in the conversation or drifting off into a fog. "Thank you. I appreciate that. I didn't mean to be a Debbie Downer on your birthday."

"Let's tell each other about happier times," Hadley said. "I think it will help both of us."

"I like that idea," Rachel said. "One year my parents rented a cabin on a lake in Maine. It took two days to drive there, but I remember how we stopped at every single Dairy Queen along the way. Chocolate-dipped ice cream cones, Oreo Blizzards, pineapple sundaes, chili cheese dogs . . . we must have gained ten pounds just on the drive." Rachel laughed. "Your turn."

Hadley pressed her lips together and squinted. She pointed a finger in the air and started. "One time, when I was in high school, my best friend Olga and I jumped our neighbor's fence and went skinny-dipping in their pool." A slight blush covered her cheeks.

"You?" Rachel asked. "You went skinny-dipping?" *Another side of her.*

A tall, good-looking waiter approached. "I understand it's someone's birthday." He looked at Hadley and placed a bowl of green tea ice cream with a birthday candle in front of her.

Hadley looked at Rachel. "My birthday?" she said, looking to Rachel for confirmation.

Rachel nodded. "Yes, make a wish and blow out the candle."

Hadley closed her eyes, then exhaled to extinguish the tiny flame. *A wish for the children.*

Rachel paid the bill. "Sorry to end our little party, but I need to let Princess out. Since we're going in opposite directions, do you want me to get you a cab?"

Hadley wasn't sure where they were. She shrugged.

Rachel sensed her disorientation. "We're on Fifty-Third between Park and Lex. It's probably less than a mile to your place." *Can she find the place alone?*

Hadley said, "I'll walk. I'll be fine."

Rachel kissed her friend on the cheek. "Happy birthday, friend."

Once Hadley turned the corner, Rachel set out behind her. She didn't trust her to get home on her own. She wanted to be sure she'd be okay. When Hadley was on her block, Rachel felt assured that she was safe. Rachel turned around and headed toward home.

CHAPTER 26

The alarm startled Hadley awake. She didn't usually set the alarm unless she had an early morning appointment. She put on her robe and walked to the kitchen. Thank God for Sydney, she thought. There hanging on the wall was a calendar. Although Hadley did not know the date, she could see that the first two rows of June dates were crossed out with a black X, and BROOK'S GRAD was in big, red letters. She smiled at the significance of the day.

Bergen was already up and dressed. Brook's graduation was important, but for Hadley's sake, he was hell-bent on getting to the school ahead of the other families. After coordinating their rendezvous point, he instructed Sydney to bring the others to the school and then took off to secure four chairs in the front row in the gymnasium. Hundreds of white folding chairs were set in rows on either side of a center aisle. The stage was festooned with school pennants and a maroon backdrop with FALCONS emblazoned across the front. Championship banners hung from the ceiling. Flanking the entryways were glass trophy cabinets. Bergen perused them and quickly found Tucker's MVP wrestling cup. Other parents filed in to claim their seats. Sydney arrived with Hadley and Tucker in tow, and they took their seats.

Bergen beamed with pride as he greeted Brook at the reception. She unzipped her gown and removed her cap. The gown was hot, and she searched the room for her mom.

"Restroom," he said and nodded in the direction of the line forming. Brook shrugged, then took her dad by the arm and guided him toward the front of the room to meet her teachers.

Bergen heard his name. He turned to see a short, plump woman dressed in a flowery caftan hurrying toward him. "You're Bergen Stanton, right?"

Bergen nodded. *Do I know this woman?* He looked at Brook.

"I'm Lacey Montrose, a friend of Hadley's from the PTO."

Bergen quickly looked around for his wife.

"I hope I'm not overstepping, but Hadley is outside on the quad near the middle school. I wouldn't normally stick my nose into her business, but she's standing there and looks confused."

Bergen immediately rushed through the crowd. "Which way is the goddamn quad?" he said. One of the students pointed in the other direction. Bergen ran down the hall. From the window, he could see her standing in the middle of the grassy field. The look on her face reminded him of when Brook got lost in the mall. She was five and playing hide-and-seek, sitting amid a rack of clothes. Bergen was shopping for Mother's Day gifts. When he turned around, she was gone. He panicked and ran around the department store, frantically calling her name. After five minutes, Bergen saw a salesgirl holding Brook's hand, keeping her safe.

"Hads, honey, over here," he shouted. The look of panic quickly changed to relief. Bergen approached slowly, not wanting to alarm her. He took her hand. "Honey, let's go inside."

Later that evening, Hadley stood in a circle with other parents at the graduation party. She was dressed in a sleeveless peach dress. Tied loosely around her neck, she wore a colorful scarf attached at her shoulder with a round pearl pin. Sydney helped her pick out a coordinating outfit. Bergen stood in line at the bar while keeping a watchful eye on Hadley. Two women to the side gossiped viciously about other parents. Bergen half-listened as they chattered about the O'Malley's divorce, that Carolina Spieler was caught cheating on her husband, and "poor, demented Hadley Stanton." *Demented? Is that what people think?* Bergen got his drink and walked over to the gossiping women.

"Excuse me, I'm Bergen Stanton," he said, extending his hand. The ladies stepped back, looking at each other with wide eyes. "I couldn't help but overhear you talking about my wife, Hadley. Hadley has Alzheimer's disease, which causes memory impairment. She is not demented." He paused, giving them time to recover from their embarrassment. "The word demented negatively colors the perception of the disease and leads to harmful stigma. My wife graduated summa cum laude and until recently was the chief marketing officer at a law firm. She has raised three beautiful children, and I am the luckiest man alive to have her. Perhaps you'd like to meet her?" The two busybodies shook their heads and quickly walked away. Bergen joined the other dads at the bar.

The lights flickered several times, signaling guests to be seated for dinner. Fortunately for all concerned, the graduates were eating in a separate room downstairs, complete with balloons, a lavish buffet of "kid" food, and loud music. The adults made their way to the Montauk Room, one of the private dining rooms at the country club. The dark walnut walls were decorated with archival black-and-white photos. On the north wall was one of two men wearing long white slacks and white polo shirts, holding wooden tennis rackets. Next to it was another picture of women in one-piece bathing costumes on a dock. Above the fireplace at the head of the room was a round plaque made of wood, painted with the silhouette of a Montauk Indian. The yellow chintz drapes brightened the otherwise dark room.

Hadley and Bergen took their seats next to Jenn and Mark, longtime friends. Hadley waved to her Pilates buddy, Karen, and pointed to the seat next to her. Karen took her seat and reached up to touch her friend's ear. "You're missing an earring."

Hadley felt her ear and around the collar of her dress. "Oh no. They were my mother's."

Did she lose it or forget to put it on? Bergen thought.

Karen and Hadley looked on the floor. When the earring was nowhere to be found, Karen offered to tell the manager, suggesting maybe it had fallen off at the reception.

After several rounds of toasts for their children's success in graduating and their own success for surviving those years, Hadley pushed her chair back and smoothed the front of her dress. "I'll be right back. I want to go downstairs and take some pictures of the party."

"Want me to come?" Bergen asked cautiously.

She rolled her eyes. "No. Excuse me."

Once Hadley was out of earshot, Karen looked at Bergen with sad eyes. "We are honored that you have included us in your circle of trust. We were and are devastated. We respect your privacy but have heard rumors. How is she, Bergen? How is she really?"

Bergen put his palms on his forehead and sighed. "It's hard to say. Sometimes she's fine, and you'd never know anything was wrong. Other times she's confused, loses things, can't find the right words. She got lost going to the ladies' room today."

Karen reached across the table and put her hand on Bergen's forearm. "I'm so sorry."

"Last week Tucker found her missing wallet in the pantry," he explained.

"You'll tell us when you need help," Jenn said, as more of an order than a request.

"Thank you for your concern. I am doing just fine. If I need support or someone to talk to, I'll reach out." But he felt guilt and shame, always ignoring friends' calls. Even Rodney's.

"And the kids?" asked Jenn. "How are they?"

"We're lucky that Sydney has taken the semester off. She knows the most so far. She has chosen not to find out if she has the mutation."

"I don't blame her," Mark said. "Especially given there's nothing—"

Jenn cut in, "So, how are the youngest fairing?"

Bergen was anxious, helpless. Jenn put her hand on his shoulder and told him to take a deep breath. Bergen inhaled and exhaled slowly.

His shoulders relaxed, his jaw unclenching. "Brook will be fine. She's looking forward to school and living in the dorms. But Tucker . . . I don't know. Lately, he's been odd, touching objects repeatedly, that kind of thing."

"Mmm, I recognize that. They're called compulsions," Jenn said. "My grandmother did that after her brother was diagnosed with cancer. I don't know a lot about it, but they are brought on by bad thoughts. Obsessions. Does Tucker have someone to talk to?"

"With the appointments and challenges, we haven't had family therapy, but Tucker has talked to the wrestling coach. He's been supportive and available. His father had Alzheimer's."

Hadley returned to the table. "Bergen, I have bad news. I was in the ladies' room, and I noticed that I've lost an earring." Her tablemates looked down without saying a word.

"It's okay, dear," Bergen replied. "We'll find it."

CHAPTER 27

The jury sat on brown wooden benches. Only three of them. A man with a stern face. A woman with a cheap shell necklace peeking out from the folds of fat in her neck. And a child. It was a jury, right? And they were here to judge her. Rachel looked for the judge, but all she saw was the high desk, the top of the judge's chair. She felt small, frightened.

A preppy man entered the room. He had an enormous, oversized watch on his right wrist. He took the stand, and Rachel realized that she was not the one on trial. But who was?

She could make out a shadowy figure at a table. She strained to get a better look but could not make out a face.

An elegant woman entered the room and read from a large piece of paper. Rachel strained to hear her. "Can you speak up?" she asked.

The preppy man shifted uncomfortably. *I'm not on trial. He is.* A new woman, a blond, questioned him, shouting at him, and Rachel wanted to come to his defense. The words felt like lead in her mouth as she cried out, "He is innocent."

The preppy man smirked at her. He didn't care. He put his feet on the table. He wore Gucci loafers. With his eyes on Rachel, he took another watch out of his pocket, then another and another. They were gold and silver, with chunky wristbands. One had diamonds on the bezel. He offered them to her, and she took them. They were heavy.

"But you didn't do it," she said. "It wasn't your fault." He looked sorrowful. He touched her cheek. The child in the jury box was now a teenager. His mouth was snarled. He wagged his finger at the preppy man and shook his head. Rachel turned to the blond woman, the shadowy figure. A strong wind blew through the courtroom, and clouds threatened to open. The teenager popped a beer. She strained to see his face, squinted. *Was it—*

She gasped, struggling to sit up in her bed. There was no jury or judge. There were no attorneys. There was only Princess. She eased back down. Dr. Blanzaco had discussed dreams, especially now that her nightmares were receding. "Our unconscious sends us messages in imagery. It's easy to forget them as the day progresses," she'd said. Rachel reached for her journal, and more details surfaced. They were trying to blame the man with the watches, but he wasn't guilty. He hadn't done anything wrong. Rachel pulled back the covers and sat up.

"What are you smiling about?" Mandy asked, surprised at her unusually good mood.

"I just had the best dream," Rachel replied. "I dreamed about a man accused of inviting a robbery just because of the way he was dressed," she said.

"Wait, you had a good dream about a robbery? Not one of your nightmares?"

"Exactly," Rachel replied. "I don't know, maybe my therapy's working. I'm going to talk to my shrink about it. But in my dream, a man gets robbed in Central Park, and a woman in a courtroom is accusing him. As if it's his fault he got robbed. It was so weird. He gave me all these expensive watches and then looked so sad."

"What do you think it means?" Mandy said.

"I dunno. That's why I see a shrink." Rachel laughed. "But this dream was different, Mand. I mean, just because he wore an expensive watch doesn't mean he encouraged the robbery. Maybe that's it. And just because I only wore a T-shirt and underwear to bed that night doesn't mean I invited the rape." Rachel let out a long breath.

She felt her body loosen and lighten. "It wasn't my fault." It was a breakthrough, and this time she believed it.

Mandy smiled and hugged her friend tightly. "You're going to be okay, Rach. Everything's going to be okay."

"I hope so," Rachel said, and they both laughed.

CHAPTER 28

Hadley sat in the den, paging through a magazine and singing Streisand tunes. *How can I know all the words to my favorite songs and not remember my email password?* Hadley checked the gardenia candle she thought she had lit earlier. She breathed in deeply but couldn't smell the fragrance. But the candle was lit. She had burned it many times before and always relished its sweet, intoxicating scent. Images of wearing a gardenia corsage to her prom flashed in her mind.

"Brook, can you help me with my email? Someone must have changed my password."

Brook clicked on Gmail. "Oh, it's fine. You were just clicking the wrong thing."

"Thanks," she said, flustered. "How about some lunch before you go back to school?"

Brook sat by her on the couch. "Mom, you had lunch an hour ago," she said sadly.

"Oh, I know. I meant lunch for you," Hadley replied, pretending.

She's trying so hard to be okay, Brook thought. "Gotta go, Mom." She gave her a peck on the cheek and left.

Before Hadley had time to wallow in her own grief, she heard Bergen and Tucker coming off the elevator.

They opened the front door and barged into the hallway, laughing about *The Three Stooges*. "Yuk, yuk, yuk," Tucker imitated as they joined Hadley in the den.

"Guess who I talked to earlier?" Hadley asked, knowing Bergen would never know. "Olga. About our twenty-fifth high school reunion. Can you believe that?"

Bergen was bewildered. "How are you going to get there?" he asked.

"On a plane, silly," she said.

Tucker quietly tiptoed out of the room, tapping his hand along the wall as he walked.

"No, Hadley. I mean, how will you actually get there? I don't mean to be hurtful, but you get lost in the grocery store."

"Bergen," she whined. "That's cruel. I'll be fine. I am not ready to give up yet."

"Navigating JFK is a nightmare for people who don't have memory issues." He couldn't say Alzheimer's. "And when you get to San Diego, then what? You haven't been there in years."

Hadley continued to plead, bargain, and bribe, but Bergen refused to give in. "Bergen, this is so unfair," Hadley said, angrily storming out of the room like a child. She texted Olga, *No go. B is being a sh&t!* And she added emojis: a red angry face and a sad face with tears.

WTF, Olga shot back. Hadley's phone rang. "Hadley, put him on the phone," Olga demanded. "I'll talk to him."

Hadley went back to the den and pushed the phone toward Bergen. "*Hello*, Olga, nice to hear from you," Bergen said sarcastically.

"Bergen, listen," Olga started, "this is really important for Hadley! She feels like a trapped child. This trip will do her a world of good."

Bergen walked out of the den. "You don't understand," he said. "Her dementia is getting worse. She'll get lost. And a reunion? Jesus, Olga, she can't even remember our doorman's name, let alone classmates she hasn't seen or heard from in twenty-five years!"

Olga countered, "This isn't something I concocted on a whim. I thought about this a lot."

"Well, you should have said something to me first," Bergen said with a tinge of irritation.

After weighing the pros and cons, Bergen breathed a long sigh. "Okay, but I'll come too. It's too risky to let her fly across the country alone."

Although pleased Bergen had relented, Olga pressed, "That's great, but hear me out. What *if* she comes alone, you check her in and make sure she gets on the plane, and I'll be at the gate to pick her up? I'll call you immediately once she's landed. I promise, Bergen. C'mon, she needs this."

Hadley, who had been eavesdropping, screamed with joy and grabbed the phone. Bergen, half-smiling, went to his office while Hadley and Olga planned the trip.

—

BERGEN SHOWED THE letter to the TSA agent. He was allowed to escort his wife through security and to the gate. Even after Hadley had boarded, he waited until the plane taxied and was in the air before he left. Once out of the terminal, he called Olga and confirmed that she left.

Olga was ready. She had a copy of the doctor's letter and would be there when Hadley got off the plane. She thanked Bergen profusely, promising safety and a good time.

"She'll have fun, but please, she really has declined since the last time you saw her. And she's pretty good at faking it. I mean, she pretends to know what you're talking about or makes up excuses to cover. Take care of her, okay?" he said, then ended the call.

Olga arrived at the airport forty-five minutes before the plane was expected to land. She parked her car in the lot and followed the yellow walkway toward the terminal, enjoying the warm breeze that rustled the fronds of the nearby palm trees. She checked the electronic arrival board and stood in the queue for security. Olga handed the TSA agent her driver's license and the letter from the psychiatrist, which explained the need for her to meet Mrs. Stanton at the gate. She looked in the shops and browsed the magazines and bestselling paperbacks. She purchased a small bag of almonds and a bottle of water before walking to the gate. The waiting area was full of passengers ready for the next flight. Olga found a seat directly in front of the door to the gate. Anxious to see her friend, she stood and craned her neck to see the passengers as they deplaned.

Hadley was the third passenger off the plane. Olga waved her hands wildly as she rushed to hug her friend. The two had grown up on the same street. They'd gone to kindergarten, elementary, and high school together. Hadley had stayed with Olga and her family for the first month after her parents' death. Olga was also the first person Hadley called when Sydney was born and after her diagnosis. Olga had a knack for knowing what Hadley was thinking.

"You look fabulous," Olga exclaimed. "I love those shoes."

"Thank you. I got them at, oh, never mind, who cares where I got them." She laughed.

Olga lifted Hadley's suitcase into her car. She apologized for the mess, explaining that she'd been redoing her front garden with succulents because of the high water prices.

Hadley tried to remember Olga's front yard. "You're still in Poway, right?"

"After my divorce, I moved to a small townhouse in Carmel Valley. Eight years ago," Olga reminded. "What are you wearing to the reunion?"

"Rule number one," Hadley said, half teasing, "no memory questions, okay?"

"Let's get the elephant out of the room," Olga said. "Tell me how you're doing, how you're coping, then we won't talk about it for the rest of the time."

Hadley put her hands between her knees and looked out the car window. "San Diego is just so darn pretty. I loved the view as we were landing. You get to see Balboa Park, the Coronado Bridge, all the sailboats, and the USS Midway. I miss it here," Hadley said, sad.

Olga took one of Hadley's hands. "Hads, what's the hardest part of all this?" she asked.

Hadley didn't want to talk about it. She wanted to escape the doom and gloom for just a few days. Hadley eyed a billboard advertising nonstop flights to Buenos Aires. *Will I lose my chance to go?* Hadley pressed the window button. "It's warm in here. Let's get going."

Olga started the car and backed out of the parking space. She put her ticket and credit card into the parking kiosk and exited the airport.

"The hardest thing," she said, then paused. "There is no *one* hardest thing. Knowing I won't see the children and Bergen again. I won't be there for their graduations, weddings, pregnancies. I'm going to forget how to change my own damn clothes or use the bathroom."

Olga put her free hand on Hadley's arm. "Are you on medications? Going to therapy? How are the kids coping?"

"I take two meds, one to slow the disease and an antidepressant. I see a shrink once a week and a neurologist. Bergen is doing his best, but he doesn't like to talk about it, to face the truth. Soon, I'll be gone, and if he hasn't accepted it . . . it will be more devastating. Ugh. The funeral. I worry about my funeral. I think about Mom and Dad, two caskets. I don't want my kids to remember me like that."

Olga didn't know what to say. She had opened Pandora's box and had no idea how to make it better.

Hadley pushed the window button down again and breathed in the warm autumn air. "We rarely have sex. It's my fault, not his. I don't feel sexy. I feel like a broken-down old woman. I told him to date again." Hadley sighed. "It's hard for me to picture him with another woman, but in my heart, I want that for him. He deserves it. So do the kids."

Hadley stared out the window at the cacti and fuchsia

bougainvillea growing in the median of the street. *New York City is a frenetic, sleepless town. Certainly not like San Diego, America's finest city. Where else can you find miles of white sand beaches, year-round temperate weather, skiing, and sunbathing, all within a few hours' drive? Why did I leave?* She couldn't remember. "You know the hardest part? I may have passed on this horrible illness to the kids."

Olga had researched it. She talked to friends whose parents or grandparents succumbed to it and called the local Alzheimer's Association chapter. She knew about the horribly grim prognosis and the fifty-fifty odds for Hadley's children. What she didn't know was how to help. How to really, really help. Offering support and a listening ear wasn't enough.

The sand-colored townhome is more garage than house, Hadley thought as Olga pulled into the driveway. A lone date palm flanked by white oleander bushes stood in the small patch of grass that was Olga's front yard. Hadley suddenly remembered the acrimonious divorce after learning Peter was cheating with his secretary. *Her new place is small, but at least she has her health. I'd trade all my material goods for my health back.*

"Did you know those oleander flowers are one of the deadliest plants in the world?" Hadley asked. "Remember when we were in fifth grade? A preschool brother and sister ate the flowers and died. It was all over the news. The mom thought her twins just had the flu." After a pregnant pause, she added, "You know, that might not be a bad way for me to go."

Olga's eyebrows bunched. "You're not serious, right?"

"I'm kidding." Hadley winked.

"Hads, you'll tell me if there's anything I can do, right? I can take Tucker on a school holiday if you and Bergen need a break or help around the house. You name it, I'll be there."

Hadley smiled and kissed Olga's cheek. "I know, Olga, thanks. It helps just hearing you say that." She got out of the car. "Okay, now can we get on with it and have some fun?"

Olga gave Hadley a quick tour. After explaining how the hot and cold shower handles were switched, she left Hadley to unpack. "We'll go in two hours. Take your time getting ready."

—

THE TWO FRIENDS walked arm in arm into the ballroom and checked in. Hadley put her name tag on. She was thankful that the reunion committee had them. She looked around the room, wondering if she'd recognize anyone. Hadley stared at an overweight woman in a tight red dress. Her face was familiar, but after twenty-five years, everyone had changed. Once young, carefree, and gawky, the class of '84 was portly, balding, and in serious need of filler and Botox. *Do I look that old?* Hadley and Olga played the name game for the next three hours. They visited with friends from the cheerleading squad, old crushes, and teachers.

Other girlfriends joined them and reminisced about the fun and mischief they'd had. Hadley yawned. It was still early but after midnight in her body. "I'm sorry to break up our party, but I need to get some sleep," she said, stretching her arms. The girls hugged goodbye.

"See you at our next reunion," a few of the women called out.

Hadley gave Olga a sad smile. *Probably not*, she thought.

—

BERGEN AND TUCKER waited by the big glass windows outside of gate thirty-eight. Tucker held up a sign: Welcome Home, Mom. He drew a heart around the words. The plane arrived. Bergen picked up the bouquet of red roses and smelled them. He thought about how relaxing the last five days had been. There had been lightness at home. He slept soundly each night. Even the children seemed more relaxed, and he felt guilty.

Passengers filed out of the gate. Harried parents with screaming children hurried off while others anxiously checked their phones. Tucker was giddy. More and more people left the plane. Bergen tried to look down the ramp but couldn't see around the bend. When there was a break in people, he checked his phone. Four uniformed flight attendants and two pilots came out. "Are you the last on the plane?" Bergen asked in an urgent voice.

"Yes sir, this is the termination of this flight," a young male steward replied.

"There's no one else on the plane?" Bergen asked.

"No sir, are you expecting someone?" the young man asked.

"My wife, Hadley Stanton. She was flying here from San Diego," Bergen insisted.

"I'm sorry, there are no more passengers on the plane," the steward replied.

"What about in the bathrooms?" Bergen asked.

"No, I'm sorry. This flight did stop in Dallas. Perhaps she got off there?"

"I knew this would happen," Bergen said. "My wife, Mrs. Stanton, has Alzheimer's disease. She was unaccompanied," he explained, with shame.

"Dad, is Mom okay? Where is she?" Tucker asked, trying to sound brave. He walked seven steps away, then returned, counting quietly to himself. *One, two, three, four, five, six, seven.* He walked in the opposite direction. *One, two, three, four, five, six, seven.*

The attendant looked quizzically at Tucker. "I'll find her. My supervisor will call Dallas."

They followed him to the airline's customer service desk. Tucker counted as he walked.

"Mrs. Britton will assist you," he said. "Good luck. I'm sure she's fine."

Bergen explained the situation, feeling another stab to his gut. "Her friend took her to the gate in San Diego and made sure she got on. I had no idea she'd get off the plane at a stopover. She's petite, about five-five, with blond hair." Tucker tapped his right heel on the ground seven times; then he did the same with his left.

"I'll just call the desk in Dallas. I'm sure she's fine, sir," Mrs. Britton said. After a short dialogue, Mrs. Britton nodded and smiled. "They have her. Your wife thought she was in New York, so they kept her at the desk, figuring someone would call once the flight landed at JFK."

"Thank God!" Bergen sighed, practically falling to his knees.

Tucker stopped counting. *It worked*, he told himself. *Mom will be okay.*

"Mrs. Stanton will be on the next nonstop flight to JFK, landing just before nine-thirty." Bergen and Tucker got takeout and hunkered down in the waiting area for three hours.

They arrived home at 11 p.m. Tucker went to bed. There were yellow sticky notes everywhere. By the alarm clock read, *Did you turn me off?* On the front doorknob read, *Do you have your keys?* The contents of the drawers, cabinets, closets, and cupboards in the kitchen, office, and den were labeled: *silverware, wineglasses, coffee cups, paper goods, DVDs, office supplies, vases, good china, candles, games.* Hadley stared in disbelief. *My memory's that bad?*

"Hads, Tuck was *really* scared when you didn't come off that plane," Bergen said. She was too. Bergen held her in his arms, rocking back and forth.

Hadley gently pushed away. "Have you decided about the pact?" she asked.

"Pact?" Bergen asked, unsure what she was referring to.

"It's only going to keep getting worse. When the time comes, you have to help me end the misery. You promised."

Bergen squeezed his wife tightly and kissed her neck. The smell of her Chanel No. 5 brought back sweet memories of earlier days. "To tell you the truth, I still have the same reservations. Don't you think it's more appropriate to talk about what you want to do in your remaining years instead of planning your death?"

Hadley cut him off, "It's really the same as deciding to pull the plug on a person in a coma or the doctor ordering not to resuscitate a terminal patient," Hadley explained. "I've got a pretty good plan. There are three factors, which will determine when it's time."

Bergen didn't want to talk about it. Not now. Not ever. He was just glad she was home.

"Now, Bergen, please. You can't keep avoiding the situation like you did with Angelica."

Bergen froze. He was stunned. Her name hadn't been said for over a decade. Hadley was right. It was too painful. He shoved it somewhere deep inside.

"It will bring me peace of mind," Hadley said. "It's important to me."

Bergen put his arm around his wife, and they walked to the bedroom. "If I can no longer use the bathroom or feed myself, it's time. If I don't know who you or the kids are, it's time."

"Go on, dear, I'm listening," he said softly.

"When the time is here, you will give me sleeping pills. That's it. I'll lie down and go to sleep. It will be peaceful." *I just need a way to get sleeping pills . . . Dr. Kopple?*

Bergen paced. As he passed by the dresser, he slammed his hand down, startling Hadley. "I can't do it. I just can't. You make it sound so easy, like a fairy tale, happily ever after."

"It's not easy for any of us," Hadley responded with an edge. "If you love me, you will honor my last wish. Please, Bergen, don't make this any harder than it is already."

Bergen exhaled. He was spent. The fight was gone. "Fine, I'll do it." He left the room.

Hadley stared in the mirror, barely recognizing her vacant eyes. She was tired. Not only had the reunion worn her out physically and mentally, but ending up in the wrong airport had exacerbated her feelings of vulnerability. She picked up her heart box and sat on the floor. *I get lost. I am just going toward a void. Nothing good. Only worse.*

How much crueler can this disease get? Maybe I should do it now. Why put everyone through so much inevitable pain?

Hadley placed the heart next to the golden retriever box and smiled. *What was his name again?* "What was I going to do?" she said, then brushed her hair back and found Bergen.

Bergen was leaning against the bar, holding a bottle of McCallan. He took a long swig.

"Bergen, darling, what are you doing?" Hadley called. "It's almost midnight. Why are you drinking from the bottle?"

Bergen spun around, frustrated, quickly changing moods. His reservoir of patience was tapped. "Goddamn it, Hadley. Do you really not remember you just asked me to murder you?"

Hadley raised her eyebrows and stepped back. "Bergen, are you upset with me? I'm sorry, I don't know what you're talking about." The look in her eyes was empty.

Bergen put down the bottle and closed his eyes. *There's no predicting when she's here and not here. This isn't on purpose.* His stomach rolled, and his throat tightened as a poker of hot guilt flowed through him. "I'm sorry, honey. It's just been a long day. It's late. Let's go to bed."

Bergen turned off all the lights, checked on Tucker, and set the alarm. By the time he climbed into bed, Hadley was asleep. His mind was spinning. The dementia was getting worse. *Is this when I'm supposed to hire outside help? How do I cope with her changing personalities? The smart, organized marketing executive is gone. How much longer will I have the sweet, loving wife I married? Who will she become?*

The woman lying next to him scared him. *Does she already have sleeping pills?* He would find them and flush them down the toilet. He would call the social worker, ask for help.

Bergen scooted closer to her. His arm brushed against her breast as he leaned in to kiss her. *How long has it been? My birthday, maybe, two months ago?* He looked desirously at her. Bergen kissed her again, this time parting her lips with his tongue. He hoped she might rouse and return the caress. His breathing increased, and he felt the warmth of blood flowing to his genitals as he imagined pulling her on top of him.

When they had first made love, Bergen was surprised she wasn't the demure Catholic girl he expected. Hadley kept their sex life exciting.

Bergen rolled onto his back. He wondered if they'd ever have sex again. His mind wandered as he pictured his life after Hadley. Would well-meaning friends set him up with the divorcée down the street? Bergen slid his hand under the sheets. He fantasized about going to a bar and leaving with a big-busted brunette. They'd slip into an alley, and he'd press her up against the wall. She would thrust her tongue deep into his mouth. He'd yank her dress up and pull down her panties. He'd unzip his pants.

Pangs of remorse tore through him as he went to the bathroom to clean up. He stared into the mirror and splashed cold water on his face. *It's a primal need.* The thought of never making love to Hadley again was terrifying. He didn't want to be with any other woman. Bergen brushed his teeth and went back to bed. He wanted it to be like it had been.

He started thinking. He'd arrange for Tucker to have a sleepover with a friend. He would order dozens of bouquets of red roses. He'd call Chef Jean Maurice and have their favorite meal brought in. He'd buy her some sexy lingerie. There would be carefully selected wines, romantic music, and lots of candles. Bergen's guilt dissipated. It felt good to imagine a future of happier times with Hadley.

He wasn't willing to give up. He would still go through all this with her. He loved her. And that's what you do for someone you love. You go through it. He turned onto his side and tried to sleep.

CHAPTER 29

Rachel entered the Yoku Japanese restaurant. "You have reservation?" a timid voice asked from behind her. A petite Japanese woman dressed in a traditional kimono greeted her.

Rachel shook her head.

"You sit at counter, okay?" the hostess asked, showing her to an empty seat. The restaurant was filled with young people. Japanese fans and silk cherry blossoms decorated the walls. A large gong separated the sushi bar from the entrance. Rachel glanced at the menu and ordered a Kirin beer. Small plates of sushi rolls, sashimi, seaweed salads, and pickled carrots moved on a conveyor belt in a steady stream. Rachel plucked a plate of edamame and another with a spicy tuna roll. A lady with two young children sat to Rachel's right. To her left were three Japanese men expertly handling their chopsticks. Rachel mixed the wasabi and soy sauce and placed a tender pink piece of ginger on top of her roll. Then, she heard a familiar voice.

"Do you have uni today?" the young man asked. Rachel craned her neck and saw Will. "Oh my God," she said under her breath. She turned in the other direction and took a long haul of her beer. *Of all the restaurants in New York City, he had to pick this one!*

Several skipped heartbeats later, she combed her fingers through her hair, tucked her blouse into her jeans, and smeared gloss across her lips. "No time like the present," she said and took another gulp of beer.

"Will?" she asked cautiously. Caught off guard, Will looked up with an edamame between his teeth.

"Rachel," he answered, "hi."

She was surprised and pleased. *He remembered.* "I don't mean to interrupt your dinner, but I wanted to come over and apolo—"

"Water under the bridge," Will interrupted. "No worries."

"No, really," Rachel insisted, "if not for you, at least let me apologize for me. I feel bad. Several years ago, something terrible happened to me." One of the men sitting next to Will stopped slurping his miso soup and turned toward Rachel. "When I saw you that night, it brought up my past. I'm so sorry. It was childish and rude to just leave."

"I figured something was up," Will replied. "Your neck turned red, like hives, so I figured you were having an allergic reaction or couldn't stand the sight of me." He laughed. "Why didn't you text me after?"

"I wondered the same about you," Rachel answered, "but figured since I didn't hear from you, you probably thought it best to just stay away from me. Well, I just wanted to apologize."

"Are you here alone?" Will asked.

"Who, me?" Rachel said, blushing. "Yes."

"Come sit with me," he said.

Rachel's heart skipped. *He's so handsome.* She joined him with her beer and plate.

"So, if you don't mind me asking, what was the really bad thing I reminded you of? I hope I didn't look like one of them," Will said, pointing to the scary pumpkins in the window.

Rachel giggled. "It wasn't really you. It was. . . . You're gonna laugh. Your aftershave."

"My what?" Will said, confused.

"The smell of your cologne was the same smell of a guy I used to know," she said.

Will tilted his head, trying to smell his aftershave. "Am I wearing the same one now?"

"Yes," Rachel replied, "but I'm better prepared this time." She smiled coyly.

Will dipped his napkin in his water and vigorously rubbed his neck. "I'm so sorry. I'm not sure I can get it off." Rachel smiled.

"I was raped," she blurted. Rachel was surprised she opened up so easily to him. They were both quiet for what seemed like a very long time.

Will grabbed a passing California roll and finished his beer. Then he put his hand on hers and looked her in the eyes. "My sister was almost raped," he said. "She was only fifteen."

Rachel looked away. "I'm really, really sorry," she said. "I hope she's okay now."

"Thanks," he said. "She's doing pretty good. Hey, let's get out of here and go for a walk." The server counted the colored plates and handed them the bill.

"Let me treat," Rachel said. "It will make up for our missed pizza dinner."

"Thanks—and for telling me the truth about what happened. I know it was probably hard. There aren't many people I've told about my sister, and it didn't even happen to me." The two walked through the Meatpacking district and climbed the stairs to the High Line. Mothers with strollers, joggers, and tourists crowded the park. The sycamore and oak trees were a riot of fall color. A young boy ran back and forth, trying to catch the rust and gold-colored leaves that pirouetted toward the ground. "My sister was spending the weekend at my grandparent's house. They were supposed to go to Boston for the weekend, but my grandma was sick."

"You don't have to tell me about it, Will, unless you want to."

Will shook his head. "Anyway, some guy broke into the house at night and tied up my grandma and grandpa. The guy ransacked the house, filling pillowcases with their silver and electronics, and he took my grandma's wedding rings and watch right off her. They thought he was leaving, but he went upstairs. My sister heard the commotion and was hiding in the closet."

Rachel could feel the fear stick in her throat like a wad of dry cotton balls. *What is it with closets?* she thought and then reminded herself the story was not about her.

"Do you prefer I don't talk about it?"

"I'm fine," Rachel replied. "You can tell me what happened if it will help."

"The guy went into her room. I guess when he saw the bed had been slept in, he screamed for her to come out or he'd kill her. He opened the closet door and pulled her out by her hair. He threw her onto the bed. Sammy was fighting to get him off her when my grandpa charged in and hit the asshole with a fire iron. So, she wasn't, you know, technically raped, but—"

Rachel tried to slow her breathing. This was difficult. "I understand," she said softly. "I'm glad she wasn't, but assault is assault. It's all traumatic. How did your grandpa get untied?"

"Force of God, luck, adrenaline? He just ripped the wrist ties right off."

"So, they caught the guy?" Rachel asked, hoping so.

Will raised one eyebrow and smiled. "My dad heard from the detective who covered the case. While the guy was in jail, he got shanked and died from infection."

"Serves him right," Rachel said under her breath.

Will pulled Rachel toward him as joggers ran by. "Did your guy go to prison?" he asked.

Rachel took a deep breath and stared at the New Jersey lights rippling across the water. "He was never caught," she said. "He wore a mask, so I couldn't ID him."

"Wow, that's gotta be tough not being able to get revenge or have closure."

"I never thought of it that way. I feel lucky to have avoided the whole courtroom scene."

Rachel and Will sat on a concrete bench. Rachel shivered. "You can feel the change in the air. October would be my favorite month if it weren't for Halloween."

Will put his arm around her shoulders. *It feels good being with Will*, she thought. The universe had brought them together again.

"My memories are always infringing on my privacy, my time, my well-being. They follow me. It's the stupid little triggers, like aftershave, that are the worst, they're so unpredictable and ordinary."

What am I doing? I don't even know Will that well. "I never saw his face. But he was young, I think, early twenties. He had a black tattoo of a dove on his neck. A *dove*, can you believe it? I can describe what he tastes like and the roughness of his hands. I know the size of his freaking feet. At first, I tried to fight him off, but he held my arms down. I was so paralyzed with fear, I didn't even try to remove his mask." Rachel looked out at the water. "He ruined me for life," she said and buried her face in Will's chest. Will stroked her hair.

"We better go," Will said, interrupting. "The High Line closes soon."

Rachel blew her nose. "When he was done, he got off the bed, climbed out the window, and then had the audacity to turn around and tell me to have a nice night. *A nice night.*"

Will rose from the bench, helping Rachel to her feet. She felt frail after confessing, but she found herself saying, "I feel better now. Believe it or not, I actually feel better."

He kissed her on the forehead. "I'm glad," he said. "No one should have to go through what you and Sammy endured." She could not believe what an unbelievably kind and sensitive person Will was. And much to her surprise, he kept his arm around her as they walked in silence to the subway.

CHAPTER 30

Sydney returned from the hardware store. She was alone while the family was at Tucker's wrestling match. Like her mother, Sydney was a striking young woman, tall, thin, with butterscotch-blond hair that fell just past her shoulders. If one had to choose her best feature, it'd be her long, graceful legs. They'd win any beauty pageant hands down.

Sydney replaced all the candles in the house with battery operated ones. Then she replaced the tea kettle with an electric version that turned off automatically. She checked the batteries in all the smoke and CO_2 detectors.

Now for the fun part. Sydney opened iPhoto on her laptop and dragged family photos onto her desktop. Brook entered the room, catching Sydney off guard.

"Oh my God, you scared me to death. Knock much?"

"Sorry, I thought you heard me," Brook said.

"Is everyone back?" Sydney asked, worried her mom would be home before she finished her photo project.

"I was bored, so I left early." She looked at Sydney's desktop. "What are you doing?"

Sydney explained, "I'm setting up a calendar. This way, Mom will see the dates, and hopefully the pictures will help her remember who we all are."

Brook stood as still as stone. "Help her remember who we are?

Why would you say that?"

Sydney closed her laptop. "Come sit with me," she said, patting the quilt.

Terrified, Brook shuffled over to the bed and sat by her.

"Brook, do you understand what's going on with Mom?"

Brook squinted and scratched her head. "Sure, yeah, I think I do. She has Alzheimer's. It affects her memory, and she's getting worse. I know it's a bad disease and usually affects old people. Dad hasn't told me too much about it."

Sydney put her arm around her little sister. "Brook, do you want to know the truth? I can tell you if you do, but it doesn't have a happy ending."

Brook looked up, and Sydney saw tears welling in her lower lids. "I guess so," she said.

"Mom and Dad will kill me if they know, so you have to pinky swear you won't tell I told you. Tell them you read it in a book, okay?"

"Okay."

"Pinky swear, Brooklynn."

Brook hooked her right pinky into Sydney's. "I swear."

"Mom has Alzheimer's, but it's early-onset, which can strike as young as thirty-five. People with Alzheimer's usually only live five to seven years after diagnosis, but it can also go more rapidly—especially with her type." Brook stared wide-eyed, in a trance. "Do you understand what I'm telling you, Brook?"

Brook nodded. Tears made salty tracks down her cheeks.

"Five to seven years?" Brook asked. *How old will I be when she dies?* "Go on."

"Well, you're already seeing her short-term memory disappearing, in fits and starts. She'll seem fine one minute and then totally lost the next. But then it progresses to the long-term, like forgetting our names or who we are." Sydney lowered her voice and tried to sound less like a medical dictionary. "The memory thing goes even deeper. Since you've been away at school, you don't see the day-to-day decline.

She's getting worse. Eventually, difficulty remembering how to walk or swallow can occur. I'm not telling you this to frighten you, Brookie, but you're gonna see her get worse, so you need to be prepared."

Brook put her head on Syd's shoulder. "I love her so much. I don't want to lose her."

Sydney sighed and stroked Brook's hair. Although they had never been particularly close, Sydney had never lied to Brook. Honesty was instilled by their mom at an early age. *But maybe this time I should have lied.*

The girls sat on the bed, holding each other, without saying a word. Finally, Brook lifted her head and pushed her wet hair away from her face. She forced a half smile. "Can I help?"

The front door slammed, and Sydney jumped. She grabbed her laptop.

Bergen tapped on the door and entered his daughter's room. He looked from Sydney to Brook and back again. They looked guilty. Then he saw Brook's face. "Honey, are you okay?"

"I'm okay, Daddy. I was just talking to Sydney about Mom."

Sydney mouthed *you promised* and held up her pinky. "Brook looked up Alzheimer's online and was confused, so she asked me about it," Sydney told him, feeling guilty for lying.

Bergen looked down at the floor. He felt ashamed that his daughter had to learn about the disease from a computer. "Brook, your mom and I should have told you more about it, but it's just been so painful. I'm so sorry. I'm here if you want to talk. Mom's already talked to Syd about the heritability, but I can answer any questions."

Sydney shook her head wildly and gave her father a stern warning look.

"Heritability?" Brook asked. She glared at Sydney. "You didn't tell me that part! So what? We all get this too?"

Bergen put his hand to his mouth, pulling on his lips, and closed his eyes. "Come in the den and let's talk before Tucker and Mom get home. Syd, you come too," he suggested.

"I'm good, Dad. You talk to Brook. I think she needs this more than I do. I'll stay here."

Bergen wondered, *How scared must Sydney be? Knowing she will lose her mother and one day might succumb to the same disease that took her. I'm ill equipped for this goddamn shit. I can't raise three children alone.* "Are you sure, Syd? We can all talk and share our feelings."

Sydney returned to the project on her laptop. "I'm good, Dad."

Brook's eyes darted between Bergen and Sydney, searching for clues. *What else don't I know?*

"Go," Sydney encouraged. "It will be okay. You can come help when you're done."

Brook bit her lip and followed Bergen out to the den. He leaned against the large picture window. "It's a gorgeous New York fall day. Did you know it's my favorite time of the year?"

"Dad," Brook said, questioning his sudden pensive mood, "are you okay?"

Bergen snapped to attention and shook his head. "Come, let's talk," he said and sat on the chair next to the fireplace. Brook took the chair opposite him. "I should apologize," Bergen started. "I, I, well, I just haven't done a very good job helping our family get through this." Brook started to interrupt but Bergen continued, "This isn't easy, my sweet girl. Not for your mom, not for me, and certainly not for you and your siblings."

"I know Mom will slowly lose her memory." Brook thought about the discussion with Sydney. "I've seen movies about people with it. It's so sad."

"What would you like to know, honey? I'll do my best to answer your questions."

Brook chewed the inside of her cheek. "Will Mom really stop knowing how to eat?"

Bergen nodded slowly. "It's a possibility." He dropped his chin to his chest.

"Sydney said"—her neck reddened—"I mean, I read she will

forget who we are. Is that true too?"

"Lots of people forget their loved ones, but some don't. So, it's our job to help your mom, in a fun way, to remember us—and not leave her alone. Dr. Boswell says the more we're with her, the more we remind her who we are, and the more we keep our routines the same, the longer she'll remember. You coming home on weekends is exactly what Mom needs now. I'm proud of you, honey. I know this isn't easy—your first year of college."

"You mentioned *heritability*," Brook said, breaking the word into syllables.

Bergen rolled his neck. "Mom's type unfortunately does have a . . ." He stopped, reaching out for Brook's hands. "It has a fifty-fifty risk of passing on the defective gene." He paused to allow Brook time to process.

Brook stiffened and pulled her hands away. *An hour ago, life was pretty good. A break from school, time with family, Tucker's match, maybe dinner and a movie with Sydney. Now my world is upside down. Millions have Alzheimer's. I've accepted Mom's diagnosis. But now this? My mom could die before I graduate from college, and now we could all inherit what kills her?* "So, let me get this right," she said matter-of-factly, "I have a fifty percent chance of getting the same disease as Mom?" Bergen nodded. He wanted to give her hope. *But would it be false hope?*

"Did you want a boy or a girl for your first child?" Brook asked.

Bergen tilted his head. "What do you mean, honey? We didn't care. We just wanted a healthy baby." Bergen bit his lip. *Do we have three healthy children?* he wondered.

"I was just curious where Sydney landed on the roulette wheel." Brook walked to the aquarium. She placed a flat hand on the cool glass and traced the movement of the clown fish. "Okay, Dad, so what's next? I mean, not only for mom but me and Tuck and Syd?"

Bergen joined his daughter at the fish tank. He put his hands on her shoulders and faced her. "You can get a genome test if you want. That's how your mother found out."

"Genome?" Brook repeated. She didn't remember much about that from science class.

"A blueprint of your DNA. It identifies all kinds of things, like the color of your hair, ancestry, and predictions for illnesses. It's a personal decision. You must be prepared to handle bad news. I was hesitant at first."

Brook's eyes widened with panic. She felt dizzy. *Were his results carrying bad news too?*

"Sweetie, I'm fine. I have a mutation that prevents gaining weight from high-fat diets. I can eat tons of pizza. This is up to you. Sydney doesn't want it. It's a huge decision."

"Why did she decide not to get tested?"

"We're not sure," Bergen replied. "I think Syd isn't prepared to deal with the results."

"And Tuck?"

Bergen was tormented by the what-ifs. "Tuck doesn't know. Are you okay with that?"

Brook nodded and hugged Bergen. "I'm okay with whatever you decide to tell him. I'm going back in with Sydney. I love you, Dad."

Bergen watched his eighteen-year-old daughter walk out of the room. Bergen wondered, *What would I do in her shoes?* He knew Tucker would behave with a lot of emotion; he was still young and attached to his mom. And Brook would be levelheaded and rational about the future. Bergen knew he could count on Sydney to step up to the plate and try to help, but he was surprised at her unwillingness to look at her own destiny. The treatment team advised him that he and Hadley should have not one but several conversations with their children. People process grief differently. Bergen thought about the changing dynamics in his family as Hadley slowly slipped away. *We need a family meeting so we can get through this together.*

CHAPTER 31

Rachel stood in front of her mirror in her underwear. She turned sideways and examined her figure. Her black lace bra revealed a deep cleavage, and her curvaceous hips punctuated her thin waist. "He's gonna think I'm fat," she said to Princess.

Mandy tapped on the door. "Can I come in?"

Rachel invited her in and asked for help with what to wear.

"Another date?" Mandy asked, winking. "This is getting serious, eh," she teased.

Rachel broke into a huge smile and blushed. "I *really* like him, Mand. He just *gets* me." They were going to a special restaurant tonight. Rachel pulled out two dresses. Mandy pointed to the black crepe dress and suddenly dashed out of the room, returning moments later with tall silver high heels, dangly earrings, and an ornamental clip to put in Rachel's French twist.

Rachel turned to the full-length mirror and stared as if a stranger looked back at her. Her cheeks flushed. Princess wagged her tail approvingly and licked Rachel's leg.

When they got to dinner, Will gazed across the table at his date. "You are stunningly beautiful, Rachel." For the third time, Rachel blushed and looked away. She hadn't worn revealing clothes in years. The catcalls and glances unnerved her, but she enjoyed his attention. She forgot how good it felt to be admired. They sat mesmerized, barely touching their plates.

"This wine is nice," Rachel said. "I've never really been a big wine drinker. I think mostly because I never know what to order."

"This is an Italian Chardonnay from the Umbria region. My dad is a big collector. My parents go to Europe every year and bring wine back. As kids, Sammy and I were allowed to have a juice glass of red wine with dinner."

Will saw her astonishment on her face. "Honestly, being allowed to drink, even a little, I think it kept us from going crazy with booze when we got older."

Rachel nodded. "That makes sense. My friend Hadley likes wine a lot too."

Will looked up and cocked his head. "Hadley? I don't think I've met her yet."

Rachel said, "We met outside our therapists' rooms, became friends, got Princess together, and go to lunch sometimes. We talk every day now."

Will smiled. *She looks relaxed, peaceful.*

"Shall we go?" Will asked. "I'll get the check unless you want something else."

Will paid and escorted her outside. Turning onto Madison Avenue, he faced Rachel, took her face in his hands, and gently kissed her. "Do you want to walk or go back to my place?"

Rachel met his gaze and kissed him harder. "Let's go to your place."

Rachel felt tingly, a thrilling sensation. The ten-minute walk felt like forever. Will unlocked the deadbolt and turned on the lights. "After you," he said. "Welcome to my humble abode and our greeter, Tiger." Will scooped up the small tabby cat. "Tiger's a stray I took in a year ago. He's the sweetest cat ever. The vet says he's probably five. He's had his claws removed. Someone must have had him as an inside cat. Maybe one day Tiger and Princess can meet." Will smiled and led Rachel to the couch. "Can I get you a glass of wine or a beer?"

"You choose," she said. Will disappeared to the kitchen. Rachel sat on the brown leather couch and looked around. It was certainly a guy's place. A huge flat-screen TV, a DVR player, loudspeakers, and an Xbox. Framed posters of Jimmy Hendrix, Bob Marley, and Kiss. In the corner by the window was a large iron chin up bar and weight-lifting bench. A poster of Arnold Schwarzenegger in his prime was taped to the wall. She imagined Will's place might be more professional and a little less college dorm, but it was clean and neat, so it passed.

Will returned with a bottle of wine and glasses. "This is called a wine key," he said, holding up the opener. He showed her the label, a Washington state Pinot Noir, then poured the wine into the glasses and sat next to Rachel. "Cheers," he said, clinking glasses with hers.

"Cheers," she responded. "I like your place, Will. It's cozy."

"Small is more like it," he replied, and they both laughed.

Rachel took a sip. She could feel her anxiety rising and wondered if her neck and face were red. She took another swallow. "Will, I'm a little nervous. Can we take it slow?"

Will placed her glass on the table. Taking her hands in his, he kissed the tips of her fingers. "We can go as slow as you like. If you want to just talk or go home, I'm okay with that."

Rachel took a deep breath. "Kiss me again," she said.

Rachel's emotions flip-flopped from utter happiness to fear to lust, then back to nervousness and joy. She allowed him to take her in his arms. They were strong yet gentle. He softly kissed her cheeks, her chin, her ears. He kissed her neck and chest. Rachel let him.

Let go, she told herself. *He's safe*.

Will reached around to her back and started to unzip her dress. Rachel stiffened, and she pulled away from his mouth. "You okay?" he whispered.

She licked her lips, tasting the saltiness from his skin, and put her hand on his thigh. "I'm good," she said. "I trust you."

Rachel and Will lay in his bed, holding each other. She stared at the ceiling, not believing this day had really come. She, Rachel Weissman, was lying naked in bed with Will Devereux. He was handsome, smart, cultured. Best of all, he was normal.

"Thank you, Will," Rachel whispered softly in his ear.

"For what?" he asked.

"For being you, so kind and gentle."

"It goes both ways, you know. I feel totally lucky we met each other, and it's working out. You're a special person."

Rachel nuzzled against Will's neck. She inhaled deeply, detecting deodorant, wine, and his new aftershave. The scents were stimulating and brought on sharp feelings of arousal. Rachel pushed the sheets and comforter away and pressed her breasts up against Will's chest. She smiled invitingly as Will moved gently on top of her.

CHAPTER 32

Brook watched the second hand on the clock, waiting for her class to end. *Why did I sign up for History of the Middle Ages? It's so boring.* As soon as the professor ended the class, Brook stuffed her books into her backpack and hurried down the corridor. Once outside, she checked Google Maps and headed toward the C train. She took the subway uptown. Two elderly women with canes huddled together at one end of the car. They wore black raincoats and scarves. Their thick beige stockings sagged around their ankles. Brook could hear them speaking in another language. Yiddish? Next to Brook was a young Hispanic woman and her baby. She pushed the stroller gently to-and-fro with the swaying of the train. At the first stop, three teenage boys entered. They wore blue jeans that hung past their boxer shorts, white tank tops, and black beanies. Brook caught their gaze and immediately looked away. She focused instead on reading the signs: DO NOT HOLD DOORS. DO NOT LEAN ON DOORS. NO SMOKING. NO MUSIC. DON'T TAKE THE RISK. RIDE SAFELY. A disheveled man stepped into the car and sat next to her. His stained brown coat was ripped, and his sneakers were held in place with gray duct tape. He muttered something about Jesus while rubbing his tobacco-stained thumb and forefinger together. Brook tried to block the offensive odor. She counted the stops to her destination.

Growing up in Midtown, she was accustomed to skyscrapers, but the one in front of her seemed intimidating. She wondered if coming here was a mistake. Brook entered the lobby.

"May I help you?" the guard asked.

"I have an appointment with Dr. Rathdrum. My name is Brooklynn Stanton."

The guard had her sign in, gave her a visitor pass, and showed her to the elevator.

Isabella greeted her and escorted her to Dr. Rathdrum, just like she did with her parents.

Brook admired the diplomas. Dr. Rathdrum, dressed in a blue, green, and white paisley dress and a white lab coat, didn't look like what Brook was expecting: a big woman, probably over 200 pounds, with dull, short, thin brown hair and lifeless brown eyes.

"I'm Dr. Rathdrum," she said, extending her hand. Brook shook hands. "Your dad tells me you would like to talk about your genetic risk for Alzheimer's. Is that correct?"

Brook nodded and questioned the sanity of her decision. Maybe it was an overreaction.

The doctor invited Brook to sit and offered to answer any of her questions.

Brook looked at the pictures of DNA strands. "I studied DNA and chromosomes in biology," Brook started. She took out a small notebook. "I wrote questions so I wouldn't forget."

"I do that too," Dr. Rathdrum replied, smiling warmly. "It always seems you have so little time, and then you're out the door and have forgotten all your concerns."

Brook smiled. *I like her.* "I've read about Alzheimer's, and my dad explained the kind my mom has, but how does this affect me and, if I have children, my kids?"

"Before I answer, I want to ensure you understand the ramifications associated with the answers you might receive." Brook nodded and held a pen to a notebook.

"Your father told you about the potential heritability of your mother's type of Alzheimer's. You understand that it carries with it a fifty percent chance that children will get it. Currently, there is no cure, although research is making massive strides. There are medications on the market that slow its progression. The only way to determine whether you are affected is to have your genome tested. Unfortunately, if you do have the faulty gene and you decide to have children, they would have the same fifty-fifty chance of getting it."

Brook listened stoically. She'd had time to process the information and do further research. "I guess where I need help is deciding whether or not I should get tested. If I don't, I'll live in fear. And if I do, I could pass it to my children, which isn't fair. And it wouldn't be fair to my partner either, right? If I do find out I have it, then there's no point in living. I mean, why go to school, get married, go on trips, do anything if I'm just going to forget it all and die?"

"We all die, Brook. And if you don't have it?" Dr. Rathdrum asked in a soothing voice.

"So, basically, I get to flip a coin. Heads I live, tails I die," Brook said sarcastically.

Dr. Rathdrum rested her arms on the table. "It doesn't have to be that way, Brook. Your mother, although still young, has lived a full, vibrant life. She has three wonderful children and a loving husband. Had she known about her disease, do you think she'd have chosen not to live?"

Brook started to cry. "I hate her for doing this to us, to me," Brook blurted. "My life was fine until this. Now what? If I do have it, I don't see the point in going to college anymore. Why would I want to acquire knowledge I'm just going to forget?"

"You have the advantage of time."

"I wouldn't call it an advantage. My sister doesn't want to know. Whenever I misplace my keys or forget something, I'm convinced the dementia has started. It's going to haunt me every waking moment until I know. But I don't want to know. I'm so confused and scared."

"I know a lady who always wanted to have a baby girl," Dr. Rathdrum said. "Her first two children were boys. She didn't necessarily want a third, but she wanted a girl. They traveled to Pasadena to have a special procedure called sex selection. She got pregnant on the fifth try. With her first two, she wanted to know the sex right away, but with this one, she told the doctor to only give the results to her husband. One evening while she was reading to her boys, her husband came home from work. As soon as the door opened, she could hear the crinkle of plastic, the kind the florists use to wrap bouquets. At that very second, she knew it was a boy. After all, if it had been a girl, he'd have called the minute he got the news. For months, she was depressed and cried all the time. She hated being pregnant and was angry with her unborn son. She wouldn't decorate the nursery or choose a name. Her husband feared that once he was born, she would sink into an even deeper depression."

"What happened to her?" Brook asked, spellbound.

"The baby boy was born prematurely, and she almost lost him. She fell in love with her son. He is grown now, the apple of his mother's eye." Dr. Rathdrum smiled.

"So, you're telling me she had a fifty-fifty chance. She rolled the dice and even though the results weren't what she was hoping for, she was, in the end, still happy?"

"Life extends past us. That woman is my husband's mother."

Brook looked up in surprise.

Dr. Rathdrum smiled. "No one can tell you what to do. You must weigh the advantages and disadvantages and know how to handle the results if they're not what you are looking for."

"I feel so selfish worrying about me when my mom is going through so much."

"There's nothing selfish about it, Brook. It's a normal reaction to want to know our own fate. You're eighteen. You're not a minor. It's a big decision. And it's *your* decision. Come back if you want to talk some more. I'm available anytime." Dr. Rathdrum smiled warmly. "Discuss it with your family if you think that will help."

Brook left and walked toward the subway. A tall gentleman

dropped his flowers and newspaper. Brook reached to pick them up and noticed a headline: "Family of Six Killed in Plane Crash." She robotically handed the man his items and murmured, "We could go at any time."

"Thank you," the man said. "I'm sorry, but what did you say?"

We could go at any time. Like my grandparents' car crash and that kid from sixth grade who died of meningitis. I've got to see what's in my head. To live life to the fullest. I'll schedule an appointment tomorrow. We could go at any time.

CHAPTER 33

Will rang the buzzer at 7:30. Rachel kissed Princess and then ran down the five flights of stairs. "Thanks for coming with me, Rach. I hope you're not too bored," Will said. "Our finance professor said we'd get extra credit. The speaker's supposed to be a guru on Wall Street."

"I'm happy to join you. 'Investments for Life' might be a pretty sexy topic," she teased.

Rachel and Will arrived at the lecture hall fifteen minutes early. Rows of brown wooden chairs faced the blackboards at the front of the room. Smeared chalk revealed shadows of the notes from an earlier lecture. In blue chalk, in the bottom corner, someone wrote MW ♥ JCR.

"My mom always told me the ones who sit in the front get the best grades," Will said.

Young businesspeople filled the room. A few were young couples, planning investments. "It's past eight," Rachel whispered to Will. "Where's the speaker?"

"Good evening," the man bellowed as he hurriedly entered the room, tossing his briefcase on the table. "I apologize for being late. I couldn't get a cab."

Rachel looked up in astonishment. The man had his back to her as he removed his overcoat and wrote his name on the board. *Could it be?* She leaned forward.

The man turned around halfway and announced, "Good evening, I'm Mr. Weissman."

Will turned toward Rachel and grabbed her hand. He saw the expression on her face and the hives spreading across her neck. "Is that your . . . dad?"

The speaker's eyes alighted on Rachel. His face flushed with shame, and he withdrew his gaze and looked out at his audience. "Shall we get started?" he asked.

The familiar acrid taste in her mouth, racing pulse, and need to run had returned. Rachel closed her eyes and tried to quiet her pounding heart. *Breathe. Slow in, slow out. You're not in any danger.* She held Will's hand throughout the lecture. Her dad looked different, but she couldn't put a finger on why. He was, of course, older, with more lines around his deep-set eyes. *Is he thinner?* But his face had a look of pain. His eyes looked sad, and the corner of his lips seemed permanently turned down. Rachel wrestled with conflicting feelings of hating her father for leaving and wanting desperately to run into her daddy's arms. *He doesn't deserve your vulnerability.*

Finally, after one of the longest hours, the room erupted in applause. Several people rushed to the front to ask the speaker more questions. Rachel grabbed her handbag and rose.

"Rachel, wait!" her dad called out, removing himself from the group. "Rachel, please wait," he said gently, taking hold of her arm. Will stood by Rachel's side.

"Dad, I, I, I," she stammered. "I didn't know you were giving investment lectures."

"Rachel, honey, can we go somewhere and talk? Just give me ten minutes," he begged.

Rachel took a long breath in. "This is Will Devereux. He's a finance major in the MBA program at Manhattan College."

"Nice to meet you," Frank Weissman said. "Please, give me ten minutes. I really want to talk."

Rachel looked to Will for the answer. He nodded but shrugged.

Will only knew that Rachel hadn't seen her dad in four years and he couldn't cope knowing she'd been raped.

"Sure, but I can't stay long. We'll be at the café across the street."

Rachel pushed open the double doors. "Well, I wasn't expecting that," she said.

"I didn't know. I'm sorry. I just didn't know." Rachel took his hand. "I never put two and two together that Frank Weissman, the author of a weekly finance newsletter, was your dad," Will said. "I'm so sorry. Believe me, had I known I would have never taken you. Do you want me to come with you? Or I can go home and let the two of you get reacquainted."

"No, please stay with me," she begged. "I don't really know what to say or what he could say. We should have met him at a bar instead," Rachel joked. "I could use a drink."

Frank Weissman stayed true to his word and entered the Coffee Bean and Tea Leaf ten minutes later. He found Rachel and Will and pulled up a chair. "Can I get anyone anything?"

Rachel and Will shook their heads. She just wanted to get this meeting over with.

Frank removed his blazer and loosened his tie. "Thank you for waiting for me, Rachel. I really do appreciate it."

"Sure, Dad, but Will and I have a late dinner reservation." Will looked at Rachel, surprised, but understood the ruse.

"You look great, honey," Frank said with a tortured look.

"You look good too, Dad," Rachel answered. The tension was palpable.

"How are you doing? Are you still living with your mom and aunt Claudette?" he asked.

The inner turmoil restarted, and she felt her whole body tense. *How dare he ask about my life. Where has he been for the last four years?* Will put his hand on her knee. She liked it. It was support, encouragement. She took a breath. "I have a roommate. I got a dog." She was sure not to mention the rape. After a few minutes, Will excused himself to go to the restroom.

Once they were alone, Rachel's dad lowered his voice. "I know I don't deserve to ask this of you, but can I see you again? I'd like to talk to you alone. I have some things I need to tell you," Frank said, looking at Rachel with the sad look of a forlorn puppy.

Rachel thought it was strange. *If we hadn't accidentally run into each other, would he have reached out?* The urge to hug him enveloped her. *I could forgive him*, she told herself, *but would he just disappear again?*

Will returned as a barista announced the store would be closing. Rachel stood.

Frank rose quickly, almost knocking over his chair. "Rachel, please, give me a chance to explain. If you decide not to see me anymore after we talk, I'll understand. Please."

Rachel closed her eyes and shook her head, then looked at Will. He smiled. It wasn't his decision to make, but he'd support her. Rachel took a deep breath. "Okay, Dad, I'll meet you, but just for lunch."

Frank moved forward to kiss his daughter goodbye, but she turned away. "Can you meet me this Monday at Hamilton's at noon?" Rachel nodded and started to leave. As they reached the door, Frank called, "Oh, and tell your mother I said hello." Rachel let the door slam behind her.

Rachel and Will walked in silence. The dead leaves scattered on the ground left the air smelling damp and earthy. The threat of a thunderstorm above. "Let's call an Uber. It looks like it's going to rain." Rachel squeezed Will's hand tightly as he opened the app on his phone.

Will checked the license plate of the approaching car, then opened the back door. Rachel slid across, and Will followed. "Thank you, Will, for staying with me. I couldn't have faced him alone." She paused. "Well, now you've met my dad. What do you think?"

"Seems like a nice enough guy, I guess. Are you glad you saw him?"

"I won't lie," Rachel said. "It certainly was a shock. Growing up, my mom used to talk about what a financial genius he was. Supposedly, he was the only one at his firm who correctly forecast the downturn in the US housing market in 2008. He was always so strong and confident. Tonight, though, he seemed timid. I mean, all his pleading. I felt sorry for him. Maybe it all came about for a reason." Rachel put her head on Will's shoulder and stared out the window.

CHAPTER 34

Bergen placed yogurt and fresh berries on the kitchen table, Hadley's favorite. He started a routine of showing her a different photo from their past each day. Today he chose one of them next to a SOLD sign in front of a red brick townhouse. "This was our first house in Brooklyn Heights," he told her. *We were so young and naive. Despite our tough times, I'd remarry you in a heartbeat,* he thought. Hadley shrugged. *Disinterest, or does she not remember?*

"Mariah can't come to clean today; she's not feeling well. I'm running to the office for a quick meeting, but then I'll be right back," he promised her as he pulled on his cashmere overcoat.

"I'll be fine, Bergen." She looked at him with a clenched jaw. "And I'd appreciate it if you would stop treating me like a child," she said, oblivious to the nerves Bergen felt every time he left her alone. Bergen nodded and kissed her head. "See you soon," he said, turning to leave.

After she finished her breakfast, Hadley changed from her nightgown to a mismatched outfit: gray running pants, a beige silk blouse, and sneakers. She looked at the oversized calendar by her dresser. The blocks for November 1 to 27 had large red Xs through them. Hadley walked to the office and retrieved the index card from the top drawer of Bergen's desk and then took the elevator to the basement. It was cold and damp, and she could not find the light switch. The cellar housed the boiler, main breaker panel, and fuse boxes. In the middle of the room were storage cages for each of the apartments. Hadley walked up and down the narrow aisles lit only by the sunlight coming in from the narrow storm windows, searching for the unit assigned to her apartment. As she rounded the corner of the third aisle, the lights came on, flooding the room.

"Mrs. Stanton, hi, it's Marvin Stein in twelve B," a voice from behind her said. "Can I help you find something?" *Who is this?* Hadley thought.

"I'm looking for my Christmas decorations." The man guided her to the end of the row and pointed to a metal plaque that read, STANTON. Hadley thanked him, then lifted the combination lock into the palm of her hand and read the numbers from the index card. "Two to the right, twenty-two to the left, and fourteen to the right." The lock did not open. Hadley tried again, getting more flustered with each attempt. "Damn it, open!" She kicked the metal door.

The man returned. "May I?" He took the index card from her. Within seconds, he opened the lock and retreated to his unit to put his bike away.

The unit was crammed full of large plastic storage bins. They were stacked on each other from the floor to the ceiling. Taped on the side of each was an eight-by-ten-inch piece of paper labeling the contents: SKI WEAR, T'GIVING, HALLOWEEN, XMAS LIGHTS, BEACH, TAXES. Hadley scanned them until she found XMAS DECS. "Damn it all, you would have to be on the top," she cursed, then pulled two smaller bins from the corner to use as step stools.

A loud crash thundered through the basement, shaking the corrugated metal unit dividers. The man from before, Marvin, hoisted his bicycle onto two hooks and instinctively ran toward Hadley's unit. Her head and left arm poked out from under the stack of spilled boxes. Kneeling by her side, he could see that her arm was badly lacerated and her face cut. A bruise bloomed on her left ear. She lay motionless. Marvin placed two fingers on her neck. She was alive.

"Mrs. Stanton," he said softly, "can you hear me? I'm going to help you, but I don't want you to move. It's important you don't move your head," he instructed. Hadley didn't answer.

Marvin took out his phone to call 911. "No reception." He ran to his storage unit and grabbed the spare tire from his bike kit. Marvin dashed back to Hadley and wrapped the rubber inner tube tightly around her bloody upper arm. Hadley cringed in pain. Marvin began carefully removing the heavy boxes that lay on top of her. "It's okay, Mrs. Stanton, hang tight. I'll be right back." He ran to the stairwell. Minutes later, he returned with the desk clerk and doorman.

The three men continued moving the boxes out of the way. Her skin was turning ashen, and there was more blood. "Oh man," remarked the doorman, "I hope that ambulance hurries."

Marvin knelt, holding Hadley's good hand. "Mrs. Stanton, is anyone home?" Hadley went in and out of consciousness but did not answer. "Go ring her place, and if no one's there, call whatever numbers you have for her husband," Marvin instructed the desk clerk.

"Yes, sir," he replied and left the basement, glad to be away from the blood and chaos.

Karilynn knocked on Bergen's office and opened it before he responded. "Mr. Stanton, pardon the interruption," she said fretfully, "but there's been an incident with your wife."

Bergen dropped the papers he was reading and jumped to his feet. "What? Is she okay?"

"Someone from your building called and said she fell and is in the ambulance. He doesn't know for sure but thinks she has some broken bones." Karilynn put her hand to her mouth.

Bergen grabbed his phone and coat. "Tell Mr. Cavanaugh I've had an emergency and will have to reschedule." He rushed out of the office. Inside the elevator, his mouth went dry, and his heart pounded wildly. "Hurry up," he said as he watched the display counting down from seventeen to L. At the lobby, he wedged himself through the half-open doors and caught a cab.

He raced to the ER and saw Hadley on a stretcher in a cubicle partitioned off with beige curtains. He cringed. The sheet beneath her was stained with blood. Her blouse and pants had been cut off, and she wore a light green hospital gown. An IV was in her right arm. Her left, stabilized on a padded board, revealed two large gashes caked in brown, dry blood. Wires peeked out from her gown as red blips on an overhead heart monitor kept a constant cadence.

"Hadley, honey," Bergen whispered.

Hadley tried to open her swollen eyes, instinctively smiling at his voice.

A stocky woman in hospital greens pulled back the curtain. "Are you Mr. Stanton?"

Bergen nodded rapidly, his eyes wide and unblinking.

"I'm taking your wife to x-ray," she told him. "We should be back in twenty minutes."

"Wait, is she going to be okay? What's broken?" Before she could reply, a doctor arrived.

"I'm the attending on duty, Dr. Singh," he said, extending his hand. "Your wife has had a very bad fall," he said. "I understand you weren't there. Is that correct?

"No, I was at work," Bergen replied. "My neighbor told me she must have been trying to reach a container in our storage unit when the pile fell on her."

"That's what I was told. She's lucky. I would have expected more injuries from the weight of the boxes and her head hitting the concrete floor. Does your wife have any allergies?"

"Yes, she's allergic to codeine and latex," Bergen replied, "and she's O positive."

The doctor jotted notes in his chart. "Thank you. We've already drawn labs and done a cross and match for a blood infusion. Has she eaten in the last four to six hours?"

Bergen looked at his watch: 11:30 a.m. "Some yogurt and berries, but I don't know if she's had anything else. Also, my wife, she has Alzheimer's disease."

Dr. Singh tilted his head. "Alzheimer's?" he asked, double-checking her age.

"Yes, I know, she's young, forty-eight, but she has FAD," Bergen explained with a tortured look. "I had a very important meeting at work and was only going to be gone for an hour. Shit, what have I done? Is she going to be okay, Doctor?"

Dr. Singh scribbled notes. "She has a concussion and soft tissue damage. I'd guess her left radius is broken, but we'll wait for the X-rays. I have paged Dr. Fattimeh Karimi, our orthopedist. Your wife is going to have quite a bit of pain and will require pain management." He paused. "I'll have to reconsider narcotics because of the Alzheimer's."

"I should call the kids," Bergen said. "They'll be worried if she's not there."

Dr. Singh asked, "Who is her neurologist?" He jotted down her name. "I know your wife will want visitors, but she'll be heavily sedated and will need her rest. Tomorrow is better."

Bergen nodded. "My oldest daughter took my son to school. I can't believe I left her alone. How fucking stupid."

Dr. Singh patted Bergen's shoulder. "It's not your fault. Your wife should be back from radiology soon," he said. "We'll have more answers then."

A NURSE CHECKED Hadley's vitals, assessed the wound, and adjusted the IV drip rate. "Quite a spill," she exclaimed. "If you need anything, my name is Lucinda. I'll be Ms. Stanton's nurse until eleven tonight. Dr. Karimi should be in soon to discuss everything with you."

An hour later, Dr. Karimi offered her hand to Bergen. She was strikingly beautiful, with large, almond-shaped eyes and thick black hair in a bun. Her curvaceous figure was obvious despite her baggy surgical greens. "Your wife is a champ," Dr. Karimi started. "We casted her arm and stitched up that nasty cut. I'm sure she's sore, but our goal is to get your wife up and out of bed as quickly as possible. Given her Alzheimer's, I am concerned about the possibility of increased mental confusion after an accident like this. The disorienting experience of pain, being in a strange place, and drugs are hard on anyone and can accentuate pre-existing dementia. I'm hoping her neurologist can see your wife while she's here in the hospital. I'd appreciate her assessment of next steps." Bergen was overwhelmed but nodded. "Do you have any questions?"

Bergen had hundreds, but his major fear was her prognosis. "What is . . . how long?"

Looking at Hadley while she slept, Dr. Karimi put a hand on his arm. "She's going to be okay, Mr. Stanton. Her wounds will heal, and the bone will knit back together. But given the dementia, I think it prudent to keep her a few days to monitor her concussion."

Bergen put his face in his hands. "I'm sorry," he choked out, "it's just—"

Dr. Karima interrupted, "Mr. Stanton, this must be very difficult for you. I assure you, we'll give your wife the best possible care. She is on heavy-duty pain meds and will most likely sleep throughout the night. I suggest you go home and get some sleep yourself." Bergen nodded but knew he wouldn't leave Hadley's side. "I'll be on call tonight. You can reach me through the hospital operator." She put her hand on his shoulder.

It was past eleven when Hadley woke. "Bergen, are you here?" she whispered. She was scared. Everything was dark, and she wasn't quite sure where she was.

Bergen immediately startled back to consciousness. "Yes, dear, I'm here."

"I can't open my eyes. My arm, it aches so much. And I need to use the bathroom. Can you help me up?"

Bergen realized Hadley had no clue what happened or where she was. "You can't get out of bed yet. Sorry." Hadley fell back to sleep. *A blessing*, he thought. *Sleep is relief from the pain.*

Nearing 8 a.m., Hadley woke to the clattering of food trays. Greasy bacon assaulted her nostrils. "Bergen, are you here?" She peered out from purple, swollen eyelids. A woman sat by her bedside in a white dress. "Where am I? Is my husband here?" She lifted her good arm and touched her face, exploring the bumps and cuts. "What happened? Why can't I see?"

"You are in the hospital, ma'am," Carly, a student nurse, replied, who was sent to watch Hadley until Bergen arrived. "You had an accident. Let me call the nurse and tell her you're awake." The student pressed the call button and placed the remote in Hadley's hand. "Push this button whenever you need something."

"Mrs. Stanton, good morning. How are we today?" the chipper nurse said.

"What happened? Why am I here? My husband, where is he? Is he here?" Hadley asked.

The nurse moved closer. "He was here all night but left this morning to freshen up. He will be back soon." The nurse pushed a button on the bed. "Carly and I are going to pull you up a little higher so you can eat. After breakfast, we can help you into the bathroom to wash."

As the bed moved, Hadley winced and clutched the side rail. "What time is it?"

"It's seven-forty-five," the nurse answered. "I'll be back in a few minutes."

Carly plumped the pillows. "Today, we have some cut-up fruit salad and oatmeal." She spoon-fed her. "And there's a beautiful vase of flowers on the windowsill."

"Sounds beautiful," Hadley said. "Is there a card? Can you tell me who it's from?"

The student read the card and then described a gift of colorful balloons tied to the bed.

Smiling made Hadley grimace at the stab of pain. "Let me guess. They're from Tucker?"

The student nurse read it aloud. "Get better soon, Mom. I love you. Tucker."

A kitchen aide entered and drew the curtain separating the beds. "Are you finished?"

"Yes, thank you. I'm not hungry," the patient beside Hadley replied.

"I think I am," Hadley said, and the student feeding her nodded.

The young girl in the next bed said, "Hi, I'm Carmen."

Hadley tenderly turned her head. "I'm Hadley. Sorry. I can't see you."

"No worries. Looks like we might've had similar injuries. What happened?"

"Well, I really don't know," Hadley replied.

The girl shrugged. "I got in a car accident last night."

Have I been in a car accident too? Hadley wondered.

Shortly after 8:30, Bergen and the kids arrived. Tucker rushed to the bedside first but stepped back in alarm. "Mom, are you okay? Does your face hurt? It's way swollen." Before she could answer, he noticed her arm. "Oh cool, you have a cast. Can I be the first to sign it?"

Hadley lifted her good arm and searched for him. "Honey, of course. Is Dad here?"

Without missing a beat, Brook and Sydney said hello and moved closer. Sydney brought her hand up to her mouth and shuddered at the nasty purple splotches around her mom's eyes. Brook swallowed hard, trying to be brave. Even though she wasn't squeamish, it was difficult to see her mom this way. "Dad's talking to the nurses. He'll be right in," Sydney assured her.

Bergen kissed Hadley gently on her head. "How do you feel today, honey?"

The chipper nurse entered. "You beat me to it. How is your pain, Mrs. Stanton?"

"I have a splitting headache, and my arm hurts. Can someone tell me what happened?"

"You had a fall, Hadley. On a scale of one to ten, with ten being unbearable, what would you assign your pain level?"

Hadley grimaced. "Probably a seven," she answered. "Can I get something for it?"

The nurse pointed to a whiteboard. "Mrs. Stanton, I know you can't see this quite yet, but all your medication times are written on a board. Your last Tylenol was at six. You can have it every six hours, so we'll wait until noon for your next dose. You're due for a Vicodin if you think you need it. It can make you sleepy, and we don't want you to be uneasy on your feet."

"I think I need it."

"That's fine. We want to stay on top of the pain," the nurse said. "The Vicodin takes about an hour to get the full effect, so let's get you out of bed sooner rather than later."

"Can't wait," Hadley said with great sarcasm.

Sydney tilted her head toward the door. "Mom, Tuck is late for school. I'll run him over now. If you're up for visitors, when Brook's done with class, we can come back."

"I'd like that. Bergen, can you stay?" Hadley asked with apprehension.

Bergen kissed her good hand. "Of course. I will stay as long as you like. I'll walk the kids out, grab a cup of coffee, and be right back."

Bergen returned with his coffee and leaned against the windowsill, reading the paper.

Carmen noticed him. "Hi, I'm Carmen. Where'd your wife go?"

"Hi, Carmen. I'm Bergen. They took her to get another x-ray," he explained.

"She's lucky," Carmen said. "She doesn't remember anything about her accident."

Bergen tilted his head. "My wife has Alzheimer's disease."

Carmen looked away, embarrassed. "Oh, I'm sorry," she apologized. "She's so young. Does she know she has it?"

"Yes, she does, but her long-term memory is starting to go too, so I'm not really sure how much she actually understands now." Bergen looked blankly at the floor. The orderly opened the door and pushed Hadley in a wheelchair into the room. Together, they helped Hadley into bed.

Minutes later, Rachel peeked inside and smiled at the girl in the first bed. Her face blanched when she saw Hadley. "Hi, Hadley, it's Rachel," she said, grateful her friend couldn't see her expression. "Brook called me last night and told me there was an accident."

"Who is it?" Hadley asked. "Who's visiting?"

"It's Rachel." Hadley didn't respond. "Your friend. We met at the psychiatrist's office. You got me Princess, the dog from Pooch Rescue."

Hadley pieced together the clues to identify this mysterious woman. "I'm glad you're here, Rachel. That was very nice of you to come," she said.

Rachel nodded, relieved by Hadley's recall. Bergen was clean-shaven, his shirt and slacks crisply pressed, but the deep, dark hollows under his eyes said it all. "I can stay until noon, Bergen, if you want to get some rest or have anything you need to do."

Bergen detested hospitals, the strong aseptic smells, and the constant beeping of monitors. But the overhead hospital codes and looming threat of death frightened him the most. They reminded him of Angelica. "Thank you so much. I'll be back by noon. Goodbye, dear."

Because of her limited vision and drowsiness from the pain meds, Hadley could only leave her room in a wheelchair. Rachel retrieved one from the hallway and pushed it into the room. "Let's go down to the solarium. I passed it coming to your room. It looks bright, cheery."

Hadley snickered. "I won't be able to see it. But let's go." A moment later, she said, "What do I look like? Do I look grotesque?"

"Hmmm, grotesque, no. Cut up and swollen, yes. You look like Rocky Balboa."

Hadley reached up and gently traced the edges of her swollen eyes. "That bad, eh?"

Rachel rolled the squeaky wheelchair into the dayroom. She parked it by the windows overlooking a sunny courtyard. Several flower arrangements adorned the sill and brightened the otherwise dull room. "I've been thinking about our pact," Rachel said. "A lot has happened since I told you I wanted to die. Now I have you and Will. I am trying to bury the hatchet with my dad. I think I can be happy. Thank you, Hadley. You've really helped me. I owe you a huge debt of gratitude. You're like a big sister, mother, friend, and mentor all rolled into one. I want you to know that, Hadley. I want you to know how deeply I care for you."

Who is Will? What happened with her father? "You taught me not to give up hope. I'm not sure what my future holds, but I am grateful for the time I do have. Right now, I just want to get out of this darn hospital and go home to Bergen and the kids."

A young girl in a red-and-white-striped pinafore entered the solarium with a cart of beverages and gently used magazines. She poured two cups of cranberry juice. Rachel lifted her paper cup in the air and lightly touched it to Hadley's.

"Cheers," Hadley responded, and the two laughed. Rachel wasn't sure Hadley knew what she was cheering for, but still, it was sweet to connect.

CHAPTER 35

Rachel stared into her closet. *Why does it matter what I wear to see my dad?* She felt fidgety and restless and hoped her grounding techniques would calm her nerves.

Hamilton's is an upscale place. I should wear a dress or a smart pantsuit. "Where are you, Mandy?" she yelled. Princess jumped off the bed and sat at Rachel's feet, attentive to the sound of her distressed voice. "I'm okay, Princess, just a little nervous. I wish you could come with me." Princess raised her fluffy ears. *She looks like she's smiling. Oh! That's it! She can come! I'll put her vest on. A diversion and unconditional love.*

Dressed in slacks, a floral blouse, and her only pair of stilettos, Rachel entered the restaurant with Princess by her side. Her heels were difficult to walk in and clicked loudly, but they were a symbol of power. "I'm meeting Mr. Weissman," Rachel told the maître d'.

"Yes, madam," he responded. "Is your dog a service animal?"

Rachel nodded and was promptly escorted to a table in the far corner of the room. Although Princess helped calm her nerves, she was still anxious. Her armpits were moist and sticky. *Are the sweat stains visible? What does my dad have to say after all this time?*

Sitting with his back against the large picture window, Frank was dressed in a blue pin-stripe suit. He stirred a bamboo stick of olives in his martini while staring at his phone.

"Your guest, Mr. Weissman," the maître d' announced.

"My daughter. Louie, this is my daughter, Rachel," he said, beaming with pride.

The maître d' bowed his head. Frank pulled out a chair for Rachel. Her seat at the table afforded her the view of Wall Street and the city below.

"Who do we have here?" Frank asked, patting Princess on the head.

"This is my best friend, Princess. She goes everywhere with me." Princess idled up to Frank and put her cold, wet nose on his outstretched hand. Then she settled by Rachel's feet.

After they perused the menu, heard the specials, and made their selections, Frank took his daughter's hand. Rachel stiffened and pulled away. "Dad, this is really difficult for me. I have barely heard from you in over four years." She watched the Adam's apple bob in his throat as he swallowed in succession. Princess, aware of the tension, rubbed against Rachel's feet.

"I know, Rach, believe me. This is hard on me too."

Does he expect sympathy? I was raped and cast aside. I was supposed to trust you.

"Leaving was wrong. I never meant to hurt you or your mother. I love you both very much," he said, his drink spilling as he twirled the stick with the olives a little too strongly.

"You have a funny way of showing it," Rachel said.

"I need to tell you something. Even your mother doesn't know," he said. Rachel looked warily. *What can he say to undo the pain of leaving when I needed him most?* "When I was ten," Frank said, looking around, "I was—"

The waiter approached and served their salads. "Can I get you anything else?" he asked.

"Thank you, no," Frank responded brusquely, anxious to continue.

"Actually, may I have a bowl of water for my dog?" Rachel said.

After the waiter returned, Frank took a deep breath. "Rachel, I was abused by a friend of my father's." He swallowed hard, trying to push the memories back down.

Rachel sat up straight and shook her head in disbelief. She put her fork down and reached for his hand. This was certainly not what she was expecting.

Frank scooted his chair closer to Rachel. "My dad, your grandpa, had a friend who came around a lot to help after Mom died. Grandpa couldn't cope for a long time. He was depressed, unable to care for himself, let alone me. His friend"—Frank swallowed hard again—"Bernie Muckim, used to stay over to help." Frank used air quotes when he said, "to help." He lowered his voice to a whisper, "Muckim, or *fuck him*, as I called him, lived with us for five years. He came to my room almost nightly." Frank took his handkerchief from his breast pocket and wiped his nose. "I don't know if my dad knew or not, and I never told him."

Rachel felt sick. She pictured her father, a little boy, being "visited" by some sick old bastard who was stealing his innocence and dignity. She felt revulsion. *Why didn't he tell his father, a teacher, their rabbi? No, don't judge him.* Rachel reached for her tea and rubbed Princess with her foot. "I'm so sorry, Dad. I didn't know."

"Of course you didn't, honey. No one did. In fact, for years I stuffed the memories away. I kept them in a safe compartment and never let them out until"—Frank hesitated, then finished his martini—"well, when you had your incident." Rachel wanted to correct him but decided to give him a break this time. "My memories started to come back." He dug his fingers into the top of his scalp, hoping the physical pain would dull the emotional hurt. "I was so busy tackling my own demons, I knew I was of no use consoling you. The more I saw how much pain you were in, the more my memories surfaced. For your sake and mine, I distanced myself. I became useless as a father and a husband. I thought it was for your good that I leave."

"Why didn't you just tell us? We could have gotten you help—both of us," Rachel asked.

"I got stuck in the shame and guilt." He wouldn't tell his daughter this, but as he got older, his body responded to his abuser. He got aroused but also felt confused and bad.

Rachel felt like she and her dad were the only ones in the room. There were no sounds other than his voice. The picture window was blurry, and the room spun. She rubbed an ice cube on the back of her neck until the wooziness passed.

Frank's upright posture reduced to a slump. His face was pale. Rachel moved her chair closer to him. "Dad, I know how hard it is, but I think I can tell you from experience that you will find healing and strength in talking about it. Have you told anyone else?"

Frank stared at his lap, avoiding eye contact, and shook his head. "At the time, Muckim threatened that if I ever told, he'd go to jail and no one would be there to help, and I'd be put up for adoption. Of course, I know now that it was his way of keeping the secret. But back then, I believed him." Frank raised his head and met her gaze with a pained expression. "As I got older, the fear was replaced by shame. I felt so dirty."

"Daddy, I'm so sorry." She squeezed his hand. "I have a great therapist who's been helping me with my memories. Part of my journey has been to embrace that none of it was my fault. It's hard to talk about it, but it really does help."

Frank closed his eyes and gave Rachel a quick smile. "Honey, I'm sorry. I didn't mean to unload so much on you. You may not believe me, but I love you and your mother more than anything in the world. I stuffed all that love away too, but when I saw you last week, I knew I had to get back in your life."

Rachel's heart swelled. "Dad, I get it. I've been there. I'm glad you told me."

Frank and Rachel sat in silence until the waiter interrupted with dessert and coffee menus. Both declined, and Frank asked for the check. *Why did I pick a public place for this?*

Frank escorted Rachel and Princess to the elevator. "I wasn't sure if I should share, but you'd never forgive me if you didn't know the truth. It wasn't you I couldn't stand to be with; it was my memories."

Rachel stood on her tiptoes and kissed her dad's cheek. "Thanks, Dad. I appreciate you telling me. I too was haunted by my memories. That's why I went into therapy."

"I'll hail you a cab."

"Nah, I'll walk. That's okay," Rachel responded.

"Could we meet again? Maybe go for a walk? There's so much I want to know about you." Rachel nodded. "Rachel, did they ever catch him?"

"No," she said as the elevator doors closed.

Rachel's heart ached for her father. Her incident was only one time, but her poor dad had endured years of abuse, as a little kid, no less. *He seems so different. He never would have cried in public before or plead for her attention. He was strong, confident, scary smart. Now he seemed meek, less sure of himself. Abuse does that to people.* She sat on a chair in the lobby.

Rachel needed to talk to someone. *Monica will be booked, Mandy is at work, and Will is in school. Mom and Claudette? No, this is too uncomfortable for them, and not mine to share.* The sidewalks were crowded, people hurrying by on their cell phones, oblivious to the outside world. Rachel pulled Princess onto her lap, stroked her soft fur, and then sent a text to Will:

> Can u meet after class?
> Need 2 talk.

Within seconds, he replied,

> Can leave now if u want?

Before she could respond, he called. "Hey, aren't you in class?" she asked.

"Are you okay?" he asked with genuine worry. "Did everything go okay with your dad?"

The nausea and dizziness had finally dissipated, and now she felt calm. *Will cared. He really cared.* "Everything was okay," she said, "but my poor dad." *Should I share?*

"Your poor dad?" Will asked questioningly. "Is he okay?"

"It's a long story. Let's meet for a beer at Dougan's after your class."

Rachel looked at her watch. Two hours until Dougan's. She kicked off her heels and massaged her sore feet. "Let's go shopping," she said to Princess. "I want to get my dad a long overdue Father's Day gift."

CHAPTER 36

Bergen sat in the den with his feet on a leather ottoman. He paged through the weekend edition of the Financial Times and then read each page of The New York Times. Hadley curled up on the couch with a mug of tea and stared at the fireplace. Her Sunday morning routine had always been to do the NYT crossword puzzle, but now even the easiest clues baffled her.

"Shit! What the fuck?" Tucker screamed. "Oh my God, *ow*," he wailed.

Bergen and Hadley jumped to their feet and ran over to Tucker. "I think it stung me," he screamed. "Oh my God, this hurts like a mother—" He held his hand above the aquarium.

Hadley was bewildered. "What happened?" she asked. "Should I call the police?"

Bergen ushered Tucker to the kitchen. "Put it under hot water."

"*Shit*, this is so f'ing painful," Tucker screamed. "I was putting the fish cubes in, and I didn't see the lionfish coming to the top. *Ow*, Dad, make it stop."

Bergen yelled, "Sydney, call poison control and ask about a lionfish sting." She did.

"Tucker, no swearing," Hadley reprimanded. "What's happening?"

"Sit down, Hadley," Bergen said sternly. "Just sit down."

"They said they don't know about fish poison," Sydney yelled.

"Who has the fish guy's number?" Bergen yelled.

Hadley walked in circles. "What happened? What happened?"

Tucker's face was bright red, his teeth were clenched, and he used his good hand to pound on the kitchen counter. Bergen held the injured finger tightly below the first knuckle, hoping to restrict the movement of the venom.

Sydney Googled lionfish stings. "You'll be okay, Tuck. You're not gonna die. It's just gonna really, really hurt for the next hour or two."

"Hour or two!" Tucker screeched. "I can't stand this."

Bergen rubbed Tucker's back. "Slow your breathing, Tuck. Get me the fish net, Syd. I'm getting rid of these stupid poisonous fish. Who puts these kinds of fish in a family aquarium?"

Hadley looked at her young son crying in pain. "We had poisonous fish in there?"

Bergen just stared at her and shook his head. He wanted Hadley out of the kitchen, out of all the chaos. "Syd," he whispered, motioning with his head toward Hadley. She understood.

Like a toddler, Hadley dutifully followed Sydney out of the kitchen. "Is Tucker okay?"

"He's been stung, but he'll be okay."

Sydney settled Hadley on the couch, turned on the television, and returned to the kitchen.

"Dad, that was so weird with Mom, don't you think?" Sydney said.

Bergen motioned at Tucker. He left Tucker at the sink and walked to the other side of the kitchen. "It's another sign." *Each change is even more painful than the last.* "I feel terrible for scolding her. I know it's not her fault," Bergen said.

Sydney rubbed his back. "It's a cruel disease, but we'll get through it, Dad."

Tucker turned the water off and joined them. He winced with pain as he wrapped a rubber band around his finger. "You can see the spine punctures," he said, showing them the red marks on his swollen fingertip. "Thanks, Dad, for helping. And sorry for swearing so much. Boy, it's a good thing I wasn't here with just Mom," he said, feeling instantly bad. "I mean, I'm sorry I said that," he stammered and began tapping the edge of the kitchen island.

Bergen reached for Tucker's hand, hoping to stop the compulsion, but Tucker slid it away and continued. The urgency to perform the ritual was increasing. He tapped harder and faster in short bursts of sevens. "It's okay, Tuck. We understand what you mean," Bergen said, fending off any guilt he might be feeling. "You bring up a good point, though. Since her accident, the disorientation seems to come on more frequently, and eventually it will be longer lasting and then—" Bergen swallowed hard, feeling a lump in his throat. *Permanent.* "I think it's time to look into some additional help."

"I can quit the team and come home right after school. Please don't send her to one of those homes." Tears bulged over his lower lids and slid down his face again, this time from emotional pain, not physical.

Bergen put one arm around Sydney and the other around Tucker. The children moved in closer, softly burrowing their chins into his neck. Although formed out of turmoil, it was a special moment for him. It felt good to comfort them. To finally be able to help. He would call Dr. Boswell tomorrow and get her recommendations. Bergen relished the private moment. He then kissed them on the forehead. "Let's join Mom in the den."

CHAPTER 37

Princess tugged at the leash, pulling Rachel toward the park. "Okay, little girl, I'm going as fast as I can."

Dog parks are communities. People gather at the same time each day. There's Mr. Brodwell and his poodle, Tripsy, at 7 a.m., rain or shine. He sits by himself and smokes cigarettes. There's the Hispanic nanny, her three-year-old, and their dachshund in the afternoons. Why do kids play in the poopy grass, with germs and worms? There are two golden retrievers, Belle and Beau, with their handler. They are worth a lot of money from their dog show days. That's the rumor, at least. There's a new Chow Chow here. I remember that time the Chow Chow attacked a Jack Russell terrier. That dog never came back.

Rachel surveyed the park for dangerous dogs. It seemed clear, so she let Princess off her leash. There were friendlier dog parks, but this one was closer to the Apple store. She had a late appointment. She read emails while Princess played in the park. Then it was time to go.

Rachel and Princess entered the Apple store. "Hi, I'm Rachel. I have an appointment." The young man with the iPad had long brown hair in a neat ponytail and tunnel earrings in each earlobe. He directed her to wait at a nearby table. Five people sat around the table, each holding their ailing electronic device. Young children sat on beanbag chairs and played games. Rachel checked the weather app. "Shoot, rain all weekend," she said. Princess looked up.

Rachel noticed a man at the side counter dressed in jeans, Converse, and a gray sweatshirt. On his neck was a tattoo of a dove.

Rachel stood abruptly and looked at the exit. A hundred thoughts bombarded her mind: *Did he see me? Is he following me? Does he remember me? Should I run? Ignore him? Call the police? Call my mom? Punch him in the face or kick him in the balls?*

Rachel's heart pounded in her throat, her ribs tightening with every breath. *The Apple store is safe. Concentrate on slow breaths.* She stroked Princess, then dialed 9-1-1, almost pressing the call button. "Rachel," a young man said, tapping her shoulder.

Rachel turned so fast, she almost knocked him over. "What?" she said in a loud, frightened voice. Everyone in the store, including the man with the dove tattoo, turned to see the commotion. Rachel's eyes met his, and she felt a deep, visceral conviction: *He is the man.*

"Are you okay, miss?" the employee asked. "I didn't mean to startle you. It's your turn."

"Sorry." Rachel walked over. She picked up Princess and held her tightly. Pretending to look at the phone cases, Rachel stared at the dove tattoo. *Could more than one person have a dove tattoo?* She sized him up and compared him to the images in her mind. Same height, approximate weight, skin color, even the same type of jeans. "You're safe, Rachel. You're safe."

"Excuse me, what did you say?" a young girl dressed in an Apple shirt asked.

Rachel fanned herself with her free hand. "Do you have any water? I feel a bit dizzy." The girl retrieved a bottle of water for Rachel. She kept her eyes fixated on the man and drank the entire bottle. "I'm sorry. I have to reschedule." She took a seat at the same counter where the man with the dove tattoo sat. She reviewed her options: call the police, leave, or confront him.

Rachel sat for thirty minutes while the man talked to an employee about his phone troubles. When it became obvious that his session was ending, Rachel knew she had to decide.

I've spent most of my adult life avoiding this kind of threat. Why risk it now? I must know if it's him or not. I have to face him.

Holding Princess under one arm, she walked over to the man and stood to his left. Purposefully, she dropped her purse by his feet. Simultaneously, they both bent to pick up the purse. Her heart raced faster than she'd ever experienced. She felt her gut convulse and was sure she would throw up. Forcing herself to meet his gaze, she looked directly into his brown eyes. The man smiled. "Here you go," he said innocently, handing her the purse.

The same voice. In slow motion, she robotically took the purse. *He doesn't recognize me, but it's him. Was it that dark in my room? Was I no one special? Just one of his many victims?* Rachel stared. She was okay. She hadn't died, exploded, or gone crazy. She had a loving mom, an awesome boyfriend, a good job, and two best friends. This man did not define her.

Rachel walked to the other end of the counter. Pretending to take a picture of the newest laptops, she snapped a picture of the man with the dove tattoo and walked out. As she walked down the street, in the store windows, she saw the reflection of a confident young woman staring back at her. "I did it," she yelled into the darkening night sky. "I actually did it." Rachel was amazed. She didn't run from the situation. *Monica will be proud.* She hurried home to share the good news with Mandy.

CHAPTER 38

Bergen thanked Dr. Boswell and hung up. He stared at the silver framed photo of Hadley on his desk and slumped down in his chair, allowing the ensuing melancholy to wash over him. He took the picture and studied her face, afraid that one day he might forget how beautiful she once was, how her eyes sparkled. It seemed almost inconceivable that in just over a year, his wife had gone from a vivacious, beautiful woman to a progressively disabled, powerless child.

Bergen sent a text to his children.

> Family meeting at 6 p.m.
> Mom will be with Rachel.

Three hours later, Bergen and the kids gathered around the kitchen table. The mood was somber, Tucker and Sydney both long-faced. Bergen interlocked his fingers around the stem of his wineglass. Tucker, sitting next to Bergen, clicked the tab on his soda can. "One, two, three, four, five, six, seven, one, two, three, four, five, six, seven," he murmured. Sydney reached across the table to quiet his hands.

"So, Dad, are you going to start?" Brook asked in a serious and unemotional tone.

Bergen sat up straight and took a big sip of wine. He watched the syrupy legs of the dark red wine drip down the inside of his glass. "Kids, I love you all so, so much. This year has been the hardest time of my whole life, which I know is just as true for you. I'm so sorry."

Brook put her arm around him. "We love you, Dad. You've been amazing—with Mom, with us, with everything."

Bergen was taken aback. *How mature is she?* "I'm sure you've all noticed that your mom is getting worse. Her memory losses have moved beyond short-term, and she's easily confused and disoriented."

"I've been noticing it a lot," Sydney blurted. "Our last lunch, she told me she didn't like scallops. They're her favorite! And another time, she told a cabbie I was her sister."

How can my parents, in their seventies, still be living a full, complete life? Playing golf, going on cruises, hosting bridge parties? I love that they're healthy, but this isn't fair to Hadley. She needs residential care? She's not even fifty. "We need a plan. A skilled nurse, more protective measures, and eventually a memory care facility."

Sydney spoke up immediately. "I can be her full-time caregiver."

Tucker pushed his chair away from the table. All eyes were on him as he stopped to touch the frame of the kitchen door before going through.

Bergen turned his head. "It's probably for the best. This is tough for all of us, but he is so young." Bergen downed the remaining wine in his glass. "I also want to talk to you two again about your option to have your genome sequenced."

"Dad, I already told you both, I have absolutely no interest in finding out," Sydney said.

"And it's your right to make that decision," Bergen replied. "I just wanted to check in with you and answer any questions you may have. Brooklynn, have you given it more thought?"

Brook stared at the refrigerator, the family photos on the door. At eighteen, she felt years beyond her age. "I haven't decided," she lied. "But if I find out I have the gene, I am going to do everything possible to keep it from affecting me." Sydney scoffed. "I have been doing a lot of research and going to Alzheimer's support groups. They even offer classes at the public library about the latest studies and how to make lifestyle choices that keep your brain healthy as you age. Even if I don't have the gene, it can't hurt, right?" *It's about maintaining control.*

Bergen was in awe. He was proud of them.

Before he could compliment them, the front door opened. "Anyone home?"

Bergen looked at his watch. She hasn't even been gone an hour. "In here, the kitchen," he yelled. Rachel guided Hadley into the kitchen and gently seated her at an empty chair. Hadley's eyes were vacant, her face waxy and expressionless.

"Hi, Bergen. Hey, girls," Rachel started. "Your mom's not feeling so well. She got very upset during dinner. She was pacing and kept saying she was going home to her mother's house. I thought it best to bring her back."

"It's called sundowner's syndrome," Brook said. "They don't really know why, but in the evening, people with Alzheimer's can get very agitated. You did the right thing, Rach. Being in familiar surroundings can help with her disorientation." Once again, Bergen was impressed.

"Thank you for bringing her home, Rachel." Bergen gently rested his hands on Hadley's shoulders. "Can I get you a drink or something?"

Rachel declined and tenderly gave Hadley a kiss goodbye on the top of her head. Bergen walked her to the door. "Thank you. You're a good friend." They hugged goodbye.

The girls sat quietly at the table, looking at their mom. Deep lines had formed between her eyebrows. Her mouth hung open, though she said nothing. "Let's get you into your pajamas," he said. Hadley rose and tottered after him. She needed help with dressing. Bergen removed her sweater and jeans and slipped her nightgown over her head.

Hadley stood suddenly and retrieved her purse. "I'll be back in an hour. I have to go to tennis," she said as she left the bedroom. *Should I correct or distract her?*

"I think tennis was canceled," he said. "Stay and join us for some supper."

Hadley dropped her purse and allowed Bergen to help her into her yellow robe. He took her hand, noticing how frail it felt, and shepherded her out to join the kids.

It was difficult for Sydney to see her mother like this. The disease had sped up quite a bit since the accident, and Hadley was falling into an abyss. Powerlessness overwhelmed her. Brook jumped to her feet and pulled out the kitchen chair. "I like that bathrobe, Mom," she said.

Hadley tugged at the sleeve of her robe. "Why the hell am I wearing this?" she asked belligerently. Brook stepped away from her mother. Bergen touched her shoulder.

"Don't touch me please. I don't know you," Hadley barked, then attempted to push her chair away from the table. Bergen was shocked. "Hadley, dearest, you're here with Sydney and Brook, your daughters, and me, Bergen, your husband. We are in our kitchen at home."

"This is not my home. Get away from me." she protested.

"Brook, did you learn what to do during this sundown thing?" he asked.

"Don't agitate them further, and give them medicine to prevent combative behavior."

"Christ," Bergen muttered. "Can I get you some chamomile tea, Hadley?"

Hadley, with sudden lucidity, answered, "I'd love some."

"Unbelievable," Sydney said.

"What is, dear?" Hadley asked.

"Nothing, Mom, nothing," Sydney said, the exhaustion in her voice audible.

Bergen poured tea into the cup and floated the bag, twisting its label around the handle. He placed the cup on the table in front of Hadley, gently reminding her it was hot.

Confused and frightened by the Jekyll and Hyde in their presence, Sydney wanted to get out of the house, away from all the pandemonium. "I have to go to the store," Sydney said. Bergen glanced at Brook, giving her a look that it was okay to leave too.

Brook looked from Bergen to Hadley and then to Sydney. She

was conflicted. Sydney was obviously stressed and could use some support. She also didn't want to abandon her dad, but mostly she wanted to show that she was resilient and could handle her mother's mental decay.

"Dad, would you like me to stay?" she asked, her stomach churning. Each episode of her mother's debilitation made her angry and sad—yet stronger in her resolve to help.

"You go with your sister," he replied. "Ask Tuck to go too. Your mom and I will sit by the fire and watch TV." He winked and lifted his chin in the air, motioning for her to go.

"Okay, Dad," Brook said. "Need anything while we're out?"

"No, dear, we're all good here," Hadley replied.

CHAPTER 39

Muddy footprints from a large dog and a squirrel covered the steps to Rachel's apartment building. The sun tried desperately to peek through the clouds and warm the unseasonably cold spring morning. Old newspapers, grocery store fliers, and Easter sale announcements had accumulated under the mail slot. Frank pushed the buzzer for Weissman and Gottard and adjusted the brown plaid scarf around his neck. Rachel answered promptly and buzzed him in.

Unlike his youthful daughter, who vowed to only take the stairs, Frank rode the elevator to the fifth floor. Princess barked happily at the visitor.

Frank entered the small apartment. *What might I learn about my daughter?* He smiled as he looked around, recognizing several pieces of furniture from their family home. Did Rachel think about him when she looked at the dining table, grandfather clock, and antique bar that had been in his family for generations? He perused the books and magazines on the coffee table.

"I love your apartment. It has so many"—he chose his words carefully—"different styles." *Translation: a hodgepodge of hand-me-downs.* It was true. He ran his fingers across the top of the finely veneered antique bar. "This was my grandfather's. I can't remember if I ever told you he was in the whiskey bottling business. This was a gift from a very important client."

Rachel looked guiltily at the bar. Its cut crystal glasses, bottles, and ashtrays hadn't been touched since she'd moved in. They were all so old-fashioned.

"Dad, you can have it back if you like. Mom never used it and thought it was better off here than in storage."

"No, no. This is the perfect place for it." Sipping coffee, the two sat on the cream-colored couch Rachel bought from Ikea. Princess, never wanting to be left out, sat at Rachel's feet, eyeing the bowl of pretzels on the table. In their silence, Frank continued to peruse the room. An artificial flower arrangement adorned the inside of the nonworking fireplace, which was flanked by two mismatched armchairs. He was surprised there were no curtains on the living room windows but glad to see the four different locks on the entry door.

Looking at his lap, in a low, timid voice, he said, "Thank you for seeing me again. I have to ask you something, honey. I hope it's okay."

Rachel took her coffee cup in both hands. The warm mug gave her comfort.

"Rachel, you told me that the"—Frank swallowed—"rapist was never caught."

Did he actually use that word?

Frank wrinkled his nose and narrowed his eyes. "I know I'm late, but do you want to talk about it? I don't mean the rape, but how you're doing now."

Rachel hesitated. "More coffee?" She weighed whether she should tell him about the man at the Apple store. She boiled water and filled the French press. While it seeped, she took out her phone and opened her photos. Scrolling through, she stopped when she came to the one of the man with the dove tattoo. The inky black dove with outstretched wings was etched into his neck.

Rachel dropped the phone when Frank stepped into the small kitchen. "I thought I might help with the coffee," he said. The two bumped heads as they reached for the phone.

"Dad, this is him," she said, showing him. "I saw him in an Apple store."

Frank studied the picture. "Where did you get this? I thought you couldn't ID him?"

"I remembered his height, build, smell, and this tattoo." Frank put his arms around her. His face reddened and his temples pulsed. After a few minutes, Rachel pushed away. "I told Mom and Mandy that I saw him, but you're the only person I've shown his picture to. It was two months ago. The tattoo gave him away. It's him."

"Why didn't you go to the police?" He was immediately sorry that he'd asked.

Rachel chewed on a ragged hangnail. "There's a part of me that doesn't want to go through everything again. It's been so long, and I can't prove it's him." Rachel paused, trying to slow her breathing. "Years ago, I Googled men with dove tattoos. I thought a photo or a parlor would pop up. I thought I could find him." Frank stayed silent. "There were, of course, hundreds of dove tattoos, with at least fifty on the neck." She paused, looking directly at her dad. "I'd never win."

Frank took in a long breath. He'd never gotten closure for his own abuse and was hell-bent on getting it for Rachel. "Let's go sit. Let's talk," he said, guiding Rachel back to the living room. "I'm not good at this. I don't know what to say. We can go to the police. Show them the photo. Have them get the DNA evidence from the rape kit. We can end this."

Rachel lowered her head and patted Princess. "I don't want to, Dad. I want to move on. I'm finally doing better. I don't want to dredge it all up again."

Frank shook his head. "I wasn't there for you then, and for that, I'm sorry, but that son of a bitch deserves to rot in hell. I can help now, Rachel. I can get the best prosecutor in town."

Rachel smiled sadly. "I used to want revenge too, Dad, but I don't know. My friend Hadley has taught me so much about how precious life is, and I don't want to waste any more energy on that guy." She paused and then added, "I'm moving forward, and I'm ready to let him go."

"You're a better person than I am, Rach. But he better pray I never run into him. I won't be as forgiving as you." Frank sat back and looked at his daughter. He smiled, welcoming the knowledge that his little girl was going to be okay.

Rachel smiled and gave him a hug. "Let's make some breakfast."

CHAPTER 40

Bergen answered the phone in the hallway. "Stanton."

"Mr. Stanton, good day. There's a guest in the lobby for you, a Mr. Beaman."

Bergen looked at his watch. "Yes, send him right up," he answered. "Hadley, come here, dear. I have a surprise for you."

Hadley walked slowly into the foyer. A slight limp from the accident accentuated her shuffling gait. She was dressed in a champagne-colored satin robe. Her face was drawn.

Bergen put his arm around her narrow, frail shoulders and opened the door.

Hadley looked at the tall stranger in the entryway. "Hello, I'm Hadley Stanton," she said robotically, extending her hand. "Please excuse my appearance. I wasn't expecting guests."

Mark blinked in rapid succession. "Hads, it's me, Mark, your brother." Hadley stood still, expressionless.

"He came all the way from Brazil to see you," Bergen assured her.

Hadley let go of Mark's hand and stood on her tiptoes to hug him. "You look so old," she said. Bergen wasn't convinced she really recognized him but silently agreed—he did look old.

"Ha, don't we all," Mark replied. "It's so good to see you."

"How long has it been?" Bergen asked. "Ten, twelve years? Come, come sit down. You must be pooped. Can I get you something to drink? Water, beer?"

"Excuse my appearance," she repeated. "I didn't know you were coming."

"Hadley," Bergen interjected, "please tell the kids their uncle is here." Hadley left.

Mark stretched his mouth into a wide grimace. He was unprepared. "Bergen, oh man, she is really bad. I had no idea. I don't think she really recognizes me."

"I think the accident progressed the dementia. It's unpredictable now, getting worse." *What's taking so long with Hadley and the kids?*

Hadley had changed into a pair of jeans and a sweater but left the satin robe on. She joined them in the den and stared at the fish chasing each other in the tank.

Mark sat in uncomfortable silence. Hadley's forehead furrowed, revealing torment and confusion. She ping-ponged between Mark, Bergen, and the fish tank. Then, images of his family at Christmas popped into her head. "How are Lori and the kids?" she asked.

He smiled sadly. *She doesn't remember the divorce . . .* "They're all fine. Speaking of kids, where are my nieces and nephew?"

Bergen looked at Hadley. *She didn't tell them.* "I'll get them," Bergen said. When they emerged, Mark stood. His expression changed to amazement and sadness. He hadn't seen them since they were little kids—and now they were grown. They welcomed him with stiff hugs.

"Young man, the last time I saw you, you were in nursery school. Look at you now. Brooklynn," he said, "I think you were seven or eight when we last visited. And, of course, you're Sydney," he said, putting his hands on her shoulders and stepping back to get a good look. "Like your sister, still the spitting image of your mother." Mark smiled.

Hadley sat rigidly on the edge of her chair, staring at her brother. Deep creases furrowed above her brow. She was bewildered. *Why is he talking about nursery school?* Bergen was pleased they would have the opportunity to get to know their uncle better. He noticed Hadley's fugue-like state. *She should be smiling, joyful*, he thought.

"Let's move into the kitchen. I have salmon in the oven. We're so glad you're here," Bergen said, patting Mark's shoulder.

Sydney set the table with the floral dinner plates, a cut crystal vase with pink and yellow tulips, and linen napkins. "Mom, can you get the glasses? Six water glasses and three wine."

Hadley repeatedly counted the number of places Sydney had set. She looked around the kitchen for clues and then finally put an assortment of highballs, cordials, and wineglasses in the center of the table. Mark was overcome with grief as he watched Hadley struggle.

Bergen apologized for the modest fare in comparison to the rich and spicy dishes Mark was used to in São Paulo. Brook helped with plating the meal, and they all sat for dinner.

"Uncle Mark, you're a doctor. What do you think about the relationship between telomeres and the rate of aging?" Brook asked in a serious manner.

Mark raised his eyebrows. "I'm impressed. I'm not that kind of doctor though. I have a PhD in engineering, nothing to do with medicine. Why don't you tell me?"

Tucker pushed his spinach around. "Do we have to talk about this stuff?"

"Your Uncle Mark and Brook are having a discussion," Bergen said with a slight edge. "If you aren't interested in learning about something other than Xbox, you may be excused."

Brook, Tucker, and Sydney looked at their dad in astonishment. Bergen wasn't one to cut someone off at the knees. "Sorry, Dad, I just thought we could hear more about what Uncle Mark has been up to," Tucker replied timidly.

Hadley made piles of food on her plate, a walnut from her salad placed on top of each one. She once enjoyed two glasses of wine per night; now, her Chardonnay remained untouched.

"Well, no one wants to get Alzheimer's," Brook began. All eyes, except for Hadley's, drilled into her. "I've been researching what we can do to keep it at bay, that is *if* we're going to get it."

Mark wondered, *Why is Tucker counting to himself?*

"Go on," Mark encouraged. Hadley was only interested in building food towers.

"We've all heard we need to exercise more and keep our brains active," Brook continued. "But there is more to prevention than just doing crossword puzzles. We must keep our telomeres healthy, and good job on the omega-3-rich meal tonight, Dad."

"How do you even know about these things?" Bergen asked with genuine curiosity.

"I'm no expert, but as I told you, I went to a few educational sessions and have read some books they recommended. A lot of my research is from scientific blogs. Did you know there are over five million Americans with Alzheimer's, and by 2050, the number could rise to twenty million? It's the sixth leading cause of death."

"Six, seven," Tucker said loudly. "I'm taking Mom to the den." He got up brusquely and took his mother's elbow. "Come on, Mom, let's go look at the fish."

Bergen raised his brows. "Those are astounding figures." *Please don't let them have it.*

"I know it sounds like all doom and gloom, but Mom's form of dementia strikes less than five percent of the millions affected. Uncle Mark, did anyone tell you about Mom's type?"

Mark looked to Bergen with surprise. Bergen read his worried look. "The girls know, but Tuck doesn't," he said.

Mark let out a heavy sigh. "Yes, sweet girl, I know. When your dad first told me, I realized I could be at risk, so I had my genome sequenced. I did not inherit those genes," he said bittersweetly. A sour note invaded his taste buds. *How must it feel to not know?*

Bergen patted Mark on the back and raised his glass in the air. The Stantons felt a complicated mix of emotions: happy for him, sad for Mom, worried for themselves.

"I still want to learn as much as I can, Brook. Not having that mutation doesn't mean I won't get some form of dementia later in life. And I want to support you and your mom. Please, go on. Enlighten us."

"Although food is important, a bunch of studies indicate that improving metabolic health could alleviate symptoms and reduce brain pathology. A recent study suggested that women are more likely to develop Alzheimer's after menopause because of estrogen reduction."

Mark and even Sydney stared in awe. Bergen thought, *How could I not have attempted to learn these things? And my teenage daughter did?*

Mark turned to Sydney. "Your dad told me you decided against the test. Is that true?"

Sydney twirled a piece of hair between her fingers. "Yup, that's right. If I'm gonna get it, I'm gonna get it. If I find out I have it, I'll just be counting the days until I die."

"I guess I worry that you'll spend years in anguish. It is certainly your right, but what if you don't have it? Won't that be a huge weight off your shoulders?"

Brook interrupted, "There's a study out of Canada where they discovered a potential brain-imaging predictor for dementia. They found that changes to the brain's structure might occur years before a diagnosis, even before people notice their memory problems. There are also lots of online tests to assess your level of memory loss."

"That's all great, Brook," Sydney said with sarcasm, "but that doesn't help those with the FAD gene. Tell the researchers to hurry up."

Bergen walked behind Sydney's chair. He put his arms around her. "I know you're scared, sweetie, but we don't know if you have it. It sounds like you've given yourself a death sentence. I will do everything in my power to help all of you. Brook's suggestions to eat healthy, play games, take supplements, and learn about our levels of memory loss are easy to incorporate into our lives. They can't hurt."

"What if you did the test and only let your dad know the results?" Mark asked.

"I'm not sure that's fair," Brook blurted. "That would be a terrible burden for him."

Mark tented his fingers and nodded, embarrassed by his callous suggestion.

"We can start protecting ourselves now. Let's play a game," Brook said, attempting to thwart the uneasiness she started. "I'll get Tuck and Mom. We can play rummy five hundred."

"Mom won't be able to play," Sydney reminded her.

"She can watch," Brook said, jumping from her seat and walking to the den.

"Grab the cards," Sydney yelled, "in the cabinet next to the aquarium."

After two hours, Mark said, "I didn't realize rummy was so exhausting." He stretched his arms above him. "All I won is fifteen cents! I think I'll turn in and take my winnings with me."

Bergen escorted Mark to the guest bedroom. "Hey, thanks for coming. It really is good to see you. I'm sorry it took this crisis for us to make time. Seems that's always the way." Mark and Bergen hugged briefly. "Bathroom's across the hall. You'll have to share with Tuck. Towels are in this drawer," he said, pulling out the dresser drawer. "Can I get you anything else?"

"Bergen, I have an idea," Mark said sheepishly. "What if"—he looked into the hallway—"what if the girls got tested and *I* got the results? I'd promise not to give them the results without their permission, but if both are negative, I'll tell them. If one or both are positive, I won't."

Bergen scratched his forehead. "I don't know. Trust is something I'd never want to lose with my kids. Let me think about it."

Mark started to unpack. "You're right, but it's an option. Sleep on it."

Bergen thought, *It's an odd idea. Something to appease his survivor's guilt? I barely wanted my own genes tested. Losing Hadley to this disease is the hardest thing I've ever had to do. Knowing the kids had it would be insufferable.*

CHAPTER 41

Brook didn't know if she should scream or cry. Should I call Dad? Should I divulge the report to anyone? No one? The news sat in her stomach like a bomb waiting to explode. Brook ran all the way to the subway, her heart beating against her chest like a flamenco dancer's heels. Once off the train, she ran to the street, darting between strolling tourists, dog walkers with tangled leashes, and men holding promotional billboards. A volunteer from the Salvation Army stood on the busy corner near Brook's building. She rang her bell, hopeful for holiday donations. "I don't have Alzheimer's!" she blurted to the woman. The woman smiled and rang her bell again. Brook groped in her pocket for change and dropped it into the volunteer's red kettle. Brook hurried to her favorite pretzel vendor for a soft pretzel.

Without asking, Vinnie took a pretzel from the wooden dowel and dipped it in water and salt. "Here ya go, Miss Brook," he said. "You look like da cat that swallowed the canary."

Brook beamed and kicked the swirling leaves around her feet. "I have a secret, Vinnie," she said, handing him a dollar bill. Without waiting for his prompting, Brook burst into tears and blurted, "I tested negative for FAD!"

Vinnie took off his blue New York Yankees baseball cap and scratched his head. He leaned across the pyramid of soda cans on his cart. *Is she happy or sad?* He smiled and lifted his shoulders in the air, revealing his bewilderment.

Brook pulled a wad of napkins from the dispenser and blotted her tears. She spread mustard on her pretzel. "It's a form of early Alzheimer's disease that I was at risk for," she said. "But I don't have the mutation, so I'm okay." Brook started to cry again. She was overwhelmed with relief and worry for her siblings.

Vinnie shook his head and looked at the people walking by. "I don't know nothin' about mutants and medical problems, but it seems you oughta celebrate what God gave you." Vinnie reached for a can of 7UP and popped it open. "To your health," he said, handing her the soda. Brook took it and reached in her jacket for another dollar bill. Vinnie put his hand up. "Fawgetta 'bout it. Merry Christmas. This one's on da house."

Brook smiled and took a gulp, letting out a little burp. "Don't tell anyone, Vinnie. It's our little secret." He nodded, confused why she would want to keep good news a secret.

Brook paced in front of her building, rehearsing what she would say to her family. For months, she had grappled with the decision to get tested. It was a Christmas present to herself. After her fifth time passing the door, Walter stopped coming out to open it. The cacophony of city noises made it difficult for Brook to concentrate. *What if Tucker and Sydney are positive? Can I tell them? Can Dad keep it a secret? Do I owe him this relief?*

Her hands and ears were cold. The temperature was dropping now that the sun was down. She opened the heavy glass doors and entered the marble lobby. Walter looked up from his magazine and nodded. Brook smiled. *Can he tell something is different about me? Relief.*

"Mom, Dad?" she called out softly inside the apartment. "Syd? Anyone home?" The apartment was quiet. Brook removed her tennis shoes and hung her parka in the coat closet. She looked down the hall and noticed a light on in the master bedroom. Tiptoeing, she went to her parent's bedroom and pushed open the partially closed door. Her mom, wrapped in a pale-blue blanket, was asleep. She had a tormented look on her face, and her hands were clasped together. *I wish I could help you, Mom. I'd trade places with you if I could.*

"Honey," her dad whispered, "why aren't you at school? Everything okay?" Brook hugged him tightly. She wiped her eyes with her sleeve, forcing a smile. They moved to the den.

Brook sat on the couch and pulled her legs up to her chest. "Daddy, I don't have FAD."

Bergen's eyes widened, and he jumped to his feet. "What?" he hollered excitedly. "You got the test?" He couldn't believe it. Such great news.

"I've been going to counseling with Dr. Rathdrum and just decided to do it. I think Syd has it all wrong. Knowledge can be a good thing. I mean, losing your keys can just be losing your keys. Forgetting to pick up the dry cleaning can be just that. The test could bring her relief. It has for me, and it's been, like, an hour since I found out." She smiled.

Bergen lowered his head and sighed. The exhilaration was replaced with fear and dread for his other children. Bergen sat next to Brook and pulled her into his arms. "Thank you, God," he said. "My little girl is going to be fine."

CHAPTER 42

Monica looked over the top of her glasses as Rachel entered the room. "You look different today," she commented. Rachel took her usual spot on the couch. Dressed in a navy jacket, matching slacks, and a white blouse, her posture exuded confidence.

"I feel different. I feel good," Rachel said. "I have a lot to tell you."

"I'm all ears," Monica said. She settled into her chair and smiled, reminding herself, *This is why I became a therapist, to listen, without judgment, to help my patients heal.*

Rachel scratched her chin. *Where do I start?*

"You remember Hadley, the lady with Alzheimer's." Monica nodded. "I told you about her accident last year and that her concussion caused the acceleration of her cognitive decline." Rachel looked out the window. "Hadley and I have become really great friends, and now I'm losing her. I see her declining daily. It's hard."

"From what you've shared, I think you helped her a lot," Monica said. "And aren't you one of the only friends Hadley really opened up to about her dementia?" Rachel nodded and smiled. "Give yourself credit, Rachel. You have helped her just as much as she's helped you."

She's right, Rachel thought. *I'm gonna miss her and our special bond. I'm losing her, but she's not gone yet.* "Right after our session, I have an interview for SUNY's vet tech program." Rachel squared her shoulders and arched her back. "Someday you'll have to meet Princess, the one responsible for me going in this direction."

"I'd like that. Bring her in next time," Monica replied. "Once again, Rachel, you're not giving yourself credit. Because of your trauma, *you* decided to get a dog. *You* got her certified, and *you* chose to work with her at the VA. These are actions attributable to you, not your dog."

Rachel smiled. She hadn't thought of it that way.

"I have another piece of news. My dad and I have been getting together every week. Last week we went for Sunday brunch, and he invited Mom. It was really nice to be together again."

Monica smiled. *So much progress*, Monica thought. "Tell me more about you and your dad. It sounds like you've been working on gaining each other's trust again."

"Yeah, we're working on the trust thing. Even though I know the rape wasn't my fault, I think I still blamed myself for him leaving. Now at least I understand why he left."

Rachel slipped off her heels and curled her feet under her on the couch, a wide grin spreading across her face. "You know, he's really trying. We talk about our feelings, good and bad. And he's sharing more about how incompetent and vulnerable he felt after I was raped. Mostly because of his own abuse." *Saying "rape" didn't make my body shake or hives appear. It's getting easier to talk about.* "I think I forgive him. I don't think I'm angry anymore."

Rachel looked at her watch. Ten minutes left. "I've been thinking," she said. "Maybe I should forgive the dove tattoo guy too. There's no way to erase the havoc he caused, but I believe in karma, and what he's done in this life will decide his fate in the future. I think he'll get what he deserves. Does that sound weird that I want to forgive him and let go of my anger?"

Monica placed her glasses on her lap. She smiled warmly. "Forgiveness is a huge step, Rachel. It transforms anger and hurt into healing. It's empowering. It doesn't mean he's right or you consented to the attack or that you'll forget about it. Forgiving that man is for *you*, not him."

Rachel smiled. "I've spent so much time and energy being angry. At the rapist, at my dad, that I dropped out of school, at what a loser I'd become. It's freeing to get out of the past and move on. I'm going to choose positive emotions so I can live the best life possible." Rachel dropped her arms by her side and relaxed. "Man, it feels good giving up all this shit."

"You've made a ton of great strides, Rachel. You should be proud." They smiled at Rachel's progress. "How are the panic attacks, nightmares, sleeping issues?"

"I wouldn't call them panic attacks, but I do have occasional anxiety. But hey, doesn't everyone? I won't minimize what I've been through, but I'm not the only one with a troubled past. And more importantly, I guess, I can go on with my life now and be genuinely happy. I don't know if Will and I will be a thing forever, but who would've thought I'd even be dating?"

"I'm happy for you, Rachel. Since you're really making progress, I'd like to suggest that we continue tapering the medication and meet every three weeks now instead of two."

Rachel softly clapped her hands together, celebrating. Then it hit her: *I don't have Hadley anymore, and I won't have therapy every other week.* "What if . . . I still need your help? I'm not so sure I can do it on my own."

Monica put her notepad down and leaned forward. "You've come a long way since we met. I have great faith in you. I want you to think about all those who have supported you along the way, not just me and Hadley. Bring me a list at our next session. Three weeks. I'll see you then."

Rachel headed to her interview. As she walked toward the subway station, she started to compile the list of her friends and supporters. *Mandy, Will, Hadley, Mom, Aunt Claudette. Oh, and Bergen, Dad, Auckland Joe, Bomber Bob, even Meghan. Wow. So many caring people in my life. How grateful am I? And how could I forget the most important? Princess.*

CHAPTER 43

Hadley slumped into the couch, staring blankly at the fish tank. Her mumbling was indiscernible. Mariah stood in the doorway and tried to make out her words. "Miss Hadley, would you like to move to your bedroom? I think you'd be more comfortable." Hadley slowly turned, with no sign of recognition. Mariah moved to Hadley's side and touched her arm.

"Get off me, Jesse. I'm calling the police," Hadley screamed. She clawed the air wildly and scratched Mariah's hands. Mariah jumped back, fearful of the sudden aggression. "You can't take my husband. Get out of here. I'm calling the police."

Mariah backed up and ran to the hall to retrieve her phone. "Mr. Bergen, please come home," she blurted the second he answered. "Miss Hadley is not well. She doesn't recognize me. She thinks I'm someone named Jesse. I'm afraid she's going to hurt me."

Fifteen minutes later Bergen burst through the front door. Mariah stepped into the hall and gestured with a single finger to her lips to be quiet. Bergen went to his wife's side and watched her chest rise and fall as she slept. He took a cashmere throw from the couch and placed it over her, then turned to Mariah.

"It was strange. After I called you, I went back into the den. Miss Hadley seemed calm and wanted to nap. I think she might have known it was me." Mariah hesitated. "I don't want to leave you in a lurch, but I don't think I can do this anymore. I know I said I'd help out with watching Miss Hadley when you have to go to the office, but I think she needs professional care. She's too much for me to handle. I'm not skilled in that way." Bergen could see Mariah was clearly shaken. He noticed the fresh red scratch marks on her right hand.

"I'm so sorry for putting you in this position. It was selfish of me to ask that of you. As you can see, her confusion is becoming more frequent. Please don't take it personally. You're like family, Mariah. Would you feel comfortable still helping with the housecleaning? I won't leave you alone with her anymore."

"Of course, Mr. Bergen. I love Miss Hadley and this family." She swiped a finger over the top of the credenza and looked at the dust on her fingertips. "The place could use a little TLC," she said, smiling. "I can come Thursday."

"Perfect. You can take the rest of the day. I'll stay."

"I'm so sorry, Mr. Bergen. For all of you. Such a beautiful family." Mariah exited.

Bergen went into the den and sat on the couch. The room was quiet except for the tranquil sound of flowing water through the fish tank. *What if this happens to one of the kids?*

While Hadley slept, Bergen retreated to his office to think. He knew it was time to put her in a memory care unit. He'd tell the kids his plans—and what happened—that night.

Tucker wondered, *How can Mom, such a gentle person, hurt anyone?* Brook expected a rebuttal or explanation from her mom, but Hadley was unaware of the conversation. Tucker offered his mother a bite of food. Nothing.

"Hads, honey, if you're not hungry, are you ready to go to bed?" She rose from her chair and walked out of the kitchen. "I'll come right back. We need to talk," Bergen told the children.

"Poor Dad," Brook said. "He looks so tired." Sydney cleared the dishes. Tucker turned on his Fortnite video game. "What?" he said, looking at his sister. "We're not officially at dinner anymore." Sydney was surprised Tucker did not start his touching routine.

Bergen returned twenty minutes later. His once commanding eyes now looked bewildered and dull. His heavy stubble—once sexy to Hadley—now made him look ten years older. Bergen filled his wineglass. He knew he was drinking more than usual. He didn't care.

"I think we know what you're going to say," Brook said.

"I'm so sorry," Bergen started. "I talked to Dr. Boswell, and we agree it's time for your mom to move into a more protected environment," Bergen said, prepared for backlash.

Tucker stood to hug him. Brook and Sydney joined him, and all stood huddled together, hanging on tightly to one another. They understood. It was the right decision.

It was too sad to watch their mother disappear in their home.

CHAPTER 44

The entrance to the Springcrest Assisted-Living Facility was much classier than Rachel expected. The manicured lawn, large porch with white rocking chairs, and sunny foyer was inviting. Compared to the VA, this place was the Ritz.

Rachel approached the desk in the lobby and signed in. "She's in room one twelve, in the Memory Care Unit," the receptionist told her. "Go down this hall, to the next building, and enter seven-six-eight-five in the keypad." It had been eight months since her last visit. A wave of conflicting emotions washed over her. Guilt gnawed at her conscience as she recalled the countless excuses she had made to avoid confronting the painful reality of Hadley's condition. Despite the demands of school and work, Rachel knew she should have made more time for her.

Rachel keyed in the code, saddened that her friend was declining and needed to be in a locked unit. She closed the door behind her, instinctively listening for the click indicating the door was secure. In the common area, people, some in wheelchairs, sat in a circle, singing songs led by a staff member. Rachel perused their faces, checking for Hadley. *No Hadley.* As she walked down the hall, she took special notice of the senior lift chairs, the sofas lined with blue disposable pads, and the ceiling painted to look like the sky with white fluffy clouds. The unit, although nice, certainly wasn't as stylish as the assisted-living building where she entered.

"You finally came to see me, Ann," a woman said as Rachel passed the dining area.

Rachel looked around. "Me?" she replied, pointing at herself. Before she could continue, a young aide approached the lady.

"Mrs. Carlotta, this is not Ann. Ann comes on Sundays. This is another guest." The aide pulled up a chair and sat beside her. "Would you like to look at your photos again?"

More trompe-l'oeil paintings of gardens, bookcases, and vases of cheerful yellow sunflowers adorned the hallway walls. Rachel stood outside of her room, a framed picture of Hadley's face on the door. It reminded Rachel of school picture day: perfectly coiffed hair, a plastered half smile, and a digitally inserted blue background. Rachel looked around at the other doors, each with a photo of the resident. In one case, she noticed two frames side-by-side: George and Elizabeth Whitacker. *I wonder if they both have dementia or can't stand to be apart.*

Entering Hadley's room, Rachel braced herself for a heartbreaking encounter. The woman in the bed before her bore little resemblance to the vibrant, fiercely independent person she once knew. "Hadley, I brought you a present," Rachel announced. The room was cheerfully decorated with a fake flowering tree in the corner and a collage of labeled family photos on the wall. A shiny, pink, swan-shaped music box sparkled on the table next to Hadley.

Her eyes opened, a blank expression on her face. "Are you here to give me my bath?"

Rachel leaned against the edge of the bed. "No, Hadley. It's me, Rachel," she said, hoping for any sign of recognition. *Sure, I'm busy with the vet tech program, but I should have visited sooner. Will I always regret this?* Rachel handed Hadley a gift.

Hadley took the gift and turned it over in her hand. "Thank you, dear. What is it?"

"Open it," Rachel encouraged.

Hadley looked at the box like it was a Chinese puzzle. Rachel opened it for her. "It's a voice-activated personal assistant. Her name is Alexa. You can ask her questions or tell her to do certain things," she explained. Hadley stared vacantly at the hockey puck-shaped disk. Rachel set it up and gave Hadley a simplified tutorial on its use.

Rachel gave the device a command. "Alexa, what time is it?"

"The time is three thirty-four p.m."

"Alexa, what is the weather today?"

"It is fifty-nine degrees, partly sunny, with a ten percent chance of rain, a high of sixty-three degrees, and a low of forty-five degrees."

Rachel smiled. "Give it a try, Hadley." She stared blankly at Rachel. Rachel put the Echo Dot on the side table and turned her attention back to Hadley. Rachel sat stiffly on the bed. *Should I stay or come back another time?* She heard a humming noise and noticed a small plastic fish tank on the dresser. Three fish darted through the castle. Rachel smiled. *Fish always offer her comfort.* "I'll just stay here with you a while," Rachel said. "Would you like to listen to music?" Hadley didn't answer. Rachel instructed, "Alexa, play classical music."

A half hour later Bergen arrived for his daily visit. Surprised to see Rachel, he tiptoed across the room and removed two yellow blankets from the linen closet for both of them.

Rachel startled as he lay it across her lap and sat up abruptly. "Oh my, did I fall asleep?" She swung her legs over the side of the bed. "Bergen, hi, how long have you been here?" She tucked her shirt into her jeans and ran her fingers through her hair, pulling it into a loose pony.

Bergen glanced at Hadley. Lately, he couldn't tell if she was asleep or not. The looks were the same. He motioned toward the door. Rachel followed him out.

"She sleeps most of the day," Bergen said as he gave Rachel a quick hug. "Let's go outside so we can talk." There was an enclosed grassy area, complete with park benches, a pretend postal box, and several bird feeders hanging from artificial willow trees. Rachel surveyed the park-like setting and noticed there was no way out except back into the locked unit. Parked in a wheelchair by a tree, a thin, elderly man muttered to himself. Next to him was a much younger woman, holding his hand as two children played tag.

Bergen walked to the far side of the courtyard and sat on a bench. Sitting side-by-side, Rachel looked at Bergen. His face was drawn, and his cheeks seemed sunken. His naturally good looks were overshadowed by a lack of sleep and stress.

"How are the kids?" Rachel asked.

"Everyone seems to be handling this as best they can. Sydney is back in school and plans to graduate this spring. She comes home once a month to see her mom. Brookie seems to be enjoying sorority life at NYU. And Tuck, well, to be honest, he's still struggling." Rachel raised her eyebrows. "He's doing fine in school and on the JV rowing team. He's seeing a therapist to help with the compulsions. Tuck believes the rituals hold magical properties. If he counts or touches something in a certain way, it will save Hadley. It's about control. I think the therapy's working. He seems to be getting better. Sometimes he even opens up to me."

Bergen exhaled. Rachel could feel his exhaustion. She squeezed his hand. Bergen gave her a feeble smile. "He still doesn't know he could have it. Sydney still doesn't want the test."

"It's got to be a hard decision," Rachel said. "I don't know what I would choose."

Bergen nodded, lost in thought. "She doesn't always remember me," he said numbly. "Last Tuesday, she did recognize me. We had a wonderful visit, and she asked me to take her to see Niagara Falls one last time." He choked up. "Did you know we honeymooned there?" Rachel shook her head. "We were in graduate school when we got married and only had the weekend. We eventually went on a real honeymoon to Jamaica." There was a hint of a smile, but it faded.

"One last time," he said. Bergen let go of Rachel's hand and covered his face. "How can I go on without her?" Rachel turned to face him and took him in her arms. The dam broke and Bergen let out loud sobs. He buried his face deeper into Rachel's shoulder.

Bergen wiped his face with his sleeve. "I thought I'd have more time with her."

Rachel and Bergen watched the interaction between the man in the wheelchair and his presumed daughter. "That's more like it's supposed to be," Bergen said.

"What?" Rachel asked.

"He's old. He has grandchildren. He lived his life." Before Rachel could respond, Bergen added, "I think I'll take her to Niagara this weekend."

"That's a great idea, Bergen. I think it will be good for both of you."

Bergen nodded. "I'm not sure if she's allowed to leave, but I might as well give it a try," he said with a far-off look in his eyes, imagining their honeymoon.

"Mr. Stanton," an aide called out. "Your wife is awake and asking for Sydney." Bergen and Rachel rose and walked arm in arm back into the unit.

Hadley sat in her chair, a blue cloth bib around her neck and a hospital tray table over her lap. "I was just about to feed her," the aide said. "But maybe you would like to instead." Hadley continued looking forward, seemingly unaware they had come back in the room. Her mouth was open like a hungry baby bird.

Rachel looked at the mush in the bowls and crinkled her nose. "May I?" she asked.

Rachel scooped small portions of the blended meat and potatoes onto the spoon. Like feeding an infant, she gently placed the food in Hadley's mouth. Hadley pushed the mixture around with her tongue, leaving most of it on the corners of her lips. Rachel gently wiped the excess with the spoon. Hadley raised her arms from under the tray table, put one hand on top of Rachel's, and turned her gaze toward Bergen. There was a noticeable sparkle. "I love you both," she said.

Bergen stepped forward and put his arms around Rachel and Hadley. "We love you too, my dear. We love you too."

EPILOGUE
SIX YEARS LATER

All eyes were on Dean Hendrickson as he rose from his chair. His red-and-black gown swayed as he approached the lectern.

Rachel turned in her seat, searching among the hundreds of guests for her parents and friends. They were all there, seated together. She smiled and let out a long breath. *My family*, she thought as she settled into her chair for the remainder of the ceremony.

After presenting the diplomas to each of the graduates, Dean Hendrickson commended those inducted into the Phi Zeta honor society and asked each to stand. Rachel couldn't hide her pride as she stood to join the fourteen other members of her class. When the applause died down, the dean continued with his presentation of awards. "It is with great pleasure that we announce a new award. This award has been generously endowed by Mr. Bergen Stanton and his children, Sydney, Brooklynn, and Tucker." Rachel's eyes widened. She twisted her head and neck, searching for their seats. She caught Bergen's gaze. He smiled and nodded. "The Hadley B. Stanton Award for Community Engagement is open to a student who demonstrates both scholarly achievement and an ongoing, deep commitment to community engagement. The student shall lead, inspire, and engage others toward positive social change." The dean paused and took a framed certificate from the podium. "It is my pleasure to present this award to Rachel Allison Weissman for her work connecting rescue dogs with combat veterans."

Rachel couldn't hold back her tears as she remembered her first day at the VA Hospital. *I wish Hadley could have been here.*

Rachel walked arm and arm with Will into the private room at the restaurant. Congratulations banners and balloons hung from the ceiling. Mandy grabbed and hugged her tightly. "We are so incredibly proud of you," she said. Rachel looked around the room in awe at the number of friends there to celebrate. She hadn't seen some of them in a long time. Her studies had kept her busy. Off to the side, she saw Auckland Joe. He was clean-shaven, dressed in a brown suit, and fully relaxed. He looked good, handsome, even. Cassie and Princess stood dutifully by his side. Princess tugged at her leash and ran to Rachel, jumping up to lick her face. Rachel hugged Joe.

Sydney rose from her seat. "It's a girl," she said, sliding her palm over her belly. Rachel put her hands to her mouth. Tears of joy formed.

"Do you have a name yet?" Rachel asked.

Sydney smiled at her husband, then looked at her dad. "Yes, her name is Angelica." She lifted her hand and touched the small angel charm hanging from her necklace. Rachel smiled. It warmed her heart to know it had been Hadley's bracelet and Sydney was keeping the memory alive.

Rachel sat down with Bergen, Sydney, and Brooklynn. The last time she had seen them together was at Sydney's wedding three years prior, though she did her best to keep up with them separately.

"Tuck couldn't come today," Brook apologized. "Cornell is in the finals of the rowing championship. He's the captain, so he couldn't get away."

A waiter walked through the room, tinkling a bell. "Dinner is served," he announced. "Please take your seats." Rachel took Princess by her leash and led her to the corner with Cassie, then found her seat. Her mom and dad were seated next to each other on her right. Will was on her left. Mandy, Monica, Auckland Joe, and Auntie Claudette filled in the remaining seats.

Bergen stood and thanked everyone for coming. He raised his champagne flute, tilting it in Rachel's direction. "A toast," he said. "As Eleanor Roosevelt once said, 'Many people will walk in and out of your life, but only true friends will leave footprints in your heart.' I believe you, Rachel, have left your footprint in the hearts of everyone here tonight. From the bottom of my heart, and of Hadley's, God rest her soul, we love you."

ACKNOWLEDGMENTS

I WOULD LIKE TO EXPRESS my deepest gratitude to those who made this book possible. My heartfelt thanks to my two writing coaches, Gay Walley and Lisa Fugard, for your invaluable guidance during this lengthy process.

Special thanks to my friends, colleagues, and countless beta readers for your insightful feedback, resources, and encouragement.

To my husband, John, for your constant love and support and for affording me full license to pursue this career as an author.

Finally, this book is dedicated to my mother, Sally, whose experience with Alzheimer's disease profoundly shaped my writing journey.

RESOURCES

Alzheimer's Association
800.272.3900
www.alz.org

Alzheimer's Foundation of America
866-232.8494
www.alzfdn.org

America's VetDogs (USA & Canada)
1-631-930-9000
www.vetdogs.org

Apollo Health
1-800-450-0805
www.apollohealthco.com

Canine Companions
1-800-572-BARK (2275)
www.canine.org

Crisis Text Line
In the USA, text HOME to 741741
In the UK, text SHOUT to 85258
In Canada, text CONNECT to 686868
In Ireland, text HOME 50808

Dementia Society of America
www.dementiasociety.org

K9s For Warriors
1-888-819-0112
www.k9sforwarriors.org

National Sexual Assault Hotline
800.656.4673
www.rainn.org

Substance Abuse & Mental Health Services Administration (SAMHSA)
www.samsha.gov/findhelp

The National Suicide Prevention Lifeline
1-800-273-TALK (8255) or dial 988

The deaf and hard of hearing can contact the Lifeline via TTY at 1-800-799-4889
www.988lifeline.org

Women's Alzheimer's Movement
www.thewomensalzheimersmovement.org

Made in the USA
Columbia, SC
15 April 2025

69cfb061-3ab8-46c0-b268-0aa5106f4d05R01